A MATTER OF
LIFE AND
DEATH

Center Point
Large Print

Also by Phillip Margolin and available from Center Point Large Print:

The Third Victim
The Perfect Alibi
A Reasonable Doubt

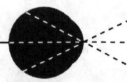

**This Large Print Book carries the
Seal of Approval of N.A.V.H.**

A MATTER OF
LIFE AND
DEATH

A ROBIN LOCKWOOD NOVEL

PHILLIP MARGOLIN

CENTER POINT LARGE PRINT
THORNDIKE, MAINE

This Center Point Large Print edition
is published in the year 2021 by arrangement with
St. Martin's Publishing Group.

The text of this Large Print edition is unabridged.
In other aspects, this book may vary
from the original edition.
Printed in the United States of America
on permanent paper.
Set in 16-point Times New Roman type.

ISBN: 978-1-64358-856-8

The Library of Congress has cataloged this record
under Library of Congress Control Number: 2020952825

DEDICATION

During the quarter century when I was practicing criminal defense, I represented clients in a dozen death penalty cases, so I know firsthand the pressure an attorney is under when a client's life is literally on the line. In two separate murder cases, I learned that horrible mistakes can be made in the most serious cases when I represented innocent clients who had been sentenced to life in prison. I was able to clear the names of both men, but I wouldn't wish on anyone the pressure I was under.

There is no more important job in the legal profession than making sure that people facing the death penalty get a fair trial. People do not get rich doing it, and it takes a toll. That's why I am dedicating this book to organizations like the Innocence Project, the Equal Justice Initiative, the Legal Defense and Educational Fund of the NAACP, and all of the attorneys who take on capital cases.

PROLOGUE

The rain pounded on Ian Hennessey's windshield with the fury of a drum solo, making it almost impossible to see the road. It seemed like Ian's bad day was never going to end.

The day hadn't started badly. It had actually started as one of Ian's best days. Shortly after court began, the young deputy district attorney had won a difficult motion to suppress. That victory had prompted the defendant to plead guilty in a case Ian was worried he might lose. His next case had resulted in another plea, ending his morning docket with two victories.

Ian left the courtroom with a big smile on his face. He was on his way to his office to boast about his victories when he received a phone call. An hour later, he was basking in the afterglow of the best sex he'd ever experienced. Then Ian's wonderful day took a 180-degree turn, and the woman he loved threatened to destroy his life.

People sometimes said that they were in hell. Ian really felt that he was as close as you could come to the real thing. He knew that he wasn't the best person. He'd listened to the podcasts and read the online articles about his generation. How they felt entitled and wanted it all right away without working for their goals like past generations. Ian fit the stereotype. His wealthy parents had indulged their only child and used their influence to get him places he didn't deserve to be. And he had taken what they'd given without an ounce of gratitude. Then he'd been given a job he didn't deserve and had taken for granted at first but had come to love; a job that could be ripped away from him at any moment, through no fault of his own.

"Turn here," said Anthony Carasco.

Ian turned onto Carasco's street, where multimillion-dollar mansions stood on large, manicured lots. Ian was surprised at how poor the street lighting was, considering the wealth of the people who lived here. Even with his brights on, the downpour was so powerful that he was having a hard time seeing the road. That's why Ian was shocked when his high beams fell on a man who was standing in the middle of the street. Ian hit the brakes. The man froze in the glare, then threw an arm across his face.

"Who was that?" Carasco shouted as the apparition shot across the street and into the woods.

"I have no idea," was Ian's bewildered reply.

"It looked like he was coming from my house," Carasco said.

Ian pulled into the driveway, and his passenger jumped out. Ian followed him inside, and his bad day got a lot worse.

PART ONE
THE OLDEST PROFESSION
TWO MONTHS AGO

CHAPTER ONE

Anthony Carasco was five seven with a slight build, dull brown hair, and bland features that made him hard to call to mind a day after you met him. When he was sober, Carasco was objective enough to know that it wasn't his looks that made him attractive to women. But Carasco had a buzz on, and that's why no warning bells went off when a stunning blonde with ivory skin, pouty red lips, sky-blue eyes, and a killer figure sat on the stool next to him in the bar in the San Francisco hotel and began making conversation.

"It's really dead in here," the blonde said.

"That's because everyone is at the bar at the Fairmont," Carasco answered.

"Why is that?"

"The American Bar Association convention is over there."

"Are you a lawyer?" the blonde asked.

"I am. How about you?"

"I thought about it once, but it's not for me. So, why are you here when your fellow lawyers are over there?"

"Too noisy," Carasco said as he flashed a drunken smile. Then he held out his hand. "Tony Carasco."

"Stacey Hayes," the blonde said, returning

the smile and holding Carasco's hand a moment more than most women would. "Noise isn't the only reason a man drinks alone," she said when she released Carasco's hand. "What's the real reason?"

Carasco hesitated. Normally, he was very private, but he was a bit tipsy, and he was certain that he would never see Stacey Hayes again.

"It's my wife. She called right before I was going down to the bar at the Fairmont, and we had another argument." He shrugged. "After she hung up on me, I wasn't in the mood to socialize."

"That's too bad."

"It's too bad we're married, but divorce is out of the question."

"With a name like Carasco, I'm guessing you're Catholic. Is this a religious thing?"

Carasco laughed. "No, it's a money thing. Betsy is loaded."

"Aah!"

"Can I buy you a drink?" Carasco asked.

"That's very nice of you."

"You're very nice."

Hayes raised an eyebrow. "How can you tell? We've just met."

"Well, first thing, you're a sympathetic listener who's kind enough to pay attention to the woes of a man twice your age."

"I doubt you're twice my age."

"See, that proves my point. I'm down in the dumps, and you're trying to cheer me up, even if it requires a little white lie."

Hayes smiled. "Maybe I used to be a Girl Scout, and this is my good deed for the day."

"Were you a Girl Scout?"

Hayes laughed. "Far from it."

Carasco grinned. "Were you a wild child?"

Hayes looked him in the eye. "I was."

"Are you still?"

"Maybe. Why do you ask?"

"I just had a crazy idea—and I don't want to offend you—but would you like to have that drink in my room at the Fairmont? It's a suite with a great view of the city."

"That idea isn't so crazy, and you make a very nice first impression . . ."

"But?"

"But I have to be straight with you, Tony. I'm a working girl."

Carasco looked confused.

"I'm a professional escort."

Carasco brightened. "Oh, I get it. I'm just a little slow, what with the booze and all. But, hey, that's not a turn-off. In fact, it's a turn-on."

He stood up. "Shall we go?"

Carasco didn't know if it was the coke he'd snorted before they got to it or Stacey's athletic and enthusiastic approach to her job, but he did know that he hadn't experienced anything like sex with Ms. Hayes in years. By the time they finished, he was drained and dizzy and feeling better than he'd felt in a long time.

Carasco rolled to one side of the king-size bed and took deep breaths.

"That was amazing," he said when he'd recovered enough to talk.

"Glad you approved," Hayes said, rolling toward Carasco so one perfect breast nudged his arm.

"Jesus! I may need an EMT with a defibrillator."

"I can always do mouth to mouth," Hayes answered with a lazy smile.

"Maybe in a bit. I'm not as young as I used to be."

"You certainly don't act like a man who claimed to be twice my age."

Carasco laughed. "Thanks for the compliment."

"It was well earned."

Carasco assumed that Hayes's praise for his performance was part of the service, but he did feel like he'd held his own.

"How long have you been living in San Francisco?" Carasco asked.

"A little over a year."

"So, this isn't home?"

"No."

Carasco noticed that Hayes's answer wasn't as playful as some of her other responses. "Ever think of moving?"

14

"Why?"

"I live in Oregon—Portland. I own some real estate, and I have a very nice apartment that's currently vacant. It's on the river with a killer view of the mountains."

Hayes smiled. "I appreciate the offer. Normally, I'd give it serious consideration if the price was right, but I'm afraid Oregon is off-limits for me."

"Oh, why is that?"

"I was busted a few times in Portland when I was new at this, and I took off. There are outstanding warrants in your hometown, and I don't need the hassle."

Carasco smiled. "If it's the warrants you're worried about, you're in luck."

"What do you mean?"

"I can get rid of those pesky things as easy as one, two, three."

"How can you do that?"

"I'm a Multnomah County Circuit Court judge, Stacey, and judges have magical powers when it comes to dealing with warrants."

CHAPTER TWO

Robin Lockwood was a lean and muscular five eight with short blond hair, blue eyes, and a face that was unmarked, despite having been a high school wrestler and a UFC cage fighter. Robin had abandoned her career in mixed martial arts after suffering a brutal knockout on a pay-per-view event in Las Vegas during her first year at Yale Law School, but she still kept in top shape by working out every weekday morning before going to her law office. This morning, Robin had skipped her workout at McGill's gym. A lengthy federal trial had forced her to get an extension on a brief, and she was running up against the new deadline.

Barrister, Berman, and Lockwood was located in a modern glass-and-steel office building in the heart of downtown Portland. Robin asked her receptionist if there were any urgent messages before walking down a hall decorated with a series of artistic cityscapes, past the offices of her partner Mark Berman, her investigator/boyfriend Jeff Hodges, and their newest associate, Loretta Washington.

Robin's spacious corner office had a stunning view of the Willamette River, the verdant foothills of the Cascade Range, and the snowcapped peaks of Mount Hood and Mount St. Helens. This morning, she was oblivious to nature's masterpiece because the deadline hung over her like the sword of Damocles.

Robin had just started working on the brief when Mark Berman walked into her office. Robin's law partner was six two, in his early thirties, and had long brown hair and bright blue eyes. Mark was married with a young daughter and had a sunny disposition that he maintained, no matter how stressful the case he was handling. While Robin was working out at her gym in the morning, Mark was rowing on the Willamette River to maintain the shape he'd been in when he was a member of the University of Washington's nationally ranked crew.

"Got a minute?" Mark asked.

Robin didn't, but she waved Mark toward a seat anyway. "What's up?" she asked.

"Erika Stassen is a CPA at Kimbro and Fong, the firm that prepares my taxes. She has a serious problem. Can you see her?"

"I'm snowed under because of the Lowenstein trial. I've got a brief due and piles of work to catch up with. Can't you handle it?"

"I would if I could, but it's a criminal matter."

"Can she make an appointment?"

"She's in my office, and she's really upset. You'd be doing me a big favor if you'd talk to her."

Robin sighed and pushed the case she was

reading to one side. Moments later, Mark ushered in a tall, well-dressed woman with glossy black shoulder-length hair, a smooth complexion, and pleasant, feminine features. After introducing Erika to Robin, Mark left and Robin offered Stassen a seat.

"Mark says you have a problem, Ms., Mrs. . . . ?"

"*Ms.* will do. I'm not married. I was for a few years, but I'm not now."

"Why do you need to see me?"

Stassen looked down. Her shoulders were hunched, and her hands were clasped in her lap. "This is very embarrassing."

"What you tell me is just between the two of us, and I don't judge my clients," Robin said with a gentle smile. "What's your problem?"

"Mark probably told you that I work at an accounting firm. The people there, well, they're very understanding, very supportive. But if this comes out, I don't know what they'll do. I . . . I could lose my job."

A tear trickled down Erika's cheek, and she stifled a sob.

"Do you want some water?" Robin asked as she handed Erika a Kleenex.

"I'm sorry. This has been very difficult for me."

"No need to apologize. Why don't you tell me why you're here so I can see if I can help you."

Erika took a deep breath. "It's prostitution. That's what they say I did."

18

Robin frowned. She'd represented prominent men who had been arrested for soliciting a prostitute and women who had been charged with being a prostitute, but a female CPA didn't seem to fit into either category.

"Why don't you tell me what the police say you did."

"Okay, but before I do that, there's something you need to know. My name on my birth certificate is Eric Stassen. Legally, I'm a man, but that's going to change in two months."

CHAPTER THREE

Ian Hennessey spent more time than usual selecting the clothes he would wear to work, because he wanted to look like a consummate professional when he met with Robin Lockwood. Hennessey, a stocky, broad-shouldered twenty-five-year-old with bright red hair and pale, freckled skin, had been a Multnomah County deputy district attorney for less than a year. His opponents in most of the misdemeanor cases he'd tried had been public defenders, who were also inexperienced, recent law school grads. This was the first time Ian would go up against an A-lister. Kicking Robin Lockwood's ass would give him a ton of street cred, and to be honest, Ian really needed a big win.

Ian had finished near the bottom of his law school class and had flunked the Oregon bar twice. His early track record reinforced the views of the other deputies that he would never have been hired if his father hadn't used his influence.

When he started his job at the DA's office, Ian resented the fact that his parents had "bought" it for him, and he had put very little effort into his cases. The deputy in charge of his unit had called him on the carpet after he lost three winnable cases in a row. Ian had several feeble explanations for his failures. He couldn't help it if the security guard in the shoplifting case was an idiot, the defense attorney in the DUII had surprised him by producing a smartphone video that contradicted his cop's testimony, and the jury in his other case was stocked with bleeding-heart liberals.

Ian's supervisor had accused him of failing to prep the security guard, not reading the list of evidence the defense attorney in the DUII had sent over in discovery, and doing a lousy job during jury selection. Ian had told the supervisor that he had too many cases and too little time to prepare, but his excuses fell on deaf ears. Ian had been faced with an unspoken threat that his days as a deputy DA were numbered if he didn't improve.

Terrified of losing his job, Ian had applied himself, and two guilty verdicts had followed. Success as a result of his own efforts was new to Ian, and he started believing that he could be a good lawyer. The Stassen case was a sure winner, and beating Lockwood would go a long way toward salvaging his reputation.

Hennessey checked his watch every couple of minutes as the time for the scheduled conference approached. Just as he was about to look again, the receptionist buzzed. Hennessey straightened his tie, buttoned his jacket, and checked himself in the mirror that hung in the cubicle he shared with another new DA. Then he took a deep breath and walked down the hall to the reception area.

"It's a pleasure to meet 'Rockin' Robin,'" Hennessey said. "I'm a big UFC fan."

When Robin walked down the aisle to the Octagon, her fans used to sing "Rockin' Robin," an old rock-and-roll song.

Hennessey puffed out his chest as he led Robin to a conference room.

"I wrestled in college. I even thought about trying my hand at MMA, but I got into law school and shelved the idea."

"You made the smart choice," Robin said. "Duking it out with defense attorneys is a lot less painful than getting your bell rung."

"You're probably right," he said as he opened the conference room door and ushered Robin in, "but sometimes I wonder how I would have made out."

Robin smiled but didn't comment.

"So," Hennessey said, "are you here to negotiate a plea?"

"I was hoping we could work out an agreement that would let Ms. Stassen avoid a criminal record. This is her first offense, and she has a good job. A conviction could lead to her losing it."

"This is the first time *Mr.* Stassen was caught." Hennessey smiled. "And yeah, I know your client is a man, and I bet *he's* offered to give blow jobs for dough more than just this once."

"I've talked to several people about men who change their sex. Erika—"

"Eric," Hennessey corrected Robin.

Robin didn't want to get in a fight over a pronoun, so she decided to refer to Erika as a male until she got what she wanted.

"He didn't engage in sex for the money."

Hennessey tuned out when Robin explained what she had learned from her research, and he smirked when Robin was finished.

"You can make that argument to a jury. Maybe it'll fly. But the way I see it, your client engaged in sex for dough. That's prostitution. The case is open and shut. Have him plead guilty and I'll go along with probation, but that's all I'm willing to offer."

Robin looked frustrated, and Ian gave a mental fist pump.

"I'm sorry you feel that way," Robin said. "I guess we'll have to go to trial."

"Guess so. See you in court, Counselor."

Ian waited until Robin left the conference room and was out of sight before breaking into a grin. That had gone very, very well, Ian told himself. This case would be an easy notch on his gun and a big boost to his reputation.

CHAPTER FOUR

Anthony Carasco stayed an extra day in San Francisco while Stacey Hayes considered his offer to get rid of her warrants, install her in an upscale love nest, and give her an allowance that would let her live a life of leisure. Two weeks after Carasco returned to his duties on the bench, Hayes moved to the Grandview, a luxurious apartment on the Willamette River with a view of the mountains through floor-to-ceiling windows.

Carasco couldn't get enough of Hayes. The afternoon after she moved to Portland, the judge told his wife that he would be home late. Then he dismissed a case on the flimsiest of grounds so he could spend the day in Hayes's bed. From that day on, Carasco was either with Hayes, fantasizing about her, or devising excuses for being away from home so he could go to her.

Sometimes, Carasco would wake up at night and sneak into the bathroom to text Hayes. That's what he was doing when the bathroom door opened and Betsy stormed in. Carasco tried to hide his phone, but Betsy caught him.

"What are you doing?" she demanded.

"Nothing," Carasco stammered. "I couldn't sleep, so I was reading sports news."

Betsy glared at her husband. "Let me see that."

"There's nothing to see," the judge said as he struggled to shut down the phone.

Betsy took a step toward her husband, and he backed into the glass wall of the shower.

"I know what you're up to, Tony. Now show me the phone."

Carasco hesitated, and Betsy lunged for the hand that held the phone. Carasco thrust out his other hand. It slammed into Betsy's shoulder and threw her off balance. She was barefoot and she slipped on the tiled floor and fell on her backside.

Betsy's mouth opened in shock. Then she flushed with rage. Carasco stuffed the phone in the pocket of his bathrobe and reached for his wife. Betsy slapped his hand away.

"I'm sick of this. If you want your whore this badly, get out of my bed and go fuck her."

"There isn't anyone, Betsy. I love you."

"Bullshit. That's what this marriage is, and I'm not putting up with it anymore."

"What . . . what do you mean?"

Betsy struggled to her feet. "You'll find out soon enough. You can sleep in the guest room from now on."

Betsy stomped out of the bathroom and slammed the door behind her. Carasco slumped down on the toilet. This could end badly if Betsy went to a divorce lawyer. But there had been blowups like this before, and he'd been able to get back in his wife's good graces by humbling himself and cutting his ties with the woman he was seeing. He could definitely humble himself to keep his opulent lifestyle and her political influence, but Carasco could not imagine giving up Stacey Hayes.

Carasco waited until he thought it was safe to leave the bathroom and go to the guest room without inciting a new screaming fit. While he waited, the judge weighed his options. There was one he'd considered in the past and rejected as too radical. But if Betsy started divorce proceedings, it might be the only viable option.

CHAPTER FIVE

As soon as Robin agreed to take Erika Stassen's case, she started reading about gender reassignment surgery, which used to be referred to as sex change operations, and the psychological problems encountered by the people undergoing them. Then she talked to the doctors, social workers, and psychologists who were working with Erika. When she felt she had enough information, she had arranged the meeting with Ian Hennessey.

Before meeting with the young DA, Robin had asked other defense attorneys about him. The few attorneys who'd had the misfortune of trying cases against Hennessey told Robin that he had an overinflated view of his abilities and didn't prepare his cases. That led to amateur mistakes brought on by overconfidence.

Robin had been frustrated when she'd left Hennessey's office, but she'd held out hope that the judge assigned to the case would talk sense into the young zealot. Then she learned that the case had been assigned to Anthony Carasco.

Robin had never had a case in Carasco's court, but the criminal defense bar in Portland was a tight-knit group, and his reputation had made the rounds. Carasco had started his career in the

DA's office, where he was known as a brilliant prosecutor who could not be trusted. There were numerous stories about exculpatory evidence that had been concealed from the defense and questionable courtroom tactics. But the most disturbing rumors concerned cases Carasco had lost because key evidence had disappeared or a witness had changed his story under suspicious circumstances. These losses were infrequent, but they usually involved high-level drug dealers, members of biker gangs, or prominent, wealthy citizens.

A year ago, Carasco announced that he was going to challenge Molly Devereaux, a very popular judge, for a seat on the Multnomah County Circuit Court. Carasco's campaign had been vicious, and there were rumors of campaign irregularities. When Carasco unseated Devereaux, he proceeded to earn the same bad reputation as a jurist he'd had as an attorney. He was a tyrant in court who was not above upbraiding an attorney in front of a jury. Though intelligent, he was also lazy and would rule on complex motions without reading the memos submitted by the attorneys. Few lawyers who had appeared in Carasco's court had anything good to say about him.

Carasco was sitting in a courtroom on the fifth floor of the Multnomah County Courthouse, a brutish, eight-story concrete building that took up an entire block between Fourth and Fifth and Main and Salmon in downtown Portland. Mark Berman, Robin, and Erika took the elevator to the fifth floor. When they rounded the corner, Robin spotted a well-dressed, middle-aged African American woman sitting on a bench outside the courtroom.

"Thanks for coming, Dr. Langford," Robin said.

"I hope I can help," Langford answered. Then she smiled at Stassen. "How are you feeling, Erika?"

"I'm pretty nervous."

"I'd be surprised if you weren't."

"Let's go inside," Robin said.

Carasco's courtroom had high ceilings, ornate molding, marble Corinthian columns, and a polished wood dais. The spectator section consisted of several rows of hard wooden benches set back behind a low wooden fence that separated the public from the judge, jury, and attorneys.

Erika's case was not high profile, so the only spectators were a few retirees who sat in on trials for entertainment. Mark Berman was along for moral support, and he and Dr. Langford took seats in the front row of the spectator section while Robin walked Erika through the bar of the court and seated her at the defense table.

"Wait here," Robin told her client. "I'm going to see if we can settle this without a trial."

Ian Hennessey was seated across from Carasco in the judge's chambers. They stopped talking when the bailiff opened the door for Robin.

"Ah, Ms. Lockwood," the judge said. "Come on in, and let's see what we can do here."

"Thanks, Judge."

Carasco studied Robin for a moment. "I don't think we've met before, but your name sounds familiar."

Robin was certain that the judge was going to bring up her career as a professional fighter. Then he smiled and said, "You endorsed my opponent, Molly Devereaux, when I ran against her. Am I right?"

The inappropriate remark shocked Robin, but trial lawyers train themselves to show no emotion when the unexpected happens.

"Molly is a friend," she answered, flashing her own smile.

"Of course," the judge said. "So, Ian, have you made Ms. Lockwood a reasonable offer?"

"I think so. We have her client dead to rights. Officer Balske is a ten-year veteran who was undercover posing as a john. He'll testify that the defendant offered to exchange oral sex for money. When Balske accepted, Ms. Lockwood's client started to unzip Officer Balske's fly, and Balske arrested him. I told Ms. Lockwood I would recommend probation if her client pleaded guilty, but she rejected the offer."

"The offer seems reasonable," Carasco said. "Why did you turn it down?"

"My client is a CPA with a good job and no priors. Very shortly, he will be going through gender reassignment surgery. I'm sure you can appreciate the stress he's under. His firm is very supportive, but a conviction, even for a misdemeanor, could cost him his job. I was hoping for a plea that involved diversion and a dismissal if he successfully completes the requirements of diversion."

"What do you say to that, Ian?" the judge asked.

"No go. I'm sure Stassen has been prostituting himself for a while."

"He told me that he has never been in a situation like this before," Robin said.

"I'd expect him to say that."

"Do you have any evidence to the contrary?"

"Look, Robin, it's plead or go to trial."

"Then we'll go to trial," Robin said.

"You might want to take some time to think about how you're going to advise your client, Robin," the judge said. "He could be facing jail if he insists on wasting the time of the court with a hopeless case."

"We don't think it's hopeless, Judge."

"From what Ian said, it sounds open and shut."

"We'll let the jury decide that."

Carasco shrugged. "Okay. Going to trial is a decision your client has to make. But you should make it clear to him that jail is a real possibility, and I don't think someone going through a sex change would do very well in jail with all those predators."

Carasco's unethical and insensitive comments infuriated Robin, but she controlled her temper. "I don't think it's appropriate to prejudge a sentence before hearing the facts."

Carasco smiled and held out his hands in a show of innocence. "I have no opinion on a sentence. How could I? As you said, I haven't heard the evidence. I'm just advising you about one possible outcome if your client insists on a trial."

Robin decided that she had to get out of Carasco's chambers before she said something she would regret.

"Let me talk to my client and see what she wants to do."

"Good," said Carasco. "Unless I hear you've accepted Ian's offer, I'll call for a jury in twenty minutes."

Hennessey waited until the door closed behind Robin. "Judge, I'm pretty new at this. After the trial, would you have the time to tell me what I did right and wrong?"

Carasco was about to turn down the request,

when he got an idea. "Sure, Ian," Carasco said. "We can talk after everyone leaves."

Hennessey walked out, and Carasco looked in his direction, but he wasn't really seeing him. What he did see was a future where he was free of his wife.

The judge and Hennessey had chatted while they waited for Robin, and Carasco learned that Hennessey was single. As soon as he'd found out that Robin Lockwood was representing the defendant, the judge had planned to punish her for supporting Devereaux by making this trial as hard for her as possible, but now he changed his mind. He decided to let the trial run its course. It might even work to his advantage if Lockwood won. After giving his idea more thought, Carasco phoned Stacey Hayes.

"What happened?" Erika asked.

"I'll tell you in a minute, but I'd like to get Mark's input before we discuss what we should do," Robin answered with a smile that betrayed none of the emotions she was feeling when she left Carasco's chambers.

Mark followed Robin into the corridor outside the courtroom. Several lawyers were in the hall talking to each other or their clients. Robin walked down the hall toward the back of the courthouse and around a corner into a deserted hallway.

Mark rounded the corner. His partner looked furious.

"What's wrong?" he asked.

"Carasco is an unethical prick," Robin spat out.

"Whoa! What brought that on?"

Robin told Mark what had happened in chambers.

"I have half a mind to report that asshole to the Judicial Fitness Commission," she said. "What if I were a new attorney and he threatened to put Erika in jail if I didn't force her to plead guilty?"

"You would have stood your ground."

"Others wouldn't."

"Look, Robin, Carasco can weasel out of any accusation you make. He'll tell the commission what he told you in chambers; that he was just informing you about a possible outcome but hadn't jumped to any conclusion about sentencing because he was going to keep an open mind until he heard the evidence."

"What about that crack about me endorsing Molly?"

"Hey, I'm not saying Carasco isn't an asshole. That's his rep. I'm just saying that you won't win if you report him, and you might have to go in front of him again. I know you're tough enough, but it's your client who'll suffer if he decides to screw you because you reported him."

Robin's shoulders sagged, and she sighed. "You're probably right."

"I am right," Mark insisted. "Carasco is bad news, but the State of Oregon is stuck with him until the next election. So, what are you going to tell Erika to do?"

"Go to trial, of course. I don't plead innocent clients."

CHAPTER SIX

"The State calls Curtis Balske, Your Honor," Ian Hennessey said.

The bailiff went into the hall and returned with a handsome, square-jawed man with wavy blond hair and a thick mustache, who looked like he belonged on a recruiting poster for the police academy. Robin had read his police report, and it seemed objective. She hoped he was an unbiased witness, because the report gave her hope.

As soon as Balske took the oath, Hennessey established that he was a decorated police officer assigned to Vice, who had volunteered to go undercover, pretending to be a man interested in purchasing sex.

"On Friday, May 13, did you encounter the defendant?" Hennessey asked.

"I did."

"Please tell the jury where you met him and what happened."

Balske turned to the jurors. "We had received information that prostitutes were operating in the Gold Piece nightclub. I went undercover to see if I could verify our intel. A little after eleven, the defendant struck up a conversation with me at the bar."

"What name did the defendant give you?"

"Erika."

"What did you believe the defendant's sex to be?"

"Female."

"When did you learn that the defendant is really a man?"

"After I arrested him."

"Thank you, Officer Balske. Please continue."

"At some point during our conversation, the defendant started talking about sex."

"He brought up the subject?"

"Yes, sir."

"What type of sex did he discuss?"

"Oral."

"Go on."

"The defendant said that I was handsome and that he felt a connection. Then he said that he enjoyed oral sex and asked if I liked it. I said that my wife didn't like oral sex but I did and that I'd paid as much as fifty dollars for oral sex. At that point, the defendant said that we should go into an alley next to the parking lot, where we could have some privacy."

"What happened in the alley?"

"As soon as we got there, the defendant started to open my zipper. That's when I displayed my badge and told him that he was under arrest."

"What did the defendant say to that?"

"He seemed shocked, and he asked why I was arresting him. I told him he was under arrest for prostitution."

"How did the defendant react?"

"He started crying. He said that he didn't know he was committing a crime and begged me to let him go. Then he said that he was a CPA and he would lose his job if I arrested him. I told him I couldn't let him go and that we had to go to the station so he could be booked in. That's when he told me that he was a man going through a sex change. He was terrified that he would be raped if I put him in jail."

"What did you tell him?" Hennessey asked.

"I told the defendant that I would make sure he wouldn't have to stay in jail. He thanked me, and I took him to my car and drove downtown, where I booked him in and let him go."

"Thank you, Officer. No further questions."

"Ms. Lockwood?" the judge said.

"Officer Balske, I want to thank you for the compassion you showed to Ms. Stassen . . ."

"Objection," Hennessey said. "The defendant is a man."

"That's true, Your Honor," Robin said, "but Ms. Stassen identifies as a woman, looks like a woman, and has done everything to become a woman except have an operation, which is scheduled for two months from now."

"Nevertheless, Ms. Lockwood," Carasco said, "right now, in this courtroom, your client is legally male. So, I am going to sustain the objection and order you to use male pronouns."

"Very well," Robin said. Then she addressed the witness. "If I understand your testimony, my client asked if you liked oral sex?"

"Yes."

"You said you did and that you'd paid as much as fifty dollars for oral sex?"

"Yes."

"So, you were the first person to mention money."

Balske hesitated, then agreed that he had mentioned the money first.

"Did Mr. Stassen ask you for fifty dollars?"

Balske's brow furrowed, and he took a moment to answer. "No."

"Did money ever change hands?"

"I arrested the defendant before it could."

"So, your answer is that my client never asked you for money and no money changed hands?"

"I . . . Yes."

"Thank you. I have no further questions."

Hennessey's pale complexion reddened. "Officer Balske, it was obvious, wasn't it, that Mr. Stassen expected to get paid for oral sex?"

"Objection, Your Honor. The officer can't read minds."

"Sustained."

"You are an experienced Vice officer, aren't you?"

"Yes, sir."

"And you've been involved in many pros-titution cases and arrests?"

"Yes."

"In your experience, did what happened in the Gold Piece conform to the actions of prostitutes in the cases in which you have been involved or have learned about in your capacity as a Vice officer?"

"Objection, irrelevant and prejudicial. We are talking about this particular case. Not cases in general."

"No, Ms. Lockwood. The officer qualifies as an expert, so I'm going to let him answer."

"What happened between me and the defendant is similar to what happens in the typical prostitution case."

"No further questions, Your Honor."

"Ms. Lockwood?" the judge asked.

"Officer Balske, isn't it true that men and women go to bars all the time to meet partners who will agree to have sex in situations that do not constitute the crime of prostitution?"

Balske smiled. "Of course."

The Golden Rule of cross-examination was "Never ask a question if you don't know the answer," but Balske seemed to be unbiased, so Robin decided to take a chance.

"Given the fact that you were the one who brought up money and my client never asked for money, couldn't what happened in the Gold Piece simply qualify as a situation where my client found you attractive and wanted a nonprofessional sexual relationship?"

Balske thought over what Robin had said. Then he nodded. "It could have."

"No further questions."

Hennessey looked upset, but he didn't ask any more questions.

"The State rests," Hennessey told the judge.

"Any witnesses, Ms. Lockwood?"

"May I have a moment to confer with my client?"

"Of course."

Robin thought about making a motion to have the case dismissed for lack of evidence, but she decided that Carasco would deny her motion because of Balske's opinion that Erika's actions fit the pattern of a typical prostitution case.

Robin leaned over and whispered to Erika, "I'm going to call you next."

"Do you have to? I'm scared to death."

"I know you're scared, but you didn't do anything wrong. The jury needs to hear from you. We went over what I'm going to ask. Remember what I told you. Just talk to the jurors as if they're friends who are having dinner with you."

"What about cross-examination? He'll try to trip me up."

"Hennessey is new, and he'll be aggressive. Jurors don't like attorneys who are mean or disrespectful. If you stay calm and tell the truth, Hennessey won't be able to touch you."

"I don't know if I can do this."

"Look, Erika, if you've got the guts to change your sex, you're tough enough to survive cross-examination. You're also innocent. Tell the truth and you'll be okay."

"Ms. Lockwood?" the judge asked.

"I call Mr. Stassen to the stand."

CHAPTER SEVEN

"Mr. Stassen, are you a lifelong Oregonian?" Robin asked after her client was sworn.

"I am."

"Where were you born?"

"In Portland."

"Do your parents still live here?"

"Yes."

"Are you close with them?"

"I am."

"Do they support your decision to go through an operation to change your sex?"

Hennessey leaped to his feet. "Objection, hearsay and irrelevant."

"Sustained. Please move on, Ms. Lockwood."

"Very well, Your Honor. Where did you go to school?"

"Wilson High School and the University of Oregon."

"What degree did you receive from the U of O?"

"I majored in accounting."

"Did you graduate with honors?"

"Yes."

"After you graduated, did you become a certified public accountant?"

"Yes."

"Where was your first job?"

"I was hired by the Internal Revenue Service to investigate cases of tax fraud."

"How long did you stay at that job?"

"Five years."

"What did you do after that?"

"I missed Oregon, so I moved home and was hired by the accounting firm where I am currently employed."

"At some point in your life, did you begin to feel uncomfortable as a male?"

"Since I was little, I had the feeling that I was in the wrong body, that I should have been a girl."

"When did you decide to go through the procedure for gender reassignment?"

"Three years ago."

"Was this decision difficult?"

"It was a terrible time for me. I was torn apart emotionally. But I was seeing a wonderful therapist, and she put me in touch with the transgender program at the medical school, and they gave me the confidence to make my decision."

"Let's turn to the events that have brought you here. On Friday, May 13, did you go to the Gold Piece?"

"Yes."

"Were you dressed as a male or a female?"

"A female."

"Why did you do that?"

"I felt like a woman. Except for the operation, I am a woman, and . . . well, I wanted to see if the men and women at the bar would react to me as if I were a woman."

"Had you ever done anything like this before, going to a bar as a woman?"

"No."

"How did you feel when you entered the Gold Piece?"

"I was frightened and excited at the same time."

"At some point in the evening, did you initiate contact with Officer Balske?"

"Yes."

"Why did you do that?"

Erika blushed. "He's very handsome, and I was attracted to him."

"How did Officer Balske respond to you when you started to talk to him?"

"I thought he was interested in me." Erika looked down. "Of course, now I know he really wasn't."

"Did you initiate a discussion about sex?"

"Yes."

"Why?"

"I wanted to see if he was attracted to me enough to want to have sex."

"Did he appear to be interested in that way?"

"Yes."

"Did you turn the conversation to oral sex?"

"Yes."

"Why?"

Erika's embarrassment was evident. "It was the only way I could do it. I couldn't let him see that I . . . that my genitals . . . I was afraid he might hit me if he knew . . ."

"Do you want some water?" Robin asked. "Do you need a short break?"

Erika shook her head. "No, please, I just want to finish this."

"Okay," Robin said. "Please tell the jury whether you ever asked Officer Balske to pay you for sex."

Erika took a deep breath and looked directly at the jury. "I didn't want money. I wouldn't have taken any money. That's not why I wanted to . . . to do it. I make a good living. Fifty dollars wouldn't mean anything to me. I just wanted to know if he thought I was attractive enough to want me."

"No further questions."

Hennessey strutted over to the witness-box and stared at Erika for a moment before beginning to question her. Erika tried to look Hennessey in the eye, but she broke eye contact. Hennessey smiled at this minor victory.

"Now, *Mr.* Stassen, didn't Officer Balske tell you that he had paid fifty dollars for oral sex?"

"Yes."

"And the next thing you did was invite him into the alley next to the parking lot, right?"

"Yes."

"When he agreed, you expected him to give you fifty dollars, didn't you?"

"No. I didn't ask him for money."

"You claim that you went to the Gold Piece because you wanted to see if you would be accepted as a woman. Right?"

"Yes."

"Wouldn't getting paid by a man for sex make you feel that Officer Balske saw you as a woman?"

"I told you, I wasn't interested in the money. I have a good job. It pays well. I didn't think about the fifty dollars. It wasn't important."

Hennessey pounced. "But your job is important, isn't it?"

"Yes."

"And you could lose your job if you're convicted of a crime, right?"

"I . . . Yes, that could happen."

"And you would do anything to keep that job, wouldn't you, including lying to this jury?"

Hennessey made a dramatic about-face and walked back to his seat as Erika stuttered her denial.

"Ms. Lockwood?" the judge asked.

"Nothing further."

Erika walked back to her seat at the counsel table with her head down, looking like a convict on the way to the electric chair.

"I feel sick," she said.

"You shouldn't," Robin said. "Hennessey just won the case for us."

"How can you say that? He made me look like a liar."

"No, Erika, he just told the jury that you would be fired if they convicted you, and that created more sympathy for your cause than anything I could say."

CHAPTER EIGHT

"Do you have any more witnesses, Ms. Lockwood?" Judge Carasco asked.

"Yes, Your Honor. We call Dr. Margery Langford."

As soon as the witness was sworn, Robin asked, "Dr. Langford, can you please give the jurors a summary of your educational background?"

"Certainly," Langford said before turning toward the jurors and smiling. "I received my bachelor of science in biology, with a minor in psychology, from Oregon State University. I received a doctorate in psychology from the University of California at Berkeley. Then I participated in the postdoctoral program at the Veterans Administration in Portland, where I specialized in the treatment of post-traumatic stress disorder."

"Thank you. At some point, did you develop an interest in helping men and women with gender identity problems?"

"I did."

"When did that happen?"

"I'd had a few patients at the VA who were experiencing gender confusion, so I started researching the area. Near the end of my stay at the VA, I saw an ad for a psychologist that had

49

been posted by the Transgender Health Program at the Oregon Health & Science University. I applied and was hired."

"Do you know Eric Stassen?"

"I do, and I prefer to refer to her as Erika for professional reasons."

"Can you explain your decision to the jurors?"

"Erika was born male and was named Eric, but he never felt comfortable as a male. It was very difficult for him to make the decision to change his gender expression. Once he did, he began referring to himself as a woman, and he has taken many difficult steps to get to the point of physically and psychologically becoming a woman."

"Can you tell the jury about those difficult steps?"

"I can." Dr. Langford turned to the jurors. "One step was coming out to his parents, friends, and coworkers. You can imagine how embarrassing and anxiety producing that was. Then Erika worked with me and the team at OHSU and began her gender transition during a two-year period. During this time, Erika dressed as a woman at work, at social gatherings, went grocery shopping dressed as a woman, and had to endure some pointed questions and a lot of abuse associated with this.

"Erika also underwent hormone replacement therapy, therapy to change her voice, and experienced laser hair removal, which is painful, lengthy, and expensive. After going through all that, I feel Eric has earned the right to be called Erika."

"What are the final steps a man takes when he transitions into being a female?"

"He may undergo thyroid cartilage reduction surgery to reduce the size of his Adam's apple, undergo breast implants, and endure face feminization surgery. Finally, Erika is planning to undergo a surgical procedure called a vaginoplasty that will remove his male genitalia and create female genitals. As you can imagine, this is expensive and not a lot of fun."

"Thank you, Dr. Langford. Now, are you aware that Erika had been charged with committing the crime of prostitution, which requires the State to prove that she offered to engage in sex with the arresting officer for money?"

Hennessey stood up. "Despite your ruling, Your Honor, Ms. Lockwood is continuing to refer to the defendant as a female. I object and ask the court to instruct the witness and counsel to follow your prior ruling."

"Mr. Hennessey," the judge said, "in light of Dr. Langford's testimony, I am going to reverse my ruling and allow counsel and her witness to refer to the defendant with a feminine pronoun."

Hennessey started to argue. Then he thought better of it and sat down.

Robin was surprised by Carasco's ruling, but she didn't show her feelings. Instead, she repeated the question, and Dr. Langford said she was aware of the charge.

"How long have you treated Erika?"

"It's been three years."

"How many times a week do you and she talk?"

"Three scheduled meetings, but she calls whenever she needs my help."

"You've heard Erika testify that she had no interest in receiving money when she volunteered to engage in sex with Officer Balske. In your expert opinion as a professional who treats men who are transitioning to being female, and as someone who has worked closely with Erika, does that sound reasonable?"

"Definitely. Any transsexual wants to have his or her gender expression validated, and one of the best ways to do this is to have a person of the opposite sex attracted enough to want to engage in sexual relations."

"Thank you, Dr. Langford. No further questions."

"Dr. Langford, during your three years treating Mr. Stassen, have you grown to like him?" Hennessey asked when he began his cross-examination.

"Yes. She's very sincere about her goals and has sacrificed to reach them. I find that very admirable."

"You weren't present at the Gold Piece when this incident occurred, were you?"

"No."

"So, you only have the defendant's word that she wasn't trading sex for money?"

"Yes."

"Since you like Mr. Stassen, do you feel that you want to help him by telling this jury you believe him?"

"Of course, but I think her explanation makes perfect sense in light of what I've learned about Erika during our professional relationship."

"Tell me, Dr. Langford, have you heard of men transitioning to women who have engaged in prostitution to validate their sexuality?"

"I have."

"In fact, that's not uncommon, is it?"

"No."

"No further questions."

"Ms. Lockwood?" the judge asked.

"Dr. Langford, is there a reason besides validating their gender expression that a male transitioning to a woman might engage in prostitution?"

"Yes. Survival. It's not easy being a transsexual in our society. As a result of prejudice, they have higher rates of unemployment and a greater risk of poverty."

"Does your knowledge of the reason many transgender people engage in prostitution support your belief that Erika did not engage in prostitution?"

"Yes. She has a job that pays very well, so she has a nice home, health care, and so on. Survival is not a problem for Erika, but validating her identity is."

CHAPTER NINE

The State had no rebuttal, so the judge instructed the jury after Robin and Hennessey gave their closing arguments. Robin was always nervous when the jury was out. A verdict in an MMA fight came quickly. If you or your opponent were knocked out or tapped out, the fight was over. If the bout ended with both fighters on their feet, the judge's decision was announced within minutes. But a jury could be out for days, and Robin had learned that trying to predict how jurors would vote was a waste of time.

Robin remembered a monthlong, multi-defendant murder case involving two gangs, extreme violence, and no light moments. Her client had the only viable defense, and some of the jurors had smiled at him on occasion. The jury was out for two days. When Robin heard some of the jurors laughing in the hall before returning with the verdict, she was certain that her client would walk. Guilty on all counts.

Robin, Mark, and Erika had gone for coffee in a shop near the courthouse to wait for the verdict. Robin had a good feeling about the case, but her nerves began to fray when an hour passed without a verdict. Then, fifteen minutes later, the bailiff called to let her know that the jury was back.

Robin looked calm, but her stomach was in a knot when the bailiff brought in the stone-faced jurors.

"Have you reached a verdict?" Anthony Carasco asked the foreperson when the jurors were seated.

"We have," answered a forty-two-year-old housewife and mother of two, whose husband was a pastor at a Lutheran church. Hennessey brightened. He was certain that she would be put off by a transgender woman, and he'd slotted her in as a vote for conviction.

"How do you find the defendant on the charge of prostitution?"

"We find the defendant not guilty."

Hennessey's mouth opened involuntarily, and his face flushed bright red. Erika looked stunned, and Robin squeezed her hand under the table.

"Would you like the jury polled?" the judge asked.

"We're satisfied, Your Honor," Robin said.

"Yes. I would," Hennessey said. He was certain that there was a mistake; that the foreperson had misread the verdict. But the verdict was unanimous, and several jurors nodded or smiled at Erika, who was unable to keep tears from running down her cheeks.

Robin and her client left the courtroom quickly, but Hennessey lingered. When everyone but Al Moody, the bailiff, was gone, Hennessey told

Moody that he would like to talk to the judge. Moments later, the bailiff came out of Carasco's chambers and told the deputy district attorney that the judge would see him in a few minutes.

While he waited, Hennessey rehashed the case. He couldn't believe he'd lost. The case was open and shut. People who changed their sex were freaks, so he figured Stassen wouldn't get an ounce of sympathy. Hennessey tried to figure out the specific point in time his case had gone south. Lockwood wasn't that good. His closing argument had been much better. She'd argued that Stassen was never interested in trading sex for money, but Stassen had said they should go in the alley as soon as Balske mentioned the fifty bucks. How could the jury ignore that?

"The judge will see you now," the bailiff said.

Hennessey hurried into Carasco's chambers. Carasco was talking to his secretary.

"You can take off," Carasco said.

"See you tomorrow, Judge."

"And tell Al he can go too."

"Will do."

Carasco turned his attention to Hennessey, who was visibly upset.

"Have a seat," Carasco said. "That was a tough loss."

"Can you tell me what I did wrong? I mean, Stassen was guilty as hell."

"Maybe, maybe not. Lockwood raised a

reasonable doubt about the key issue, which was whether her client expected to be paid for giving your cop a blow job. And she brought in a very convincing expert. Did you know the doctor was going to testify?"

"Yeah. I got the witness list."

"Did you try to interview her?"

Hennessey reddened. "I didn't have the time. You know how many case files a new DA gets. I gave the case a fast look-see and figured Stassen would plead or I'd have an easy win."

"There you are. First thing you need to know, if Robin Lockwood is trying the case, it's never easy. Second thing, when you see that the other side has an expert, you'd better bone up on the subject area and find an expert you can bring in."

"Yeah, I see that now."

Someone knocked on the door to the judge's chambers.

"It's not locked," Carasco said. "Come on in."

The door opened, and Hennessey forgot all about his case.

"Ah, Stacey. I was in trial all day, and I didn't get a chance to call. I'm afraid I can't have dinner tonight. I have a ton of work to catch up on and the trial ran late, so I have to burn the midnight oil."

Stacey's smile disappeared. She was so beautiful and she looked so disappointed that Hennessey wanted to comfort her.

Carasco turned to the deputy DA. "Ian, this is

Stacey Hayes, the daughter of a friend. She's in town job hunting. Stacey, this is Ian Hennessey, one of our brighter DAs."

"Pleased to meet you," Ian said, feeling instantly stupid for saying something so trite.

Stacey smiled. "Were you involved in Tony's case?"

"I was," Hennessey answered, hoping desperately that this stunning woman wouldn't ask about the outcome and think he was a loser. The judge came to the rescue.

"Say, I just had an idea," Carasco said. "Ian, do you have dinner plans?"

"Uh, no," said Hennessey, who had been resigned to a takeout dinner from one of the local food carts.

"I have a reservation for two at Bocci's, one of my favorite Italian restaurants," Carasco said. "It would be a shame to waste it. Why don't you take Stacey? She's new in town. You can give her the rundown on what to do in Portland."

Hennessey couldn't believe his luck. "Sure, if Miss Hayes . . ."

"It's Stacey if we're going to talk all evening. And I'd love to get your take on what's good in Portland."

"Then that's settled," Carasco said. "You two scram so I can get some work done."

Hennessey and Stacey left, and Carasco smiled. Everything was going as planned.

CHAPTER TEN

Erika thanked Robin over and over until they said goodbye outside the courthouse.

"You were terrific," Mark Berman said as the law partners headed back to their office.

"I was lucky the State's key witness was honest, because I don't know what I would have done if we'd lost and Carasco put Erika in jail."

When Robin returned to her office, she met with Loretta Washington, a five-foot-one African American dynamo, whom Robin had nicknamed "The Flash," because she was always in motion. The firm had been bringing in too much business for Mark and Robin to handle alone, so they had hired two associates. Loretta, like Robin, was the first person in her family to graduate from college. She'd grown up in the Bronx, graduated from Queens College in New York, and traveled to Portland when she'd received a full ride from Lewis & Clark Law School. Loretta had finished fifth in her class, had clerked on the Oregon Supreme Court, and was not only a brilliant appellate attorney but was showing promise as a trial lawyer. She was also fun to be around.

Loretta had researched an evidence issue Robin wanted to raise in a brief and had advised against it for very sound reasons. Robin accepted

Loretta's analysis reluctantly before sending her on her way. By the time she finished the conference, the sun was down, and Robin was wiped out from the trial and starving. She grabbed some sushi to go and took the bus to her apartment.

Jeff was in Central Oregon investigating a personal injury case for Mark. When she flipped on the light in their apartment, she saw that the dishwasher was open and the sink was full of her dirty dishes. A note on the dishwasher in Jeff's handwriting asked her to run it.

Living with Jeff had, for the most part, been great. Robin loved Jeff and he loved her, but that didn't mean that everything was always rosy. Robin was fiercely independent and had an aversion to being ordered around her whole life. She had sued the school board and won when they refused to let a girl wrestle on the boys' high school team. She had rebelled against going to a state law school and instead had excelled at a top law school on the East Coast, a part of the country that the people in her small farming community talked about in whispers. Her mother's fondest wish was for Robin to come home, marry a nice, local boy, and have children, but Robin had moved to Oregon. Her independent streak extended to her career as a lawyer, during which, to Jeff's dismay, she had risked her life for a client or friend on more than one occasion.

That wasn't the only trait of Robin's that upset Jeff. He was a neat freak, and Robin was not. She left newspapers scattered around after she read them, she didn't make the bed, and she, as Jeff had duly noted, tossed dirty dishes in the sink without rinsing them off or taking the time to put them in the dishwasher.

Jeff had tried to impose his sense of order on Robin soon after they'd started living together. Robin resented any effort to control her, no matter how small, and this had been a source of tension in an otherwise happy relationship. Robin ignored the note. She would run the dishwasher when she was good and ready.

Thinking about her mother made Robin feel guilty. Her father had always supported her. He was the one who hired the lawyer to fight the school board when it had ruled that she couldn't wrestle on the boys' team, and he encouraged her to go to law school at Yale, but her dad had passed away, and Robin felt bad about living so far from her mother. Her three brothers still lived in town. They were married, had kids, and visited often. Sometimes, Robin felt like the black sheep in the family because she wasn't there for her mom, even though she was the most successful child.

Robin thought about calling home, but she was too exhausted to put up with her mother's questions about when she was going to visit and whether she still enjoyed her job, and her lengthy play-by-play of the incredible accomplishments of her grandchildren.

Robin took her sushi and a cup of green tea to the sofa and turned on the television. The Blazers were playing the Knicks. Robin pecked at her food while the ball bounced back and forth across the hardwood. Somewhere in the third quarter, she fell asleep.

PART TWO
NO HOLDS BARRED

CHAPTER ELEVEN

Portland had a notorious homeless problem, and over the years, tent cities had sprung up. Some were permanent, but others existed only until they were shut down by the authorities. Some of the homeless were mentally ill or addicted. Others had lost their residences when they had their rent increased, or they lost their jobs and could not find another. Joe Lattimore had been unfortunate on both counts.

Joe's skin was the color of anthracite coal, his right cheek was decorated with a reminder of a teenage knife fight, and he was five feet eleven inches of sculpted muscle. Joe had fought professionally, and he'd fought for survival in the housing project where he grew up. As far back as he could remember, his life had been one long struggle.

Joe had a wife he loved, a baby girl he adored, and temporary housing in one of the tent cities. Living in the homeless enclave was safer than the streets, but there were crazy people and junkies living nearby, so Joe worried constantly about Maria, the baby, and earning the money he needed to move his family somewhere safe.

There were two things Joe did well—cook and fight. He was a decent fighter, but his manager had trouble getting him fights, and the purses, minus expenses, never amounted to much. Joe had stopped fighting when Maria told him she was pregnant, and he decided that he needed steady work to support the baby.

Joe had learned how to cook in the army and he found a good job that paid a decent wage at the Imperial Diner. Unfortunately, Joe could not control his temper. At the Imperial, he was often the butt of jokes. That led to more fights and the loss of his job.

Joe's reputation as a troublemaker followed him, and he couldn't find work. Out of desperation, Joe had called his manager to see if he could get him a fight. His manager was sympathetic, but Joe hadn't fought in a while and he'd never been a big name. The manager said he would try, but he told Joe not to hold out much hope. Joe knew a payday from fighting was a long shot, but he would have to be in shape if something came through, so he'd started working out again.

This morning, Joe kissed Maria goodbye and started running at a steady pace. Joe's route took him onto a bike path that ran along the river for five miles before he ran back to the homeless enclave along city streets. He was four miles from the tent city when the black car passed him. A half a mile later, he saw it again, this time parked at the curb. A rail-thin white man was standing beside it, smoking. He wore his greasy black hair in a ducktail that had been popular with juvenile delinquents in the 1950s, and his black leather jacket and tight jeans made him look like an extra in a teen movie from that time.

When Joe got closer, the man dropped the cigarette into the street and held up his hand. Joe slowed down. The man walked toward him. Joe stood sideways, ready to fight. The man smiled.

"It's Joe, right? Lattimore?"

"Yeah."

"I'm Sal. I saw you fight Reilly a few years back. Good fight. I thought you got robbed," Sal said.

"What's this about?" Joe asked.

Sal grinned. "No need to get defensive. I know you're down on your luck, and I'm here to give you an opportunity to make some money doing what you do best."

The mention of money got Joe's attention. "I'm listening."

"I have a friend. He puts on fights. The fights are no-holds-barred, winner takes all."

"Is that legal?"

Sal laughed. "You know the answer to that one. The important thing is you get three hundred dollars for a few minutes' work, the first time you fight. If you look good, you get asked back, and the next time you get a bigger payday. You interested?"

Joe was desperate to move Maria and the baby someplace safe. Three hundred dollars would get them a few days at a motel while he hunted for work.

"When would this happen?" he asked.

"End of the week. You in?"

Joe hesitated. Then he nodded.

"There's a vacant lot near the on-ramp to the interstate a few blocks from your camp. Be there at eight on Sunday. A van will drive up. That's your ride. Got that?"

"Yeah. Eight, Sunday."

"Good luck, Joe," Sal said. Then he got in his car without looking back and drove away.

Joe watched the car until it disappeared. His gut was in a knot. The type of fight the man had described was usually run by gangsters, and he couldn't afford to get arrested. His brain told him that he shouldn't get involved, but he needed the money. Going up against untrained fighters seemed like an easy way to make some.

Joe started back toward Maria and the baby. He had a few days to make up his mind. Three hundred dollars was a lot of money for someone who was depending on food kitchens to feed his family, but getting involved with criminals . . .

Running usually relaxed Joe, but he was uneasy all the way back to the camp.

CHAPTER TWELVE

The sun had set by the time Joe found the trash-filled lot near the on-ramp to the freeway where he'd been told to wait for the van. When the van stopped next to the lot, a bald, three-hundred-pound giant with gang tattoos and a cauliflower ear got out and slid open the rear door. Joe hesitated.

"Get the fuck in or don't," the driver said. "I ain't waiting."

Joe overcame his fear and climbed in. There was a bench on either side of the van's interior, but no windows. When the door slammed shut, the interior was almost completely dark and Joe had a hard time making out the other riders. He took a seat next to a grossly overweight woman with narrow-set eyes and an odor that made it hard to breathe. Across from Joe was a lanky six-footer whose foot tapped incessantly and whose knee jerked from nerves. He glanced at Joe, then looked away quickly. Seated beside the nervous passenger was a muscular African American who weighed a tight two hundred pounds.

Joe smiled at him and asked, "Any idea where we're headed, bro?"

"I ain't your brother, motherfucker."

Joe knew you never showed fear, so he glared at the man to show that he wasn't intimidated, but there was a knot in his stomach, and he hoped that this wasn't the person he would have to fight.

The trip started on pavement. After three-quarters of an hour, the van began bouncing, and Joe guessed that they were somewhere in the country on an unpaved road. After twenty-five more minutes, the van stopped, and the giant opened the door. Joe hopped out and found that he was staring at the side of a barn. He looked around and saw cars parked in a field and a gravel lot. Suddenly, a roar went up inside the barn.

The giant opened the barn door, and Joe stepped into an open area surrounded on two sides by stalls and hay bales. Screaming men and women were crowding around a cleared space where a blond woman and an Asian woman were fighting. The Asian had her hands up to fend off a furious assault. One eye was swollen shut, and she was bleeding from her nose and mouth. The other woman landed a ferocious kick to the stomach, and her opponent collapsed on the dirt floor. As soon as the bleeding woman hit the ground, the blonde dropped on her, pinned her shoulders to the ground, and began raining punches on her unprotected head as the crowd cheered.

Joe recognized the referee as Sal, the man with the fifties retro look who had recruited him. He thought that the fight should have been stopped, but Sal let the carnage continue for a while before stepping in and pulling the blonde off her unconscious opponent. Two men with bouncers' builds dragged the defeated woman away and dumped her at the side of the barn. Joe felt sick. He'd bled and watched opponents bleed in fights, but the referees and the fighters' corners stepped in whenever a fighter was in real danger. Sal had let the fight continue well past the point of serious injury.

A well-dressed man in tan slacks, a white silk shirt, and a navy blazer walked over to the new recruits. He was Joe's size, and bulging muscles strained the seams of his jacket and pushed out his shirt front. The man smiled, revealing pearly-white teeth.

"Welcome to fight night, boys and girls. As you've just witnessed, we don't expect mercy and our attendees love to see blood, so do your best. There are no rules here. Gouging, kicks to the nuts, and every other form of mayhem is allowed. Winners get money, losers go home broke. And that's all you need to know."

The man handed out a clipboard and told the new arrivals to print their first names.

"I'll be pairing you up soon, so do whatever you need to do to get ready. Best of luck."

Joe was wearing a T-shirt, sweatshirt, and pants over shorts. He stripped off the tee, sweatshirt, and pants and stuffed them in a duffel bag. He would fight shirtless so his opponent would have nothing to grab.

Joe started to work up a sweat to loosen his muscles and make it even harder for his opponent to get a hold on his slippery skin. As he warmed up, Joe scanned the crowd. Some of the women wore jewels and designer clothes and were with men who would have been at home in a country club. Others in the crowd looked like they would never have been allowed on the country club grounds. There were bikers, sharp-dressed men with wads of cash, and men and women who looked like they belonged in a movie about drug cartels.

While he was surveying the crowd, Joe saw the Asian woman get to her feet and stagger out of the barn. She was in bad shape, and Joe wondered if there was a doctor present. He stopped thinking about her when the referee stepped into the cleared space and called the names of the muscle-bound black man from the van and the lanky, nervous man who'd sat beside him. The black man laughed as he walked through the crowd. His opponent looked frightened.

"Next up," the referee said into his handheld microphone, "we have Mustafa and Alan. Place your bets, and we'll get started."

There was a flurry of activity as the fighters warmed up. Mustafa flexed his muscles and smiled at his opponent, who didn't make eye contact. When the bets had been placed, the man in the blazer nodded.

"Okay, fellas," Sal said. "Let's get it on."

Mustafa charged. Alan slipped to one side and slammed a foot into Mustafa's knee. A look of shock crossed Mustafa's face as the knee buckled. Alan torqued his hips and followed the kick with a vicious elbow strike to Mustafa's temple. The big man sagged to the ground. Alan leaped on his back and threw on a choke hold. Mustafa lurched backward, but his tormenter rolled with him. Mustafa threw a wild punch, but Alan buried his head behind his victim and ground his teeth into Mustafa's ear. The black man screamed, and Alan tightened the choke hold. Mustafa grabbed Alan's arm and tried to loosen the hold, but he was weakening, and moments later, he was unconscious.

While Sal was raising Alan's hand, the man in the blazer walked over to Joe.

"You're up. Good luck."

Joe walked into the open space and tried to block out the crowd. He always had prefight jitters, but they were worse tonight. He ran to keep fit, but he worried that the lack of sparring would affect his timing.

Joe was rotating his neck and loosening his shoulders when Sal led his opponent out of an office near the back of the barn. Joe thought it was odd for the referee to bring a fighter into the ring, but he needed to concentrate on the fight, so he tossed the thought aside.

Joe's opponent was taller and heavier than Joe, but he was flabby and looked older by several years. Joe knew better than to underestimate an opponent, but the man looked out of shape, and that gave him hope. He decided to box at a distance and wear the man out, then finish him when he got tired and his hands started to drop.

Sal stepped between the combatants and spoke into the mic.

"Next up, we have Joe and Carlos. You fellas ready?"

Joe nodded, but Carlos just stared. His eyes looked glassy, and Joe frowned. When the spectators finished laying their bets, the man in the blazer signaled the referee.

"Okay, gentlemen. Let's get it on."

Joe was a professional boxer, and boxers were only allowed to use their fists in a fight. But Joe had been in more than his share of street fights, where you used every part of your body in an effort to stay alive. In a boxing match, you only had to worry about the reach of an opponent's arms, but Carlos could use his legs, and Joe made a mental calculation of the reach of both sets of limbs as he stepped forward with his hands up.

Carlos charged, but he was slow. Joe sidestepped and landed a punch to his opponent's neck. Carlos staggered. Joe was tempted to step in and land another punch, but he didn't know how much the punch had affected Carlos.

Carlos shuffled toward Joe and threw a few ineffectual jabs. Joe kept just out of range. Carlos lunged forward and threw a slow, looping roundhouse right that Joe blocked easily before kicking Carlos in the shin. Carlos dropped his hands, and Joe threw a vicious hook. Joe wasn't wearing boxing gloves, which would have blunted some of the force of a punch. His knuckles were wrapped in tape to protect them, and the tape ripped open the skin over Carlos's eye. Blood ran down, blinding him. Joe moved to his opponent's blind side and hit him in the jaw.

Carlos staggered back and raised his hands. He looked groggy. Joe shot a kick to the bigger man's groin. When Carlos sagged, Joe broke Carlos's nose. Carlos flailed in defense, but his punches were very slow. Joe's next flurry sent Carlos to the ground, and Joe leaped on him, landing punch after punch to the head.

The crowd roared with bloodlust. Sal kept his distance. Joe raised his hand to land one more blow when he noticed that his opponent's eyes were closed. Fear gripped him, and he leaped to his feet. He'd lost himself in the fury of the fight. Boxers wanted to win, but most fighters never wanted to seriously injure another fighter so badly that it would affect his livelihood. Carlos looked like he might be in very bad shape.

"We need a doctor!" Joe shouted.

Sal rushed to the fallen man. Then a skinny

man in a gray suit carrying a black bag knelt beside Carlos. The man in the blazer joined Sal and the doctor, and they conducted a whispered conversation. After a minute, the man in the blazer walked over to Joe.

"Wait here while I clear the barn."

"What's wrong?" Joe asked nervously.

"I'll explain in a minute," he said. Then he took the microphone from the referee.

"Ladies and gentlemen, we have a situation that needs attending to, so I'm afraid our evening is at an end. Please leave the barn in an orderly manner, and thanks for coming. We'll notify you about the time and place of our next event in the usual way."

The crowd rushed out. Joe heard car engines starting and the crunch of tires on gravel as the parking area emptied. The man in the blazer moved Joe far away from Carlos.

"Is he okay?" Joe asked nervously.

"I'm afraid Carlos is dead," the man in the blazer said.

"Oh no," Joe whispered as his knees buckled.

The man with the blazer laid a gentle hand on Joe's shoulder.

"You're going to be okay. I'll see to that."

"But I . . ."

"You didn't do anything, and you didn't see anything. Forget you were ever here. Understand?"

Joe nodded. He felt numb.

"Give me your hand wraps."

Joe gave the hand wraps to the man, who handed him an envelope stuffed with cash.

"There's a little extra in here for your troubles. Now, go outside and we'll get you home."

Joe left the barn in a daze. Maybe they had made a mistake, he thought, and Carlos was just unconscious. He hoped that was the case, because it would be hard to live with himself if he'd killed Carlos.

"He's hurt bad, Kevin," the doctor told the man in the blazer when the crowd and the fighters were gone.

"Okay, Doc, thanks."

"He should go to a hospital."

Kevin smiled. "Great advice. I'll take it from here. Why don't you take off?"

"But—"

Kevin handed the doctor an envelope filled with cash. "I appreciate all you do for us. Go home, get some rest."

The doctor left, and Kevin knelt next to Carlos. He was emitting rasping breaths but wasn't doing much more. The truth was that Carlos never stood a chance after he drank the drug-laced water Kevin had given him before the fight.

Kevin stripped naked to keep blood, which would be trace evidence, off his clothes. After wrapping Joe's hand wraps around his knuckles, he pounded Carlos until the breathing stopped. Kevin checked for a pulse. When he didn't find one, he called over the men who had carried the Asian woman out of the ring.

"Get rid of this sack of shit where I told you to dump him," Kevin said as he took off the hand wraps and put them in a plastic bag.

The men carried Carlos outside through a back door while Kevin dressed. Kevin had recruiters in the homeless enclaves who scouted talent for him. When the recruiter told him about Joe, he knew he'd found the perfect patsy and the key ingredient in a big payday. When he was alone, Kevin took out his phone and sent a text that read, "ALL GOOD."

CHAPTER THIRTEEN

Joe paced back and forth next to the van. Fifteen minutes later, the giant who'd driven Joe to the fight walked out of the barn and opened the van door. Joe climbed in, expecting to see the other people who'd driven to the barn with him, but he was the only passenger.

Joe felt sick during the ride to town. He kept picturing Carlos's battered face. When the van stopped, the door slid open, and the driver sat down across from Joe.

"We need to talk," the giant said.

"About what?"

"About your future."

The driver showed him his gun. Joe tensed.

"Stay calm. This is just to get your attention. The last thing I want to do is shoot you."

"What . . . what do you want?"

"I want to help you."

Joe was confused. If the giant wanted to help him, why did he have a gun?

"Here's what you need to know. There's a recording of your fight that shows you beating a man to death. The recording will be given to the cops along with the location of the body, unless you do what you're told."

Joe thought he might throw up. If he went to

81

prison, how would Maria and the baby survive? The driver could see that he'd lost Joe.

"Hey, snap out of it and pay attention."

Joe took a breath and stared across the van. The driver was holding out his hand. There was a phone in it.

"Keep this with you at all times. Someone will call you and ask you to perform a service. Do it and the recording disappears forever. Plus, there will be a nice payday for you."

Joe took the phone.

"Now count the money you got at the barn."

Joe opened the envelope and counted the money. Instead of the three hundred dollars he'd been promised, there was six hundred dollars.

"We take care of our people," the giant said. "We know you got a wife and a kid. They shouldn't be living here. It ain't healthy. You get them and your stuff, and I'll drive you to a decent motel. You ready to do that?"

Joe had dreamed about moving his family to safety, but he was certain that he would be asked to do something really bad in exchange.

"I can read people, Joe," the driver said, "and I know you're thinking about running. You don't want to think that way. We'll be watching you 24-7. Try to run, and bad things will happen to your family." The man smiled. "You've got a cutie-pie for a baby and a looker for a wife. Cross us and you won't like what happens to them."

Joe flushed with anger, but he tamped down the urge to attack. It would be useless. Even without the gun, he would be no match for the giant.

The driver waited until he was certain Joe had his temper under control. He smiled.

"Now you're thinking. That's good. Go get Maria and Conchita and your things. I'll wait for you, but don't take too much time. You don't want to make me nervous."

Joe weaved his way through tents, tepees, and a few shacks constructed from wood or corrugated metal until he found the tent where his family was living. Maria was sleeping, but everyone in the homeless encampment slept lightly. She looked up, alarmed, when Joe ducked in. Then she smiled and placed a finger to her lips.

Conchita was curled up beside Maria. Joe knelt beside them.

"Pack everything," he whispered. "We're moving to a motel."

"We can't afford a motel."

Joe opened the envelope with the cash and tilted it toward Maria.

"Where did you get the money?"

"I didn't rob anyone. I earned it."

"How—?" she started to ask, but Joe shook his head.

"I'll explain later. Right now, we got to move fast. Pack our stuff. Then get Conchita ready. I'll pull down the tent."

Fifteen minutes later, Joe led Maria and the baby to the van. Maria stopped when she saw the driver.

"He's okay. We'll be fine," Joe told Maria.

The driver smiled. "Pleased to meet you, ma'am. I'm glad we can help you and your family. Now hop in back, and I'll drive you to the Riverview Motel. It ain't fancy, but it's a real step up from where you're staying."

Maria didn't look convinced, but she carried the baby into the back of the van.

"What's going on, Joe?" she asked as soon as the door slid shut. "How did you get that money?"

"Fighting," Joe told her. "They have these fights in the country . . ."

"Are they legal?"

"I don't know," Joe lied, "but I won and got paid enough to move us out of the camp to a safe place while I try to find work."

"What if the police—"

"The police won't be a problem, and I won't do it again, but I had to get us to someplace safe."

The driver checked them into the Riverview Motel at three in the morning. The idea that there was a river view was pure fantasy, but Maria was thrilled that they were someplace safe. They put Conchita on a sleeping bag on the floor and got into the queen-size bed.

Maria was exhausted by the time they settled in, and she was asleep minutes after she closed her eyes, but Joe was still tossing and turning at 5:00 a.m. He couldn't forget that he had killed Carlos, and he was terrified of what would happen to Maria and the baby if he went to prison. But would he go to prison? Carlos had agreed to fight him. He had died during a fair fight. Had he committed a crime? He had to find out. He remembered the name of someone who could tell him if he was in trouble.

Joe put on a dark hooded sweatshirt and dark jeans and slipped out of the room. There were cars parked across the street, but the van wasn't one of them. Joe hoped that the giant had been bluffing about the around-the-clock surveillance. If not, Joe would say he was going on a training run. He went to the far end of the second-floor landing, walked down the stairs, and ran into the night toward McGill's gym.

CHAPTER FOURTEEN

Robin ran to McGill's gym at five in the morning every weekday to work out before going to her office. When she walked out of McGill's on Monday, she thought a man in a dark sweatshirt, hoodie, and jeans was watching her from an alley across the street. She crossed the street, and the man fell in behind her. Robin made some random turns and noticed that the man was still behind her. When she found a street crowded with people, she stopped and turned.

"Are you following me?" she challenged.

The man raised his hands and showed open palms. "Please, Ms. Lockwood, I just need to talk. I'm Joe Lattimore. You've seen me at McGill's. I used to box professionally."

Robin stared at Joe. She did recognize him.

"Why are you following me?"

"Barry McGill says you're a good lawyer. I was hoping we could talk and you'd give me some advice. I'm homeless, but I'm married and I have a little girl. I can't pay you now, but I will when I get a job."

Joe seemed desperate. Robin made a decision.

"The advice will be free, so don't worry about the money. Let's get something to eat and we can talk over breakfast."

Joe looked embarrassed. "I don't have the money for breakfast."

"Don't worry about that either. It's on me."

"Why do you need my advice?" Robin asked when they were seated in a booth and the waitress had taken their orders.

Joe leaned forward and lowered his voice. "This is just between us, right?"

"Anything you say is protected by the attorney-client privilege and is completely confidential."

"Okay, then. I used to box until Maria got pregnant. I wasn't making much money boxing, so I got a job as a short-order cook, but I got fired, and I haven't been able to get steady work since, so I was hoping my manager could get me a fight. I was on a training run when this guy came up and told me I could make good money fighting in a no-holds-barred fight. I knew it was probably illegal, but I was desperate. We were living in a tent city, and I was scared all the time that something would happen to Maria and Conchita, so I did it."

Joe looked very upset. He took a sip from his water glass.

"I killed the guy I fought."

Robin thought that Joe might cry.

"I didn't mean to. I never meant to hurt him bad. I just wanted to win and get the money for Maria and the baby. But he agreed to it. The fight,

I mean. We both knew what we were getting into. So, I want to know if I'm in trouble if we both agreed to fight?"

The waitress brought their order, which gave Robin time to think. Joe had asked for coffee, scrambled eggs, and toast, but he barely touched his food.

"You probably are in trouble," Robin said. "I can't remember the number of the statute, but there is one that says that you aren't justified in using physical force on someone even if you both agree to fight, if the fight isn't authorized by law. I don't think you can be charged with murder, but you might be charged with manslaughter or criminally negligent homicide."

Joe was quiet. Then he stood up. "Thank you, Ms. Lockwood."

"Don't go. Sit down and finish your breakfast."

"I don't have much of an appetite," Joe said. Then he thanked her again and left.

CHAPTER FIFTEEN

Ian Hennessey's Friday-morning docket had wrapped up by eleven. Both cases had been resolved with a plea. The only thing left on his calendar was a late-afternoon hearing in Judge Carasco's court concerning a case that originally had been assigned to another judge but had been transferred to Carasco's court that morning.

Hennessey was walking up to his office when his phone vibrated. There was a text from Stacey Hayes. The young DA's heart rate accelerated.

The dinner at Bocci's had been amazing. Ian had been enchanted by Stacey's beauty and the unmistakable interest she had shown in everything he had to say. There was no question in his mind that he and Stacey had instant chemistry, and what happened after their second date proved beyond a shadow of a doubt that she felt it too.

During the dinner at Bocci's, Ian had asked Stacey if she would like to go to a movie on Saturday, and she had agreed. After their Saturday-night date, Ian had driven Stacey to her riverside apartment, and she'd asked him in for a drink. Things had moved quickly after that, and Ian had woken from a deep sleep on Sunday morning thoroughly exhausted from the most explosive sexual experience of his young life.

Ian had spent Sunday in Stacey's bed, and he'd been thinking of her all week long, but frequent calls to her cell phone had gone to voice mail, and she hadn't returned any of them. Ian had become frantic. Had he done something wrong? Had she moved? He'd driven by her apartment several times, but there was no sign of her car, and she hadn't answered her door.

Ian hurried to a corner of the corridor and phoned Stacey.

"Ian, I'm so glad you got my message," Stacey said.

"I've been trying to get in touch all week. Where were you?"

"I was out of town visiting a friend. I'm such a ditz," she said with a self-deprecating laugh. "I forgot my cell phone. I just heard your messages and I felt awful. I hope you didn't worry too much."

"I did. I thought something had happened to you, that you'd been in an accident."

"That's so sweet that you worried, but I'm fine, and I'd like to prove how fine. Do you think you could come over?"

"You mean now?"

"If you're not busy."

Ian's mouth went dry, and he felt a stirring in his nether regions. There were trials to prepare for Monday, but he had the weekend to do that. He did have the short court appearance in Judge Carasco's court, but that was a few hours away.

"I'll be there as fast as I can."

"Good, because I'm naked and very horny."

Ian stared at the ceiling in the bedroom of Stacey Hayes's apartment and tried to remember what had happened during the last hour and a half. It was a blur, and he was certain that the mind-blowing sex he'd had with Stacey had given him short-term memory loss. Ian grinned. Life was great. No, his life was greater than great since Stacey had come into it.

The toilet flushed, and Stacey came out of the bathroom. She walked to the bed slowly, which gave Ian an eyeful of her perfect breasts, flat stomach, long legs, and the shaved place between her legs that had occupied his full attention since they had stripped and tumbled into bed. Life didn't get any better than this!

Stacey pulled back the covers, and Ian felt a soft hand begin to stroke him. After what they'd been doing, Ian was astonished that he could get another erection. He closed his eyes, barely able to concentrate on what Stacey was whispering in his ear.

"I need a favor, Ian. Will you help me?"

Ian grunted. Right now, he would do anything for Stacey.

"I have something to confess," Stacey said, her voice low and shy like a little girl. "I lived in Portland a few years ago. And I did something bad."

Ian opened his eyes. "What happened?"

"I was down on my luck, and I was going to be kicked out of my apartment. I was forced to do it."

"Do what?"

"I slept with men for money, and I was arrested."

"What?"

"I got scared, Ian. I ran away."

Ian sat up. "What are you talking about?"

Stacey moved away. "I knew you'd get upset."

"No, no, I'm not upset. I just . . . Are you in trouble?"

Stacey cast her eyes down. "I could be, but you can help me."

"How? What can I do?"

"There are warrants. You can—I don't know—maybe make them go away."

"I could look at the file. Maybe there's not enough evidence."

"What if there is? I mean, I did do it." Stacey trembled, and Ian thought she might cry. "I'm scared, Ian. Can't you get rid of the warrants so no one would know?"

"What do you mean?"

"Can't you go into the computer and erase them? Or take the file and make it disappear?"

"That's illegal, Stacey. I could be fired or arrested."

"If you were caught. But you're supersmart. You'd do it right. No one would ever know."

"I'd know. I think the world of you, but I can't break the law. I'll talk to the DA who has your case."

"Then he'd know I'm in town, and he'll arrest me."

"I'm not going to break the law."

Stacey smiled. It wasn't a nice smile. She got out of bed and took something from the drawer in her nightstand.

"Aren't you breaking the law by paying me for sex?" she asked.

Ian was shocked. "What are you talking about?"

"What would your boss say if she learned that you're paying a prostitute who has warrants out for her arrest? Do you think she'd be open-minded?"

"I haven't paid you to sleep with me. It would be your word against mine."

"Not exactly," Stacey said. "I've got a sex tape for show-and-tell. But I don't need the tape. Look at you. You're a pathetic loser, Ian. What are you going to say in your defense? That I gave myself to you because I love you?"

"Goddamn it," Ian said as he started to get out of bed.

Stacey pointed the gun she'd taken from the nightstand. "Whoa, Ian. Control yourself."

"You're going to shoot me?"

"If you try to hurt me. I've done it before when a man tried to take advantage."

Ian felt sick. This had all been a scam, and he was the sucker who'd fallen for it. Stacey was right. He was a loser, and he'd been a fool to think that someone like Stacey would fall head over heels for him. But he'd wanted to believe so badly that Stacey could love him that he'd put himself at her mercy.

"Pay attention, Ian. You're going to put on your pants, go to your office, and make those warrants go away. Do you understand me?"

Ian glared at Stacey as he got out of bed.

"I didn't hear a yes," she said.

"Yes," Ian forced himself to say.

"Good boy. Now run along and call me when you've done what I've told you to do. And don't take too long. You don't want to upset me."

Ian left Stacey's apartment in a daze. If he did what Stacey wanted, he would be committing a crime. If he disobeyed her, he would be ruined.

Ian had just started his car when he remembered that he had a hearing in Judge Carasco's courtroom in an hour. Carasco was the person who'd introduced him to Stacey. He wouldn't be in this mess if it weren't for the judge. Maybe Carasco could talk to Stacey or help him figure out how to get out of this predicament.

CHAPTER SIXTEEN

The court appearance lasted longer than Ian thought it would. As soon as it wrapped up, Hennessey asked to see the judge. The bailiff came out of Carasco's chambers and told Hennessey that the judge was tied up on a conference call, but wanted him to wait.

Hennessey had brought the case files for his Monday trials. He tried to work on them, but he couldn't concentrate. It was almost six when the bailiff told Ian that the judge could see him. When he walked into the judge's chambers, Carasco flashed a big smile.

"Come on in," Carasco said.

"Thanks for seeing me, Judge."

"Thanks for showing Stacey a good time," Carasco answered.

"That's who I want to talk to you about," the young DA said.

Carasco looked at his watch. "It's late and I missed lunch. Let's get out of here and get a bite to eat. We can talk over dinner. Bocci's is only a few blocks away."

The mention of the restaurant where he'd had his first date with Stacey made Hennessey want to throw up. He was certain he wouldn't be able to eat a thing, but the trip to the restaurant would give him more time to think about how he was going to approach Carasco.

The weather outside was as dark as Hennessey's mood. He hunched his shoulders to ward off the damp, chill wind that was gusting off the river and walked to the restaurant lost in thought.

Bocci's was an old-fashioned Italian restaurant with red-and-white-checkerboard tablecloths, melting wax candles squeezed into the necks of Chianti bottles, and an endless tape that played songs like "That's Amore." Carasco was well known, and the maître d' brought him to a booth in the back with dark-stained wood and red leather banquettes. Carasco ordered veal parmigiana, a side of pasta, and a glass of wine without looking at the menu. Hennessey ordered tortellini in brodo, a thin soup with pasta, which was all he thought he could digest. When Carasco kidded him, he lied and said he'd had a big lunch.

After the waiter left, Carasco talked about an appeal from one of his cases that the Oregon Supreme Court was deciding. Hennessey pretended to be interested, but he was just paying lip service as he tried to think of a way to bring up Stacey and her warrants.

The meal came. Carasco took a few bites of his dinner. Then he gave Hennessey the opening he needed.

"So, what did you want to talk about?" Carasco asked.

"I . . . It's Stacey, Judge."

"Yes?"

"She's not what she seems," Hennessey blurted out.

"How so?"

"How well do you know her?"

"Not that well. She's the daughter of a friend. He told her to look me up when she got to town."

"Did she tell you that she's lived in Portland before?"

"No."

Hennessey swallowed. He felt nauseous, but he decided the best thing to do was close his eyes and jump off the high board.

"Stacey has warrants for prostitution from a few years ago."

Carasco was lifting a piece of veal toward his mouth, but he stopped his fork in midflight. "What!?"

"She's a prostitute."

Carasco placed his fork on his plate. "How did you find out? You didn't . . . ?"

"No, no." Hennessey reddened. "We did sleep together, but I never paid her. Only, she's going to say I did if I don't get rid of her warrants."

"Did you do what she asked?"

"No. It's a crime. That's why I need to talk to you. She said she'd tell Vanessa Cole I slept with her for money if I don't get rid of the warrants."

Hennessey flushed with embarrassment at

the thought of the Multnomah County district attorney seeing the sex tape.

"I don't know what to do. I thought, maybe, you could talk to her."

"I could, but I don't really know her. There's no reason she'd listen to me."

"You're a judge. You could threaten her with something. Get a detective in the room. Have her arrested on the warrants or for extortion."

"That wouldn't stop her from involving you."

Carasco's phone rang. He looked at the screen. "Sorry, I have to take this. It's Betsy, my wife."

Carasco talked at the table, and Hennessey heard the judge's side of the conversation.

"Hi, honey. No, I'm having dinner at Bocci's with one of the new DAs. Mentoring. Yeah, I'll be home soon." The judge looked at Hennessey. "Do you have the time?"

"It's seven fifteen."

The judge nodded his thanks. "It's seven fifteen, honey. I should be back by eight thirty, latest."

The judge listened for a moment. Then he said, "Love you." He disconnected and looked across the table. "This is very serious, Ian."

"What should I do?"

"I need some time to think. Did you drive to work?"

"Yes."

"Can you drive me home? I took a Lyft in. We can talk on the way."

CHAPTER SEVENTEEN

The cell phone rang. Maria looked up when Joe answered it.

"One second," he said before going onto the landing that fronted the second-floor motel room. Joe pressed the phone to his ear and backed against the wall to get away from sheets of rain that were being driven onto the landing by gusts of frigid air.

"I'm gonna be on the street in five minutes," the voice on the other end said. "Be there."

The call disconnected, and Joe went inside.

"I've got to go," he told Maria.

"What's wrong?"

"Nothing's wrong. I have a job."

"What job?"

"The people who are paying for the motel need me to do some work."

"At this hour?"

"I've got to go," Joe answered.

"It's legal, right?"

"Of course," Joe said, kissing her cheek as he slipped into a hooded rain jacket. "I won't be long," he assured Maria, even though he had no idea how long he would be.

The giant was behind the wheel of a dull brown Ford. Joe ran through the driving rain and jumped into the front seat.

"Where are we going?" Joe asked after they'd driven in silence for several minutes.

"You'll find out soon enough. Give me the phone."

Joe did as he was told. Then he watched the scenery as they drove out of the seedy part of town where his motel was located, across the river, and into affluent Portland Heights, which loomed above the city in the hills on the west side of the Willamette.

The road wound upward past large houses with spacious lawns. Joe had never been in this part of town, and he couldn't help staring. After a while, the car turned onto a side street with larger lots where the houses were even bigger and hid behind high hedges. The car pulled to the curb in a shadowed area between the glow cast by lights that bathed parts of the street in weak light. The driver pointed at a large Tudor two lots down.

"That's the house. There's no one home, and the alarm's off. The safe is in the living room on the ground floor behind a seascape on the wall across from the entrance to the room." He handed a slip of paper to Joe. "This is the combination to the safe. Memorize it."

Joe did as he was told, and the giant crumpled the paper and put it in his pocket.

"There are jewels in the safe. Bring them to me. If there's cash, you can keep it as a tip. Get in, get out. I'll be waiting."

"I don't have gloves," Joe said.

"Don't worry about it. Just get me what I want."

Joe had a million questions, but he knew he would get zero answers, so he pulled up his hood and sprinted for the house, trying hard to keep out of the light. There was a break in the high hedge that hid the Tudor from the street. As Joe ran up the brick path to the front door, he looked for lights behind the windows and didn't see any.

Joe ducked under the portico that shielded the front door from the downpour. He was breathing hard, and he felt shaky. "It's nerves, just like before a fight," he told himself and took deep, slow breaths. When he was calmer, he slipped the edge of his jacket over his hand and opened the door slowly, half expecting an alarm to sound. When none did, Joe took another deep breath and walked into a large entryway tiled in a black-and-white checkerboard pattern. A staircase wound up to the second floor. The darkened entrance to a living room was off to the right.

Joe listened for any indication that someone was home. All he heard was his own labored breathing. "Gotta go," he whispered as he started toward the living room. He was almost to it when something caught his eye. He took a step and squinted. It looked like a foot. Joe stopped and stared. Shadows cloaked a body. As his eyes adapted to the dark, a leg and the bottom of a bathrobe materialized. Joe hesitated, terrified of what he knew he was going to see. Then he gathered himself and flipped on the light.

A woman was sprawled on a Persian carpet that was discolored by blood and spatter from the gashes in her battered face. Joe jumped back, appalled by the carnage, and placed his hand against the wall to prop himself up. It looked like someone had used their fists to beat the woman's face to a pulp.

Joe panicked. He ran from the living room, threw open the front door, and raced into the night. When he reached the street, he looked for his ride, but the car wasn't there. Joe had never been this scared. That's when he remembered that his prints would be on the light switch and the wall where he had placed his palm. The prints were near the body. He started to go back to the house when a car turned into the street and the headlights illuminated his face. The car stopped, and Joe froze in the glare. Then he threw up an arm to shield his face and raced away from the car. He cut across a lawn and through a gap between two houses. A narrow lane led into woods.

Joe tripped over a root and fell before bouncing to his feet. He had no idea where he was or how to get out of the woods. All he knew was that his freedom depended on getting as far from the body in the living room as he could.

CHAPTER EIGHTEEN

Hennessey's racing wiper blades were only giving him brief openings in the sheets of rain that smashed into his windshield. Even his high beams weren't much help.

"Turn here," Carasco said.

When Hennessey rounded the corner, he saw a man standing in the street. Hennessey stomped on the brakes. When the high beams hit him, the man froze. Then he threw an arm across his face before racing away from the car.

"Who was that?" Carasco shouted.

"I have no idea," Ian said.

"It looked like he was coming from my house."

Hennessey drove to the far end of the hedge and up to the garage. The only lights he could see were in a room at the front of the house. Hennessey followed the judge to the front door. It was wide open, and the wind was blowing rain into the entryway. Carasco stepped inside and flipped a switch. The light from a large crystal chandelier illuminated the foyer.

"What's that?" Hennessey said, pointing toward the living room.

Carasco turned. Then he took a few tentative steps before stopping at the entrance to the living room. Hennessey looked over the judge's shoulder. He tried to understand what he was seeing. When the full horror registered, Hennessey turned away and put his hand over his mouth, praying that he would keep down his dinner.

The judge backed out of the living room. He took Hennessey's arm and led him to the other side of the entryway.

"Are you okay?" Carasco asked.

"Hell no," Hennessey managed.

"Well, pull yourself together. I'm going to call the police. When they get here, they're going to talk to us. It may not come up, but if they ask why we were together tonight, you can't mention Stacey and the warrants. That's for your own protection. Do you understand me?"

Hennessey nodded.

"If they ask, tell them that I've been mentoring you and you were asking me to tell you what you did right and wrong in the case you had with Lockwood."

"Okay."

Carasco pulled out his cell phone and dialed 911. Hennessey wondered how Carasco could be so calm moments after seeing the hideous way his wife had been murdered.

Detectives Carrie Anders and Roger Dillon were next up in the homicide rotation, so they donned their rain gear, grabbed takeaway cups of black coffee, and headed up the winding roads that led to the most exclusive section of the West Hills. The rain had faded to an annoying drizzle by the time they parked in front of the Carasco home. A uniform was waiting at the sidewalk and handed them a pen so they could log in on the sheet that listed everyone who visited the crime scene.

Carrie was tall, heavyset, and as strong as some men. She had sleepy brown eyes, a lumpy nose, and shaggy black hair. Her lumbering gait and slow drawl often fooled some criminals into thinking that the college math major was slow-witted. That usually worked to their disadvantage.

Roger Dillon was a lanky African American with close-cropped salt-and-pepper hair, who was several years older than his partner and just as wise. They were the most effective team in Portland Homicide.

Dr. Sally Grace was waiting for them in the entryway. The assistant medical examiner was a slender woman with frizzy black hair, sharp blue eyes, and a macabre sense of humor that was a psychological requirement for someone in her line of work.

"What's up, Doc?" Roger asked. Neither woman seemed to recognize the Bugs Bunny reference, and Roger felt his age.

"The victim is Elizabeth Carasco."

"Judge Carasco's wife?" asked Dillon.

Dr. Grace nodded.

"She was killed in the living room," Grace said, pointing toward a doorway blocked by lab techs in Tyvek suits. "She was beaten to death, and her face is a mess. The judge found her. He's in the den with Ian Hennessey, the deputy DA who drove him home. The den is at the end of that hall. They're both pretty shook up."

Roger and Carrie walked to the living room doorway and studied the corpse. Years of experiencing the sickening ways people treated their fellow humans usually inured them to the horrors one person could inflict on another person, but they could not help being affected by the thought of what Betsy Carasco had endured.

"We'll get out of your hair," Roger told Dr. Grace. "Let us know if you find anything interesting."

"Will do."

Grace headed back to the living room, and the detectives walked toward the den.

"I never thought I'd feel compassion for Anthony Carasco," Roger said, "but seeing what was done to that poor woman makes me sad."

"You don't like Carasco?"

"Did you ever work with him when he was a DA or appear in his court?" Roger asked.

"A few times." Carrie paused. "Yeah, I get you. Do you want me to take the judge?"

"No, I'll do it. I'll pretend we have rapport."

They found the judge and the prosecutor sitting

side by side nursing glasses of scotch in deep armchairs that stood in front of a marble fireplace with a carved wood mantel. Roger studied Ian Hennessey. The prosecutor's normally pale complexion looked completely drained of color, and the detective wondered if Hennessey had seen Mrs. Carasco's corpse and thrown up. He turned his attention to Carasco.

"How are you doing, Judge?" Roger asked.

Carasco clasped his glass with both hands. "I don't know what I'm going to do without Betsy." He shook his head. "I can't imagine what she went through."

"Do you feel up to talking?" Roger asked.

Carasco looked up. His face was a portrait of rage. "I want this bastard found, so you bet I want to talk." He pointed at Hennessey. "We both saw him. I can tell you exactly what he looks like."

"You saw Mrs. Carasco's killer?" Carrie said.

"He was standing in the road. We caught him in our headlights," Carasco told the detectives. "I can also narrow down the time of death."

It was bad procedure to interview witnesses together. Roger didn't want the judge influencing the young DA's version of events and vice versa. Getting Hennessey out of the study would also give Carrie a chance to see if he needed help.

"Is there someplace quiet where Carrie can talk to Ian while you tell me what you saw?" Roger asked.

"I don't think anyone is in the kitchen. It's in the back of the house."

As soon as Carrie and Ian left, Roger sat in the armchair Hennessey had vacated and angled it so he could look at the judge.

"I'm really sorry, Judge. I can't imagine what you're going through."

"Thank you, Roger. I still haven't gotten my head around the fact that Betsy is . . . that I'll never see her again." The judge took a deep breath. "Ask your questions. I know how crucial the first hours of an investigation are."

"They are. But I respect your situation. If you want to stop at any time . . ."

"I'll be okay. What do you want to know?"

Roger was old-fashioned, and he took out a notebook and a pen instead of using technology for note-taking.

"How can you narrow the time of death?" he asked.

"I was in court all day. Ian had an afternoon hearing before me. After the hearing, he told my bailiff that he wanted to see me. I had a conference call, so I couldn't see him then, and I told him to wait.

"After the conference call, I suggested that we talk over dinner at an Italian restaurant a few blocks from the courthouse. The reason I can narrow the time of . . . when Betsy died is because she called during dinner. I can confirm the time she called with my cell phone's call log. Betsy was alive at seven fifteen."

"How did she seem when she talked to you?"

"Fine, normal. If you're asking whether she sounded like she was under duress, the answer is she did not."

"Thank you. That's very helpful. Go on."

"I'd taken Lyft to work, and I asked Ian to drive me home. We finished our meal and drove onto my street sometime after eight. That's when we saw the man who . . ."

Carasco looked down. His hands balled into fists.

"Are you okay? Do you want to take a break?"

Carasco shook his head and drank some more scotch. "No. I just . . ."

"I understand."

Carasco took a deep breath. "Ask your questions."

"You said you saw a man outside your house. Can you describe him?"

"I was sitting in the front seat of the car, and he was a few houses from us, but he was definitely black, and he seemed to be average height."

Carasco closed his eyes and tilted forward, deep in thought. When he opened his eyes, he looked triumphant.

"He had a scar! It was on his cheek. His right cheek."

"You could see this from that far away?"

"Ian had his high beams on. It was like he was standing in a spotlight on a stage. I'm sure of the scar."

"How was he dressed?"

"He was wearing a black rain jacket with a hood."

"I assume that the hood was up because of the rain."

"Yes."

"And you could still see the scar?"

"When we turned into my street, he turned and stared at our car. The hood slipped back."

"Okay. This is very useful," Roger assured the judge. "Can you think of anything else that might help?"

Carasco thought for a moment before shaking his head.

"There are going to be people in and out of the house all night. Do you have someplace you can stay?"

"I'll make a reservation at a hotel near the courthouse."

"That's good. Maybe Ian can drive you. Pack up your stuff, and I'll see if Carrie is through talking to him."

Roger put his notebook away and walked to Carasco's kitchen, which seemed to be as big as Roger's house. It was a large, open area dominated by a granite island. Roger spotted two dishwashers, two sinks, and a massive refrigerator-freezer. Carrie was talking to Hennessey at a rustic wooden table in a breakfast nook. She looked at her partner when he walked in.

"You finished with the judge?" she asked.

Roger nodded.

"We're pretty much done here." She turned to the prosecutor. "Is there anything you want to add, Ian?"

"No. Not now. If I think of anything else, I'll call you."

"Do that," Carrie said as she passed Hennessey her card.

"The judge is going to stay at a hotel until we're finished with the house," Roger said. "Can you give him a lift?"

"Sure. No problem."

"He's packing. Why don't you wait for him in the entryway?"

Hennessey looked shaky when he stood up.

"Is he okay?" Roger asked Carrie when Hennessey was out of earshot.

"He got a good look at Mrs. Carasco, and it really got to him."

"Did he say anything useful?" Roger asked.

"The guy he saw leaving the house was black, medium height, and medium build, which fits a lot of the African American males in Portland."

"Did he mention the scar?" Roger asked.

"He didn't say anything about a scar."

"The judge is certain the man he saw had a scar on his right cheek."

Carrie frowned. "Ian said that it was raining hard when they turned into Carasco's street. The wipers were going, and they were a few houses away from the man when they saw him. In other words, the visibility was shit."

Roger shrugged. "Carasco says he saw the scar. He said Ian had his high beams on and the guy's hood fell back."

"That's definitely going to help, if we have a suspect."

"This looks like a robbery gone bad. If we're lucky, the perp was stupid and we'll get some juicy latents," Roger said.

"From your lips to God's ears."

Roger smiled.

"Did Ian mention a phone call around seven or so from the wife to the judge, while they were eating?" he asked.

"He did. I checked when he told me. They bagged the victim's cell phone. There was a call to the judge's cell phone at seven thirteen."

"I guess we can cross Carasco off our list of suspects."

"Yeah," Carrie agreed. "The husband's usually the first person I look at when a wife is the victim, but Carasco was in the courthouse until six or so and with Ian the rest of the evening, so he's got a solid alibi."

"Let's check with Sally and the lab techs," Roger said.

Dr. Grace was leaving when Carrie and Roger returned to the entryway. She told them that she'd found nothing to contradict her initial impression that Betsy Carasco had died from blunt force trauma and that she would call if the autopsy turned up something else.

Ian Hennessey and Judge Carasco were preparing to leave while the detectives were talking to the medical examiner. Carrie talked to them briefly, then the two of them left the crime scene and made their way to Hennessey's car. When he saw the judge and the prosecutor leave, the head of the team from the crime lab walked over. He told the detectives that they had found some muddy sneaker prints in the hall and many latents in the living room, which was to be expected. He agreed to call when they had been analyzed.

The rain had stopped when the detectives walked out of Carasco's house. Roger looked at the horizon. The sun was rising behind Mount Hood, spraying the sky with vibrant reds and yellows. That lifted his spirits, and they rose higher when a policewoman ran over to them and told them about a call from headquarters.

"Detective Hammond at Homicide received an anonymous tip about the murder," the officer told them. "The caller said a guy named

Joseph Lattimore did it during a robbery." The policewoman showed Carrie a mugshot that had been scanned to her. "The caller said that Lattimore is staying at the Riverview Motel on Division."

Roger frowned. This was very convenient, but then again, a lot of crimes were solved by anonymous tips.

"He's got a scar on his right cheek," Carrie said.

Roger sighed. "I was counting on solving this case through brilliant detective work."

Carrie smiled. "Don't look a gift horse in the mouth. Let's get some backup and head to the motel."

CHAPTER NINETEEN

Joe staggered through the woods with no idea where he was going. Tree limbs raked his face, and tree roots tripped him. When he fell, mud caked his legs and soaked his pants.

In the beginning of his flight from the crime scene, adrenaline kept Joe moving, but it wore off after a while, and all he felt was despair. Maria and the baby meant everything to him, and he was certain that he would lose them. What a fool he'd been. He had known that illegal fights were run by gangsters, and he'd fought anyway. Now he might pay the ultimate price if he was arrested for a murder he had not committed.

At some point, Joe found a trail and followed it down until it ended at a road. The rain had let up, but he was cold and exhausted. He checked a street sign and learned that he was on the west side of the Willamette, miles from the motel.

Joe rested until he had his breath back. Then he started jogging toward the closest bridge. As he ran toward Maria, he thought about the fight. Something had been wrong with Carlos. He had moved so slowly, and there was the glazed look in his eyes. He was certain that Carlos had been drugged, which meant that the fight had been fixed and he'd been set up. Once he'd killed

Carlos, they had him, and they'd made him the perfect fall guy.

The sun was starting to rise when he knocked on the door to the motel. Maria opened the door and stared at her husband. Joe had fallen more than once, and his jeans were soaking wet and covered with mud. His shoulders sagged, and he looked exhausted.

"Where have you been?"

"Pack up," Joe said without answering her.

"We just got here."

"It's not safe."

Maria stared at Joe. He averted his eyes.

"Why isn't it safe? What did you do?"

Joe was about to answer when he heard several cars pull into the lot below his room. He pulled back the shade. Armed police officers were getting out of the cars and following a large woman and slender black man up the stairs.

Joe felt like crying. He'd failed his family. Maria and the baby would be lost to him and thrown on the mercy of the state. He doubted that he'd ever get them back again.

"Stay inside," he said. Then he opened the door and walked onto the landing with his hands in the air.

"I give up. Don't shoot. My wife and my baby are inside. Please don't hurt them."

CHAPTER TWENTY

During the drive downtown, Ian Hennessey and Judge Carasco barely said a word. Hennessey was exhausted from answering Carrie Anders's questions and in shock after seeing Betsy Carasco's mutilated body, and nothing he thought of saying to comfort the judge seemed appropriate. A little after two in the morning, the young prosecutor dropped the judge at a hotel a few blocks from the courthouse.

Hennessey lived on the fourteenth floor of a new condo in northwest Portland. Wraparound floor-to-ceiling windows gave him a spectacular view of the city lights, the river, and the mountains. He could afford to live in luxury because a hefty trust fund supplemented his salary.

Hennessey collapsed onto his king-size bed shortly after entering the condo, but he had a hard time getting to sleep. The horror at Carasco's house had made him forget his ordeal at Stacey Hayes's apartment, but the threat she posed came flooding back as soon as he closed his eyes.

What was he going to do about the warrants? He'd been counting on Judge Carasco to help him, but the judge would be preoccupied with his wife's murder and her funeral, and this wasn't the time to approach him. That meant he would have to make a decision that could destroy his career, and his career meant a lot to him.

Ian's parents were A-plus-plus personalities. His Princeton and Harvard Medical School–educated father was a brilliant, highly compensated physician. His mother was a very successful stockbroker. Ian had never been able to live up to their expectations, and his parents had done a poor job of hiding their disappointment.

In high school, Ian had finished with a B average only because no one at his exclusive prep school received a grade below a B. He had flunked out of the top-ten college his parents' pull and donations had gotten him into, and he had graduated with a low-B average from a state college. Ian knew that he would never have gotten his job with the district attorney's office if his parents hadn't pulled some strings, but he'd come to love his job, and he was desperate to make a success of this chance. Now, through no fault of his own, he was once again on the brink of failure.

Eventually, Hennessey fell into a nightmare-plagued sleep. When he woke up, it was still dark, and he was still exhausted. Hennessey tried to get back to sleep, but failed miserably. A little after six, he scarfed down a breakfast of black coffee and toast, which was all he could tolerate, and drove to work. Only a few people were in, and the deputy with whom he shared his cramped cubicle wasn't there yet.

Hennessey logged on to his computer and typed in *Stacey Hayes*. He couldn't find any outstanding warrants, but he did find an order from circuit court judge Wilma Malone dismissing two prostitution cases and two warrants for failure to appear. The order had been put in the system shortly after Stacey moved to Portland.

Hennessey had tried a case in Malone's court. She was new to the bench and had practiced insurance defense in one of Portland's big firms. Why would Malone get rid of Stacey's warrants? It made no sense. Then Hennessey wondered if Malone knew about the order. It would be pretty simple to slip an order of such little consequence into a pile that had been sent to the clerk's office. If that's what happened, who had authored the forgery?

Anthony Carasco, the only person Stacey knew in Portland, was the most likely suspect. And that led to more questions. When they were in Carasco's chambers and at dinner, Carasco had acted surprised when Hennessey told him that Hayes was a prostitute who had warrants out for her arrest in Oregon, but he had to know if Carasco was the person who had gotten rid of them. How did Carasco learn about the warrants? The obvious answer was that Hayes told him. But if Hayes knew the warrants didn't exist anymore, why did she threaten Hennessey?

The young prosecutor remembered his case that had been shifted to Carasco's court on the morning Hayes lured him to her apartment. Hennessey had thought the switch to Carasco's court had been odd, but he also thought it was fortuitous because he got along so well with Carasco. But what if he'd been set up?

Stacey was a professional, and professionals were adept at using sex to manipulate men. Stacey had made Hennessey think she liked him, then she'd cut him off for a week so he would be aching to see her. Stacey had lured Hennessey to her apartment in late morning with the promise of sex. Then she had threatened to destroy him if he didn't make her warrants disappear. Did Carasco lure him to his courtroom later that day because he knew Hennessey would seek his advice? Why would he do that?

There was an answer to that question that made Hennessey's mouth go dry. The judge had made certain that Hennessey was with him when his wife was murdered. Was that part of a plan? Had Carasco hired someone to kill his wife and used Hennessey to provide a cast-iron alibi?

Ian closed his eyes and took deep breaths. Carasco had introduced him to Hayes and set up their first date knowing that Hennessey would be easy prey for a woman like Stacey. It had been a classic honey trap. Hennessey felt dizzy and disoriented. If he was right, Carasco had masterminded his wife's death, Stacey Hayes was his accomplice, and he was the dupe they were using to get away with murder.

PART THREE

A MATTER OF
LIFE AND DEATH

CHAPTER TWENTY-ONE

On Saturday morning, Robin opened her eyes slowly and stared at the bedroom ceiling for a moment before forming her lips into a sleepy grin. She didn't go to the gym on the weekend, but an hour earlier, she had engaged in another, very satisfying type of exercise before falling back to sleep. Robin turned her head toward the other side of the bed. It was empty. The aroma of fresh-brewed coffee and the sound of plates rattling on the island in the kitchen provided clues to Jeff Hodges's whereabouts. It took a supreme act of will to get out of bed, but she managed to do it. She showered and threw on jeans and a Trailblazers T-shirt. By the time Robin wandered into the dining area of their apartment, Jeff was putting the finishing touches on an omelet.

Jeff was six foot two with shaggy, reddish-blond hair, broad shoulders, green eyes, and pale, freckled skin. He had been a police officer in Washington County until he'd suffered serious injuries during an explosion in a meth lab he was raiding. When they'd first met, Robin had been fascinated by the faint tracery of scars on his face, but they barely registered now.

"I was just going to check on you," Jeff said. "I was worried that you were dead."

Robin smiled. "There are worse ways to go."

"Too true," Jeff answered as he flipped the finished product onto a dish that was sitting next to another plated omelet.

Robin sat at her place and sipped the glass of orange juice Jeff had thoughtfully placed there. A steaming cup of coffee stood beside the juice glass.

Jeff tucked the newspaper under his arm and carried the omelets to the table. He put one on Robin's place mat before handing her the sports section.

"Did you know about this?" he asked as he held up the front page.

The headline read JUDGE'S WIFE SLAIN IN HOME INVASION. Robin read the first sentence. Then her head jerked up, and she stared at Jeff.

"Anthony Carasco!"

"Mark told me you had a run-in with him recently," Jeff said.

"Yeah. The guy's a jerk, but he didn't deserve this."

"Judges have a human side," Jeff said. "Even the ones who are jerks."

Robin finished the article before handing the first section of the paper back to Jeff. He turned his attention to the editorial page, and Robin read an article about the Seahawks. They both missed the story on the bottom of page 7 about the two ten-year-old boys who had found a man's body

126

in a weed-covered lot not far from the tent city where Joseph and Maria Lattimore had lived.

Carlos Ortega was a fifty-eight-year-old ex-marine. The VA had a file on him. He had PTSD and was addicted to heroin. He was also no stranger to the justice system and had been in and out of jail on minor assault and possession charges. An address for Ortega's wife was in the VA file, and she was notified two days after her husband's body was found.

Not mentioned in the article were the results of a blood test, which found a tranquilizer in Mr. Ortega's system, or the similarity of the injuries to those of Elizabeth Carasco.

CHAPTER TWENTY-TWO

On Monday morning, Robin was editing a memo she was writing in support of a motion to suppress when her receptionist told her that Harold Wright was on line two. Judge Wright, a brilliant jurist with a great judicial temperament, was one of Robin's favorites.

"Hi, Judge," Robin said. "What's up?"

"I'm acting as the presiding judge this week while Nancy is on vacation, and a man charged with aggravated murder appeared in my court an hour ago. A public defender appeared with him, but he says you're his lawyer. He's indigent, so you'd have to be paid on the court-appointment fee schedule if you take the case."

Robin frowned. "What's the defendant's name?"

"Joseph Lattimore."

As soon as she heard Joe's name, Robin assumed that Lattimore's case involved the illegal fight, but she had no idea why it would be charged as a death penalty case.

"Before you tell me whether you'll accept the case," Wright continued, "you need to know that the victim is Tony Carasco's wife."

"Lattimore is charged with killing Judge Carasco's wife?"

"You sound surprised."

"I am."

"Why?"

"I'm afraid I can't tell you. Attorney-client."

"So, you do represent him?"

"Let me talk to Mr. Lattimore. I'll tell you if I'll take the case after I meet with him."

The Multnomah County jail was on the fourth through tenth floors of the Justice Center, a modern, sixteen-story building in downtown Portland that was separated from the courthouse by a park. When Robin got out of the jail elevator, she found herself in a narrow concrete hall. She pressed the button on an intercom that was affixed to the wall next to a thick metal door that sealed the elevators from the area where defendants were housed in the jail.

After a short wait, Robin heard electronic locks snapping in place, and the door was opened by a corrections officer. The guard led her into another narrow hallway that ran in front of three contact visiting rooms that she could see into through large, shatterproof windows. The guard opened the steel door for the first visiting room, and Robin entered a concrete rectangle whose sole furnishings were two molded plastic chairs and a table that was secured to the floor by metal bolts.

Moments after Robin sat down, a second door on the wall opposite the window opened, and a guard escorted Joseph Lattimore into the contact visiting room. Lattimore was wearing a loose-fitting jail-issued orange jumpsuit. His shoulders slumped, and he looked at the floor when the guard guided him onto his chair. As soon as the guard left, Lattimore raised his head. He looked exhausted.

"I didn't kill her," he blurted out. "She was dead when I got there."

Robin held up her hand. "Stop! I'm not your attorney, Joe. All I did was answer a question for you."

"You've got to help me," he pleaded. "I was set up."

"You have a public defender. I know her. She's experienced. She'll do a good job."

"I don't want someone who'll 'do a good job.' Maria and the baby have no one but me. If I'm convicted . . ."

Joe shook his head back and forth slowly.

"This was planned. Getting me to that house . . ." There were tears in Joe's eyes. "They knew I was desperate. You have to hear me out. Once you understand what they did, you'll see that you have to help me."

Robin studied Lattimore. He sounded hopeless. More important, he sounded like he might be telling the truth.

"I'll listen to what you have to say, but I'm not promising to represent you. Do you understand that?"

"Yeah. I get it. I'm sorry. I have no right to ask you to do this. You have big clients—important people with money. I'm broke. I don't have anything to offer you. But I didn't kill that woman. I was set up."

Robin sighed. She had never been drawn to the practice of law for the money. Helping people motivated her, and anyone accused of killing the wife of a judge would need a lot of help.

"Talk."

"Remember I told you about the illegal fight?"

Robin nodded.

"What you don't know is what happened after I . . . after I killed the man I fought."

"Let's do this in order. Start at the beginning."

"Okay. I was running to keep in shape when this guy passed me in a car. A little bit later, I saw the car again, and the man was standing beside it. He said that his name was Sal, and he knew I was a boxer. He asked if I wanted to make some money by fighting in a no-holds-barred fight. He said I could make three hundred dollars for a few minutes' work. I was almost broke, and we needed the money, so I said I was in.

"The night of the fight, I was picked up in a van. There were other people in the van. We drove for about an hour. When we stopped, we were in the country at a farm.

"The fight was in a barn, and there was a big crowd. Everyone was gambling. When we got inside, the guy who seemed to be running the show had us write down our first names. Then he paired us up. He said that winners were paid and losers got nothing. He also told us to make the fight bloody."

Joe stopped for a moment as an unbidden image of Carlos's ruined face crept into his head.

"Are you okay?" Robin asked.

"No. I can't forget Carlos, the guy I killed."

"Was he one of the people who rode to the fight in the van?"

"No. They brought him out of a room in the back of the barn. I thought that was strange."

Joe paused again and shook his head in an attempt to get rid of the vivid, blood-soaked image.

"I've thought about the fight over and over. Something was wrong with Carlos. He was old and so slow. It was easy to hit him, and I could see his punches coming from a mile away. I think he was drugged. I'm sure that's why it was so easy for me to hurt him."

Joe stopped again. He took a deep breath.

"I got carried away, Ms. Lockwood. I needed the money to get Maria and the baby somewhere safe. I couldn't afford to lose, so I kept on hitting him, but as soon as I realized how bad I'd hurt Carlos, I yelled for a doctor. The guy who ran the fight told the crowd to leave. I wanted to stay and see if Carlos was okay, but he gave me an envelope with money and hustled me out. The guy who drove me to the barn was waiting outside with the van. We'd been staying in a tent city. He drove me there after the fight."

"Did you get the driver's name?"

"No. I didn't get anyone's name, except for Sal's, who refereed the fights."

"Okay, go on."

"When we stopped, the driver told me they had a recording of me killing Carlos and they'd give it to the cops with the location of the body if I didn't do what I was told. He gave me a cell phone and said I'd get a call about a job. If I did good, I'd be paid, and no one would see the video. He said they were watching me. If I tried to run, they would hurt Maria and the baby. Then he took us to the motel where I was arrested."

"Did they call you?"

Joe nodded. "Friday night, the driver called. He was outside the motel. He drove me to the house where the woman was killed. He said that no one was home and there was no alarm. He gave me a combination that was supposed to be for a safe in the living room. He wanted the jewels in the safe and said I could keep any cash. When I went into the entryway, I saw a body in the living room. It was a woman. I put on the lights to see if she was okay. One look at her face and I knew I couldn't help her. So, I ran."

Joe shook his head. "I'm so stupid. I should

have seen it coming. The driver was gone. Then another car came around the corner and lit me up with its headlights. I took off and went back to the motel to get Maria and Conchita. We were going to run, but the cops came before we could go. They must have called the cops and told them where I was."

"Do you know the location of the fight or how to find any of the people you think set you up?" Robin asked.

Joe shook his head. "The back of the van had no windows, and no one but Sal used names."

"What about the phone? Do you have the one they gave you?"

"No. The driver took it back."

"Can you describe any of the people involved in organizing the fight?"

"The driver who took me to the barn was a giant, over six feet tall—six five maybe—and three hundred pounds or more. He was bald, and his head was twice the size of a normal human's."

"Race?"

"White, and he had a cauliflower ear and gang tattoos."

"Can you tell me the gang?"

"No."

"What about the people who were running the fight?"

After Joe described the man who seemed in charge, the doctor, and Sal, Robin sat back and thought. Joe watched her, knowing that his best chance for surviving his ordeal was weighing the pros and cons of taking his case.

Robin stood up and rang for the guard.

"Will you help me?" Joe asked. He sounded desperate, and Robin wished that she could give him an answer.

"I don't know. I have to think about this."

"Yeah, I get it. But can you do one thing for me? Can you find out where Maria and Conchita are? No one will tell me. If I know they're safe . . ."

"I'll see what I can do. And I won't make you wait long for my decision."

On the way to her office, Robin realized that she could be plunged into a defense attorney's worst nightmare if she accepted Joseph Lattimore as a client. On television, every client is innocent, and every defense attorney is excited to represent an innocent man. In the real world, there were two cases a criminal defense attorney took on with great trepidation: a case where her client faced the death penalty, and a case where her client was innocent.

Most people who are arrested are guilty. If you represented a guilty person, you tried your very best to get your client out of his scrape with the least wear and tear. If he pleaded guilty or was found guilty at trial and you had tried your hardest, you slept soundly knowing that your client had done the crime with which he'd been charged.

Then there was the rare case where your client had been arrested for something he had not done. No attorney wanted to carry that weight. An acquittal only brought a sigh of relief, and a conviction brought endless, sleepless nights and agonizing days filled with the nagging thought that you had failed to do something that would have kept your client out of a cage.

Robin knew that she could avoid the anxiety and constant stress she would feel by leaving Joe's case with the public defender's office. But her conscience would not let her do that. If Joe were innocent and facing death, she had a duty to help him. How could she look herself in the mirror if she walked away?

CHAPTER TWENTY-THREE

Robin called the public defender who had represented Lattimore at the arraignment and got a briefing on everything she knew about the case. Then she called Jeff and Mark to her office and told them what Joe had told her and what she'd learned from the public defender.

"What should I do?" Robin asked.

"Do you believe him?" Mark asked.

"I do. If he's making up his story, he should be writing bestselling fiction. It's the details. He sounds like he's describing things that happened. And he did ask me about his culpability when he met me outside McGill's. I believe that illegal fight really happened."

"Oh, they hold them," Jeff said. "When I was a cop, we heard rumors."

"Did you ever do anything about them?" Mark asked.

"No. It was all very shadowy. It's not unusual for the promoters to move the location every time they hold a fight, so we weren't even certain that they were being held in our jurisdiction. Plus, the word was that some pretty important people attended the fights—people who make big contributions to the people who decide what cases should be pursued."

"If the fight was real, it makes Lattimore's story more believable," Mark said.

Robin looked troubled. "A thought just occurred to me."

"And that is?" Jeff asked.

"If Joe is telling the truth, he was set up to take the blame for Mrs. Carasco's murder. Who is the first person the police look at when a wife is killed?"

"Carasco has a cast-iron alibi," Mark said. "He was in court all day and with Ian Hennessey when his wife was murdered. According to your friend at the PD's office, Hennessey heard Carasco talking to his wife in Bocci's shortly before she was killed."

"Correction," Robin said. "Hennessey heard the judge's half of the conversation. He can't say who was on the other end of the phone. What if it was the person who murdered Mrs. Carasco telling the judge that the job was done?"

"It does seem like a big coincidence that the judge drove up just when Lattimore ran out of his house," Mark said.

"Which could have been planned if the person who killed Mrs. Carasco was also the person who called the restaurant," Robin added.

Mark looked at Jeff. "It would be interesting to know how well Mr. and Mrs. Carasco got along. But that's not something we'd be spending time learning about unless Joe Lattimore is our client."

CHAPTER TWENTY-FOUR

Elizabeth Carasco's funeral was held at St. Francis, the largest Catholic church in Portland, and there was a full house. Betsy was prominent in Portland society, politically active, a member of the best clubs, and a fixture at charity galas. Everyone liked her, and many of her friends felt sorry for her because of the man she'd married.

Anthony Carasco's reputation in Portland society was as bad as his reputation in the bar. Everyone knew about his affairs, his gambling, and his shadowy relations with the worst elements in society. No one could figure out why Betsy had married Carasco or why she stayed with him.

Carasco didn't care what Portland society thought about him. He had grown up poor and had clawed his way up. Carasco felt nothing but contempt for people who'd been born into luxury.

The front rows on either side of the aisle were reserved for family. When Carasco entered the church, he glanced toward the row on the right side. Helen Raptis had commandeered the front pew for her family and had left no room on it for her daughter's husband. When the judge walked down the aisle, Helen cast a malevolent look in his direction. She held it for a few seconds before bringing her eyes back to the coffin that sat on a riser at the front of the church. Carasco wasn't surprised by her anger. He couldn't stand the bitch, and he knew that the feeling was mutual.

Elizabeth Carasco had been born a Raptis, one of Oregon's wealthiest families. Carl Raptis had made his seed money in a general store in Portland in the 1860s when Oregon was the country's newest state. One of the sons had started a prosperous farm in Eastern Oregon. Another got into logging and struck it rich when timber became the mainstay of the Oregon economy. By the end of the twentieth century, when the timber industry was dying, the family kept ahead of the curve by investing in technology and sportswear.

Helen Raptis, the matriarch of the family, was in her sixties, but plastic surgeons, a personal trainer, and great hairdressers and makeup artists had conspired to make her look much younger. She was a shade over six feet with jet-black hair, blue eyes, and tight, tanned skin. A product of Georgetown and Wharton, she had made a seamless transition to the throne of Raptis Enterprises when her husband had died from a heart attack.

Anthony found a seat at the front on the side of the aisle across from the Raptis clan. He had no family in Oregon, and the rest of the pew was taken up by his friends and acquaintances.

The service went smoothly, and the fireworks

didn't start until it ended. Mourners blocked the aisles, and Carasco was stopped every few feet by people offering condolences. By the time he got outside, so had the Raptis clan. Carasco made a beeline toward the limousine that was going to take him to the cemetery, but Helen Raptis stepped in front of him halfway down the steps to the street. Standing behind her was Leo Boyce, an ex–Special Forces officer who was head of security for Helen and her enterprises. Boyce was tall and compact. He never said much, and his stony silence and hard, unwavering stare intimidated most people. But Boyce didn't scare Carasco. He had people he could call who were just as tough and way more ruthless than Raptis's bodyguard.

Raptis stood so close that Carasco could smell her minty mouthwash, and she spoke so softly that only Carasco could hear her.

"I know you killed my Betsy, you low-life piece of shit, and I'm going to see you pay."

"I can see that you're suffering, Helen, so I'm not going to take offense. But you should check your facts before making wild accusations. I was at dinner with several witnesses when Betsy was murdered, and the police already have the killer in custody."

"That bullshit won't fly with me," Helen said, her anger barely contained. "You're not man enough to murder my daughter yourself. You're the type of coward who hires someone to do his killing."

"Why in the world would I kill Betsy?"

Helen stared at Carasco for a second. Then she slapped him hard enough to snap his head sideways.

"You lying sack of shit."

Carasco took a step back. His fists curled, but he reined himself in because Boyce was inches away.

"That one is a freebie," he said. "Do it again, and I'll have you arrested for assault."

"Betsy told me she was going to divorce you, and I have pictures of you and your whore at that riverside apartment. I know you're counting on inheriting Betsy's money, but I will spend every cent I have to break her will. And I'm also going to see you sent to prison."

Raptis spun on her heel and walked away with her head held high and her back rigid. Carasco watched her get into the car that was taking her to her daughter's grave. He seemed unruffled, but he was afraid. Helen Raptis was a very powerful woman with many resources.

CHAPTER TWENTY-FIVE

Amanda Jaffe didn't have the willowy figure of a runway model, but she still attracted male attention when she entered a room. She had long black hair, clear blue eyes, and an athletic physique, the product of years of competitive swimming that had brought her to the brink of a spot on an Olympic team.

Amanda was a partner in Jaffe, Katz, Lehane, and Brindisi, a firm founded by her father, the noted criminal defense attorney Frank Jaffe. The firm's offices took up the eighth floor of the Stockman Building, a fourteen-story edifice that had stood in the heart of downtown Portland since 1915 and featured an ornate stone façade decorated with happy cherubs and fierce gargoyles.

When Amanda returned to the firm from an arraignment in a federal bank robbery case, she found Robin Lockwood waiting in the reception area. The women had bonded because of their athletic accomplishments while representing codefendants in a three-week federal drug conspiracy case. Amanda smiled and crossed the room.

"To what do I owe the pleasure?" she said.

"I've got a favor to ask. Do you have time to talk?"

"Sure. Let's go back to my office."

Amanda had a corner office with a view of the West Hills. The walls were decorated with diplomas, certificates attesting to her admission to state and federal bars, two abstract paintings she'd purchased from an art gallery near her condo in the Pearl District, and a photograph of downtown Portland in the years just before World War I.

"So, what's this favor?" Amanda asked when they were seated with the door closed.

"You know Tony Carasco's wife was murdered?"

"Sure. It's all over the news."

"I was just appointed to represent the guy they've arrested for it. The Standards of Practice require me to have cocounsel in a death case. Are you interested?"

"Maybe, but I should tell you up front that even though none of my death cases have ended up with a client on death row, I would personally have executed some of them, if I'd been asked."

"You're in favor of the death penalty?" Robin asked, surprised.

"No, but not because I don't think it's appropriate in some cases. You've only been in Portland for a few years, so you probably don't know that I almost died at the hands of a serial killer and a paid assassin."

"I didn't know that," Robin answered, shocked by the revelation.

"Those people were animals who needed to

144

be put down. I suffered PTSD because of one of the incidents. So, I don't have any sympathy for killers, and the only reason I'm opposed to the death penalty is because death is an uncorrectable sentence, and there have been too many innocent people sent to death row."

"Then you'll want to second-chair this case, because I think Joe Lattimore is innocent."

Robin told Amanda about the illegal fight, Lattimore's assertion that he was blackmailed into burglarizing Carasco's house, and the aftermath of finding the body.

"That's some story," Amanda said. "And you believe it?"

"I can be fooled, but he sounds like he's telling the truth."

"You realize this case could be a bear?"

"That's why I need you on my side. Judge Carasco might end up being the prime suspect, and I need someone who won't be scared to go after a powerful circuit court judge. So, are you interested?"

"There might be a problem."

"Oh?"

"You know Mike Greene?"

When they cocounseled the federal case, Amanda had been dating the best trial lawyer in the Multnomah County district attorney's capital case unit.

"Are you and Mike still an item?"

Amanda laughed. "I guess you can say that. We're living together, and we're engaged. Joe Lattimore's case is going to be front-page news, and that's the type of capital case Mike usually prosecutes. Let me give him a call to see if I have a conflict."

Amanda hit speed dial on her cell phone. Robin waited while Amanda and her fiancé carried on a brief conversation. When Amanda disconnected, she wasn't smiling.

"I'm in. We don't have to worry. Mike doesn't have the case."

"Then who does?"

CHAPTER TWENTY-SIX

Vanessa Cole was a slender black woman in her midfifties, with sharp features and fierce brown eyes. She had grown up in a wealthy family and had a law degree from Stanford. After joining the Multnomah County district attorney's office, her high ethical standards and brilliant courtroom performances had earned her swift promotions. When Paul Getty, the Multnomah County district attorney, was forced to retire because of health problems, the governor followed Getty's recommendation and appointed Vanessa to head the office, but the next election was approaching. Vanessa detested politics, but she loved being the Multnomah County district attorney. Getting her name in front of voters was imperative if she wanted to defeat her challengers, and prosecuting a high-profile, sure-winner death penalty case was one way to do that.

Leading the prosecution team in the *Lattimore* case gave Vanessa a terrific chance to grab headlines, but she was conflicted about using this particular case to further her career. Vanessa knew that it was a mistake for a lawyer to take a case if she had a close relationship with the victim or someone close to the victim, because it interfered with her ability to make emotionally detached decisions. Vanessa knew Betsy and Tony Carasco, so she had given a lot of thought to handing the prosecution of Joseph Lattimore to another DA. In the end, she'd decided that her connection to the Carascos wasn't close enough to affect her objectivity.

Vanessa did not like Tony Carasco, who'd had a questionable reputation when he worked in the district attorney's office. Rumors had made the rounds about his ties to motorcycle gangs and drug dealers, who occasionally benefited from evidence and witnesses that went missing when Carasco was involved in a case. Vanessa had her own suspicions based on a case they had worked together, but she was never able to support her suspicions with proof. After much thought, Vanessa decided that the fact that she didn't like the victim's husband would have no impact on her desire to put the person who murdered Betsy Carasco behind bars.

Vanessa had met Carasco's wife at office parties, charity galas, and political rallies, but she didn't know Betsy well. She did know that being beaten to death was a horrible way to die, and she looked forward to avenging the victim of that kind of brutality.

Vanessa had heard through the courthouse grapevine that Robin Lockwood had visited Joseph Lattimore in the jail, so she wasn't surprised when her secretary told her that Robin was in reception and wanted to see her.

"Is this about Betsy Carasco's case?" Vanessa asked when Robin was seated.

Robin smiled. "Word travels fast."

"Are you representing Lattimore?"

"I am, and Amanda Jaffe is cocounseling."

"Smart. That means I can't have Mike at my side."

"That's not why I asked her to be second chair, but it is a collateral benefit."

"So, why are you here?"

"To touch base."

"And find out what we've got."

"That too."

"Robin, we've got a very strong case, so I'm going to tell you what we have. I'll also make you a plea offer."

"Go ahead."

"Judge Carasco and Ian Hennessey, one of my deputies, saw Lattimore run out of the judge's house, but we don't need them to place your client at the scene. Betsy Carasco's body was found in the living room. Your client's prints were on the light switch and wall in the living room. The wall and the light switch are very close to the body. What's more, the tread on the bottom of your client's running shoes matches muddy shoe prints we found inside Carasco's house.

"Dr. Grace will testify that Betsy was beaten to death. We did an internet search on Mr. Lattimore and discovered that your client is a professional boxer.

"You know that we don't have to prove motive," Vanessa continued, "but your client is homeless, so breaking into the judge's house to steal makes sense."

"Has Mr. Lattimore confessed?"

"He hasn't said much of anything since his arrest."

"What's the offer?"

"If Mr. Lattimore pleads to aggravated murder for killing Betsy Carasco, I won't pursue the death penalty. He'll have to accept life without the possibility of parole."

"I appreciate the candor," Robin said.

"You've always been a straight shooter," Vanessa said. "And I do have a rock-solid case. Talk to your client. Then get back to me."

"I will. But I do have one question. Soon after Mrs. Carasco was killed, Mr. Lattimore was arrested at a motel where he was staying with his wife and baby. How did the police know he was there?"

Vanessa hesitated. The way the police found out about the motel was the only thing about her case that made her uneasy.

"It was an anonymous tip."

"How soon after Mr. Lattimore left the crime scene did the call come in?"

"I don't remember. But it'll be in the police reports."

"Okay. Thanks."

Robin left. Vanessa thought the meeting had gone well. Robin had to get her client's permission to take the deal, so Vanessa hadn't expected Robin to cave right away. A case this strong would probably be resolved by a plea. Robin would try to get a concession to life with the possibility of parole. Vanessa didn't know if she'd make that concession, but she didn't have to decide that now.

The prosecutor turned to another file on her desk and forgot about Joseph Lattimore. Why think about a case she couldn't lose any way it went? If Lattimore didn't plead, she would go to trial with a case that was a slam dunk, and the win would net her a ton of good publicity.

CHAPTER TWENTY-SEVEN

"I've decided to take your case," Robin told Joe Lattimore as soon as the guard left them alone in the contact visiting room. "I already accepted the appointment, and Amanda Jaffe is going to sit second chair. She's one of the best defense attorneys in the state."

"I don't know how to thank you."

"You don't have to. This is what I do. And I have some very good news for you. Maria and Conchita are okay. They're together in a women's shelter. I know the woman who runs it, and I'm keeping tabs on them. So, you don't have to worry."

Joe choked up and could only nod.

"But the news isn't all good. Your case is going to be prosecuted by Vanessa Cole. She's *the* Multnomah County DA, and she's very good. I met with her, and she told me everything they have. They don't do that unless they're convinced that they can't lose."

"How do *you* think the case will go?"

"It's too early for me to guess about the outcome. I haven't seen the police reports, and we haven't started to investigate. But before we talk about the evidence in your case, I want to tell you how a death penalty case is tried, because a death penalty case is very different from every other type of criminal case."

"Go ahead."

"The big difference has to do with the way the sentence is determined. In every other criminal case, the judge determines the appropriate sentence, and there are several weeks between the conviction and the sentencing hearing, so I don't think about the sentence unless my client is convicted.

"In a death penalty case, the jury that decides that the defendant is guilty of aggravated murder has to decide if the defendant should be sentenced to death. To protect the jurors from outside influences, they are brought back immediately after they convict to hear evidence on the issue of the appropriate sentence at a hearing that can be longer than the trial. This has a huge impact on how an attorney prepares a case with a potential death sentence.

"When I get a death case, I have to assume the worst and start preparing for the sentencing hearing at the same time I prepare for the part of the trial that determines guilt or innocence. If I wait, I won't have time to gather evidence that can convince the jurors that they shouldn't sentence my client to die.

"If you're convicted, the only thing the jurors will know about you is that you've murdered someone. To convince them that you shouldn't be executed, I have to show the jurors that you aren't a monster; that you may have killed someone, but you are still a decent person. I'm going to have investigators interviewing you and everyone who has ever known you. We are going to create a biography of your life from the time you were born until the day of the trial."

"Is there anything I can do to help?"

Robin smiled. "I was just going to get to that. I want you to write your life story for my investigators, starting from your earliest memory. Don't sugarcoat it. If there is something awful in your background, I have to know about it, because you can be certain that the DA will uncover it.

"What you write is protected by the attorney-client privilege, so you can tell me everything. If you experienced sexual or physical abuse as a child, include it, even if it's embarrassing. I also want a list of witnesses who will have good things to say about you and any way you can think of that we can get in touch with them. When in doubt, include the information. We'll decide who to call and who to leave out. Think you can do that?"

"I'll start as soon as you leave."

"Vanessa told me that Carasco's husband and a deputy district attorney have made a positive identification. They're the people who were in the car that drove up when you were leaving the judge's home. Vanessa also told me that they found your prints on the wall and light switch in the room where Betsy Carasco's body was found. They've also matched shoe prints inside Judge Carasco's house to the tread on your running shoes."

Joe sighed. "I knew they would. What else do they have?"

"I'll know soon. You're going to be arraigned on the indictment after lunch. Vanessa has to give me the discovery in your case as soon as she indicts. I'll get you a full copy when Vanessa gives it to me. I'll want you to go over it and tell me anything you think will help your case."

"Will do."

"Do you have anything else you want to talk about right now?"

"One thing. Are you going to see Maria and Conchita?"

Robin nodded. "I haven't talked to Maria because I didn't want to bother her until she was settled in. But she may be an important witness in a penalty phase."

"When you see them, tell them I love them."

CHAPTER TWENTY-EIGHT

When Robin entered the courtroom for Joseph Lattimore's arraignment, she noticed a tall, elegantly dressed woman sitting among the spectators. The woman stood out in a crowd composed of poorly dressed criminal defendants and attorneys wearing the suits they could afford on a public defender's salary, but Robin was too preoccupied to give the woman more than a moment's thought.

The arraignment was over quickly. The judge read the charging document, Joe pleaded not guilty, and the guards took him back to the jail. When the next case was called, Robin left the courtroom. She was heading for the stairs to the street when the well-dressed woman stepped in front of her.

"Ms. Lockwood, my name is Helen Raptis, and I am Elizabeth's mother."

Robin had run an internet search on Betsy Carasco. Her mother had featured prominently in the profile. Robin knew that Raptis was worth millions and had a reputation for ruthlessness in business affairs.

"I'm so sorry about your daughter," Robin said. "This must be impossible for you."

Raptis stood ramrod straight. "What is

impossible for me to bear is seeing the man responsible for Elizabeth's death walking around without a care. Your client may have taken Betsy's life, but that bastard is the person who ordered him to do it."

"Who are you talking about?"

"Anthony Carasco ordered my daughter's murder."

"That's quite an accusation. Have you told the district attorney what you just told me?"

"Cole doesn't take me seriously. She says she'll look at Carasco, but it's obvious that she thinks I'm a bitter, grieving mother who's striking out at the world."

"Why are you talking about this to me? I'm representing the man who's accused of killing your daughter."

"Mr. Lattimore is a puppet. That monster was pulling the strings. If your client tells Cole that Carasco hired him, he can testify for the state and cut a deal."

"I'm interested in hearing why you think Judge Carasco hired my client. Would you like to come to my office?"

"Most definitely."

Leo Boyce followed his boss to Barrister, Berman, and Lockwood at a discreet distance. Helen didn't bother to introduce her bodyguard even when everyone was in Robin's office.

"Anthony Carasco is a parasite," Raptis said. "He latched onto my Elizabeth like a leech, and he's been sucking her trust accounts dry. I tried to talk sense into her when she told me she was thinking of marrying that bastard, but she wouldn't listen."

"How did Elizabeth and Carasco meet?"

"Cocaine brought them together."

"Your daughter was a user?"

Raptis nodded. "It wasn't pretty. She was ravaged by her addiction."

Helen's icy façade cracked, and Robin glimpsed her pain.

"Very few people knew what was going on. We kept Elizabeth's problem under wraps. She was enough of an actress to fool her society friends. The visits to the rehabilitation centers were 'trips to Paris' or 'safaris in Africa.' But that bastard made sure she stayed addicted so he could control her."

"You're saying that the judge was supplying her?" Robin said.

"You sound surprised. You shouldn't be. As soon as Elizabeth started seeing that . . . that thing, I had him investigated. Anthony Carasco is a common criminal. He grew up in a slum and associated with scum all his life. He has connections to people he's known since childhood who are drug dealers and members of biker gangs. He protects them if they are arrested, and he has police officers who work with him."

"How did Carasco convince your daughter to marry him? There's a big age difference between them."

"I suspect he learned about Elizabeth from one of her dealers. When she came out of rehab a few years ago, he made sure he was at the events she attended. He's older than Elizabeth, but he can be quite charming. Once he'd convinced her to date him, he also convinced her to use again. When her need overrode her common sense, he talked her into marrying him without a prenup. When she found out about his latest whore, she told him she was going to get a divorce."

"How do you know that?" Robin asked.

"She told me. Shortly before she was murdered, she called me in tears and told me he was cheating on her again and she wasn't going to stand for it. That's why he had my Elizabeth murdered. Elizabeth had a lot of money, which that bastard will now inherit. A divorce would have turned off the money faucet."

"Do you have proof that Carasco was cheating on your daughter?"

"Give me the photos, Leo," Raptis commanded imperiously.

Boyce took a manila envelope out of an attaché case he'd been carrying and handed it to his employer. She opened it and spread a group of photographs across Robin's blotter.

One photograph showed Anthony Carasco being greeted by a very attractive blonde in skimpy lingerie at the door of an apartment. A series of photographs taken through a space between a window shade and the edge of the window showed the couple kissing and fondling each other as they crossed a room, then disappeared into another room.

"Leo, did you conduct the investigation into Judge Carasco's background?" Robin asked.

Boyce looked at his employer. She nodded.

"Yes," Boyce answered.

"Did you come up with evidence that I can introduce in court that would prove Carasco hired someone to kill his wife?"

"No, ma'am. I can show he's met with drug dealers and other criminals who would be willing to kill his wife for a price, but I don't have a smoking gun."

"Besides drugs, did you find evidence that Carasco was involved in any other type of crimes?"

"Such as?"

"Illegal fights."

Boyce frowned. "Why are you asking?"

"I can't tell you. But I may be able to show a connection between Mrs. Carasco's murder and the judge if you did have evidence of his involvement in unsanctioned, no-holds-barred fights."

"I never found anything pointing that way."

"Ms. Lockwood, I am very wealthy," Raptis said. "That wealth is at your disposal if you need it to prove that Anthony Carasco hired the man who murdered my daughter."

"Thank you. And you should know that there's a good chance that my client is not the person who took your daughter's life. In fact, he may be as much a victim in this case as your daughter."

CHAPTER TWENTY-NINE

"We have something you need to see," Carrie Anders said as she and Roger Dillon walked into Vanessa Cole's office.

Carrie set her phone on the DA's desk. On the screen was a YouTube video of two men facing each other in an open space in what might have been a barn. No one else was in the shot. Carrie pressed the screen, and the two men started to fight. There was no sound. Within seconds, one man was down, and the other man was beating him senseless. That's when the clip ended.

"That's Joseph Lattimore!" Vanessa exclaimed.

Carrie nodded. "And the man on the bottom is Carlos Ortega, whose body was found in a vacant lot not far from the tent city where Lattimore lived, before he moved to that motel. Ortega was beaten to death.

"We've got more good stuff for you," Carrie said. "Tell her about the hand wraps, Roger."

"We conducted a search of Carasco's neighborhood," Roger said. "Hand wraps that a boxer would use to protect his knuckles were found in a garbage can on Carasco's property. There was a lot of blood on them. We ran a DNA test. Some of the blood on the wraps matches Betsy Carasco's DNA, and trace evidence matched Lattimore's DNA.

"Carlos Ortega's injuries are similar to those that Betsy Carasco suffered, and there was blood on the hand wraps that didn't belong to Mrs. Carasco or Lattimore. We had that blood tested. It's Ortega's. So, we've got Lattimore for two murders, and that should be enough to convince a jury he deserves to die."

Anthony Carasco had taken a few days of sick leave so it would look like he was mourning Betsy. During the first couple of days, there had been several visitors and calls of condolence mixed with calls for comment from the press. When the phone calls became a nuisance, Carasco started letting most of them go to voice mail, but he always checked caller ID before ignoring a call.

Carasco was reading the newspaper when his cell phone rang. He accepted when he saw the caller was Vanessa Cole.

"There's been a development I thought you should know about," the DA said.

"Oh?"

"Shortly after Mrs. Carasco was murdered, the body of a man named Carlos Ortega was discovered in a vacant lot near a homeless enclave where Joseph Lattimore was living. He had been beaten in a manner similar to the way your wife was killed. We have evidence linking Mr. Lattimore to this homicide. I'm going to present the evidence to a grand jury tomorrow and ask for an indictment for manslaughter.

"The manner of Mr. Ortega's death is so similar to the way your wife was killed that I may be able to introduce it in the trial of Mr. Lattimore for your wife's death. Even if I can't, I'll definitely be able to introduce the evidence in a sentencing hearing, because it bears on whether Lattimore will be dangerous in the future. The indictment will also give me a lot of leverage to get Mr. Lattimore to plead, which will save you the ordeal of having to go through a trial and all of the appeals that would follow."

"This is great news. Thank you for calling me, Vanessa."

"I've made Mr. Lattimore a plea offer that would let him avoid a death sentence. He'd be locked away for life. Will you be upset if I don't go for a death?"

"Personally, Vanessa, I would choose death over having to live the rest of my life in a cage. Death lets you off the hook."

"I'm glad you agree. I'll let you know about developments as they happen. And feel free to call me if you have questions."

"Thank you. I appreciate the way you're handling Betsy's case."

Carasco talked to Vanessa for a few more minutes. There was a big smile on his face when he hung up. If Lattimore pled, the case would be closed. If he didn't, a conviction was assured.

CHAPTER THIRTY

The guard brought Joseph Lattimore into the contact visiting room moments after Robin and Jeff sat down. On the table was a pile of police, forensic, and autopsy reports that Robin's associate had copied.

"Joe, this is Jeff Hodges, my investigator. We need to talk about something that's come up. Then I'll leave you two to start working on the penalty phase investigation."

"How are you holding up?" Jeff asked as he and Lattimore shook hands.

"This isn't my first time in jail, so I know the ropes. And knowing that Maria and Conchita are okay really helps."

"I'm glad to hear that," Robin said. "So, I have good news and bad news. First, the good news. We lucked out. Your case was assigned to Harold Wright. He's one of my favorite judges. He's very smart, and he always tries to do the right thing."

"What's the bad news?"

"A YouTube video of your fight with Carlos Ortega surfaced. The video is all over the internet. I've seen it. The fight is brutal."

Joe looked down at the table. "I'm sorry. I just couldn't stop myself."

"Some kids found Ortega's body in a vacant lot not far from the encampment where you were living," Jeff said.

Joe looked confused. "What was the body doing near the encampment? Carlos died miles away in that barn. That doesn't make sense."

"It would make sense if the body was put there to frame you," Jeff said.

"And you have another problem," Robin told Joe. "The police found hand wraps in a garbage can on Carasco's property. There was a lot of blood on them. The lab found your DNA and DNA from Carlos Ortega and Betsy Carasco on them."

Joe's head snapped up. "They have my hand wraps and the wraps have that woman's blood on them!?"

"Yes. Why are you surprised?"

"The guy who ran the fights took the hand wraps before I left the barn. Mrs. Carasco's blood couldn't have been on them unless the person who killed her put them on to frame me."

"That makes sense. I wondered why you would keep bloody hand wraps with you, then reuse them at another homicide. I also thought that it was unlikely that you would throw away blood-soaked, incriminating evidence where the police were sure to find it."

"I never had those wraps after I left the barn," Joe reiterated.

"There was one piece of evidence we might be able to use for your defense. You remember you told me that Ortega looked sluggish when you fought? The autopsy found traces of a tranquilizer in Ortega's blood."

"He was doped!"

"I'm starting to think that the key to winning your case is the illegal fight," Robin said. "The person who ran it is probably the person who set you up. Can you think of anything that will help us figure out who he is?"

"That's all I've thought about. The only person who gave me a name is Sal, the guy who recruited me. And the only guy I can think of who we might be able to ID is the guy who drove me to the fight and to Carasco's house. If he has a record, you might be able to get a mug shot. He's so unusual looking that I'd know him instantly."

"I have a techie friend who may be able to run facial recognition software on the big guy," Jeff said. "If we get a hit, I'll bring the photo to you."

Robin stood and rang for the guard. "I'll let you two get started. Remember, tell Jeff everything, and let us decide what's useful and what's not."

"Got it," Joe said just as the door to the corridor opened.

"So," Jeff said when they were alone, "you've done time?"

"Yeah. When I was in high school, I was in a gang. I got arrested for assault. There weren't serious injuries, and my lawyer was able to get the DA to agree to dismiss the charges if I went into the army. But I did spend a few weeks in jail."

Joe smiled. "Getting arrested was the best thing that happened to me before I met Maria. The army got me away from the gang, and that's where I learned how to box and cook."

"Robin told you to prepare an autobiography. Have you had a chance to do that?"

Joe held out several pages of yellow lined paper. "This is what I have so far."

"Great," Jeff said. "I'll copy this and get the original back to you. So, your folks, are they still alive?"

Joe shook his head. "Mom passed from cancer five years ago. And my father walked out when I was two. Haven't heard from him since."

"Okay. Brothers and sisters?"

"I'm an only child."

Jeff took notes for another half hour before buzzing the guard.

"Please tell Ms. Lockwood how much I appreciate what she's doing for me," Joe said when Jeff started to leave.

"I will. You won the lottery when Robin decided to take your case. She's going to give you everything she's got, and that's a hell of a lot more than any other lawyer in this city."

CHAPTER THIRTY-ONE

Ian Hennessey was almost drunk. He figured one more scotch would bring him to a safe, warm place where the thoughts that were haunting him could not intrude. The day after he'd passed the bar, his parents had visited him at his condo, and his father had told him that he would be hired by the Multnomah district attorney's office if he applied. His father hadn't told him how he knew this, but Ian knew how much influence his family's money bought, so he didn't have to ask. Ian also had not asked why his father hadn't gotten him a job at one of Portland's prestigious law firms. It was clear that his mother and father didn't think he was smart enough to handle the complex legal issues he would be tasked with at one of them.

Ian had been ashamed that his parents didn't think enough of him to believe he could land a good job on his own. Then he faced reality. Without the Hennesseys' pull, he would never have been able to land any job, and he would be reduced to hanging out a shingle. So, he had started at the DA's office with a chip on his shoulder, surrounded by young attorneys who had earned their positions by hard work and their own achievements and resented him because he had not.

At first, Ian had been unenthusiastic about prosecuting dull cases against nobodies, and his results showed his lack of preparation. After he was called on the carpet by his supervisor, Ian had won two cases. He felt an electric charge each time the jury rewarded his efforts with a guilty verdict, and he started looking forward to going to work. Then Anthony Carasco and Stacey Hayes had come into his life, threatening to take away the only thing he'd felt he could do well and turning his life into a nightmare.

Moments before Hennessey finished his drink, someone sat on the stool next to him and signaled the bartender.

"Another for my friend, and the same for me," a man said.

Hennessey turned his bleary eyes toward the voice. It had come from a solidly built man dressed in khaki slacks, a sky-blue work shirt, and a black rain jacket. A well-groomed mustache decorated the man's upper lip and was complemented by light brown eyes and a coffee-colored complexion.

"Do I know you?" Hennessey asked, his words slightly slurred.

The man extended his hand. "Brent Macklin, Mr. Hennessey. And no, we've never met."

Hennessey frowned. "You bought me a drink."

Macklin smiled. "I did."

"Why?"

"It's something you do when you want to get to know someone."

Hennessey pulled back. "Hey, I'm not . . . If this is a pickup . . ."

Macklin laughed. "No, no. I'm as straight as straight can be. I'm also a reporter, and I think you can help me with a story I'm writing."

"What kind of story?" asked Hennessey warily.

"You were with Judge Carasco when he discovered his wife's body, right?"

"Yes."

"A man named Joe Lattimore was arrested for the crime."

"I can't talk about that. I'm a witness."

"I know that, and I'm not interested in Lattimore's connection to Mrs. Carasco's murder."

"Then why do you want to talk to me?"

"Lattimore killed a man during an unsanctioned, no-holds-barred fight. I freelance stories about boxing, mixed martial arts events, and tough-guy competitions. I saw the YouTube video of Lattimore's fight with Carlos Ortega, and it gave me the idea for a story about unsanctioned fights. They're held all over the country, but no one writes about them."

"Why talk to me? I don't know anything about that case."

"But you're in the Multnomah County DA's office. I thought you could give me a lead."

"Vanessa Cole is prosecuting Lattimore. Talk to her."

"I tried, but she wouldn't discuss the case. How about someone in the police department? Do you know the detectives who are working the fight case?"

"Carrie Anders and Roger Dillon were the lead detectives on Mrs. Carasco's case. They're probably working the manslaughter case too."

Macklin held out a business card to Hennessey. "Thanks for the names. If you think of anything else, I'd appreciate a call."

Macklin left and Hennessey noticed that he hadn't touched his drink. Hennessey hesitated. Then he pulled Macklin's glass next to his and finished them both. The double shot had the desired effect, and Hennessey's brain began to fog. But just before he passed into a happy state of drunkenness, a tiny idea began to form.

PART FOUR
THE FARM

CHAPTER THIRTY-TWO

The Honorable Harold Wright looked like he'd been put together by a blind man. He had the barrel chest of a weight lifter, spindly legs, the styled, snowy-white hair of a movie actor, a bird-beak nose that overshadowed a bushy mustache, and wire-rimmed glasses that covered piercing blue eyes, which routinely saw through the flimsy arguments of unprepared barristers.

Robin and Vanessa Cole had filed a number of pretrial motions in Joseph Lattimore's case, and it was almost five o'clock when Robin finished arguing several objections to Oregon's death penalty.

"Thank you, Ms. Lockwood," the judge said when Robin sat down. "You've made your record if you decide to raise your arguments in a federal court, but our supreme court has already ruled against you on these issues, so I'm going to deny this set of motions."

Judge Wright moved a thick stack of papers to one side and picked up Robin's last motion.

"Mrs. Cole, you've charged Mr. Lattimore in a separate indictment with manslaughter. Am I correct that you are alleging that Mr. Lattimore killed an opponent during an unsanctioned fight, and you want to introduce evidence of the incident in Mr. Lattimore's trial for the murder of Elizabeth Carasco?"

"Yes, Your Honor. In the video of the fight, Mr. Lattimore is wearing hand wraps. Hand wraps found at the Carasco crime scene had the defendant's blood on them as well as Mrs. Carasco's. They also had the blood of Carlos Ortega, Mr. Lattimore's victim from the fight, on them. We believe that the blood-soaked hand wraps connect the two incidents, and we need to tell the jury about the fight to explain the significance of the hand wraps."

The judge turned to Robin. "You believe that the fight is a completely separate incident that has no relevance to proving the murder case against Mr. Lattimore."

"Yes, Your Honor," Robin said.

"You also take the position that if there is some tenuous relevance, it is outweighed by the prejudicial effect evidence that Mr. Lattimore killed a man in an illegal fight would have on the jury."

"That's correct. I've set out all of the exceptions to the rule of evidence that prohibits the state from introducing evidence of crimes not charged in an indictment in a trial of the charged crime," Robin said. "The evidence about the fight doesn't fit into any of the exceptions."

"What about the hand wraps?" the judge asked.

"Mrs. Cole doesn't need to talk about the

fight to get the evidence in or to use it against Mr. Lattimore. The hand wraps were found in a garbage can on the Carasco property. She can have someone explain that Mr. Lattimore boxes professionally and that professional fighters use hand wraps to protect their knuckles. Someone from the crime lab can tell the jury that my client's blood and Mrs. Carasco's blood were on the hand wraps. It's not relevant to this case that Mr. Ortega's blood was also on the wraps."

Vanessa started to respond, but the judge held up his hand.

"Mrs. Cole, I'm not convinced that you should be allowed to introduce evidence of the fight in Mr. Lattimore's murder trial. I'm going to bar the evidence at this time, but I'll let you raise the issue again if you can show a stronger connection between the two incidents."

The judge looked at his watch. "It's almost time to recess. Do you have anything more we need to discuss?"

"No, Your Honor," both women said.

"Then court is adjourned."

Robin talked to Joe about the judge's rulings. When they were through, the guards escorted Joe from the courtroom. As soon as Robin was free, Vanessa walked over to her.

"Has Mr. Lattimore given any thought to my plea offer?" she asked.

"I have serious doubts about Joe's guilt,

Vanessa. He swears he didn't murder Mrs. Carasco."

"I know you're not a bleeding heart, but you should consider the possibility that Mr. Lattimore is an exceptionally good liar. Our evidence of guilt is overwhelming. Think about the impact evidence that he killed Carlos Ortega will have after he's convicted and the jury has to decide if he lives or dies. In the sentencing phase, the jurors have to decide if Mr. Lattimore will be dangerous in the future. Evidence that he beat a man to death would be relevant to that decision. There is no way you can keep the evidence away from the jury in a sentencing phase."

"I hear you, Vanessa, but I can't advise an innocent man to plead guilty to something he didn't do."

Vanessa sighed. "I respect that, and I'll keep the offer open a little longer. But it will disappear a week before trial."

The courtroom had been packed because of the notoriety the case had received, and Robin had not noticed Brent Macklin, who had been sitting in the rear of the spectators' section. She was organizing her files before heading back to her office when Macklin came up to the bar of the court.

"Ms. Lockwood?"

Robin turned around.

"Do you have a few moments to talk?"

"Sorry, I don't. I have a meeting at my office."

"This won't take long."

"I don't discuss my cases with reporters."

"And I don't want to talk about Mr. Lattimore. I write articles about mixed martial arts and boxing. I wrote a few about you when you were competing."

"That's nice, but my pro career has been over for a while, and right now, I'm too busy to reminisce."

"I'm not making myself clear. I'm gathering material for an article about illegal, no-holds-barred fights, and I saw your client's YouTube video. I'd like to talk to him, off the record, for background; how he got involved, who's running these fights, who participates, stuff like that. I won't ask any questions about this case."

"Look, Mr. . . ."

"Macklin, Brent Macklin," he said as he handed Robin his card. "You can be present while we talk."

"I am the only person my client is going to talk to until his case is over. I wish you luck with your project, but Joe is off-limits."

"Are you willing to tell me what you've found out, when you have the time?"

"I'm way too busy. You should try the police or prosecutors. They're investigating the fight. Maybe they can help you. And now, if you'll excuse me, I've got to run."

Robin had scheduled a war council in her office for five thirty. She had just finished telling Amanda Jaffe and Jeff Hodges the result of the pretrial hearing when Loretta Washington walked in. Loretta tried not to show it, but she was very excited about working on her first murder case, which was also a death penalty case.

"We have a job for you," Robin told her associate. "In most cases, potential jurors are sent to the courtroom where the trial is going to be held on the day of the trial. Then the prosecution and the defense question them in the presence of the other jurors to see who they want to put on and keep off the jury.

"Jury selection in capital cases is different. I've made a motion for individual, sequestered voir dire. If it's granted, the DA and I will question each potential juror out of the presence of the other jurors. That way, we avoid the risk of one juror's answer poisoning the entire pool.

"Another difference between a regular criminal trial and a death case is that the potential jurors in a capital case are summoned to a courtroom several days before jury selection and are given a questionnaire. After each juror fills out the questionnaire, the judge gives it to us and the prosecutors before we pick a jury. The questionnaire asks the jurors questions about their education, military and work history, the magazines they read, their views of the death penalty, and a lot of other subjects."

Robin handed Loretta a stack of papers. "These are questionnaires Amanda and I have used in other cases and a memo listing the key issues we want the jurors' views on. For example, Joe is African American. We need to know if a juror is prejudiced against African Americans. We want you to put together the questionnaire for Joe's case. When you're done, we'll review it and edit it, if necessary. Any questions?"

"No. I've been reading death penalty trial manuals and articles on trial mechanics. I think I know what you want."

Robin smiled as she handed the sample questionnaires to her associate. She wasn't surprised that Loretta was two steps ahead of her.

"You can take off. Check with me if you have any questions."

"Will do," Loretta said.

Robin suspected that Loretta would be burning the midnight oil tonight.

"Jeff, bring us up to date on what you've got for the sentencing phase," she said.

For the next twenty minutes, Jeff gave a summary of the testimony they could expect from the relatives, friends, and acquaintances he had interviewed.

"I want to talk about the illegal fight, which I see as the key to winning this case," Robin said when Jeff was through. "Any ideas on how we can find out who was behind it or the people who ran it?"

"I've got a lead on the giant Joe described. I think he's Andre Rostov. He's been arrested twice for assault, but there are no convictions. Witnesses failed to show or simply disappeared. I'm trying to find him."

"Okay, that's good. Amanda, any ideas?"

"Actually, I do have one."

"What is it?" Robin asked.

"I have this, uh, acquaintance who might be able to help."

Robin frowned. "Who is it?"

"I'd rather not say until I've talked to him."

CHAPTER THIRTY-THREE

In one of those weird coincidences that happen every once in a while, Tony Carasco was fantasizing about Stacey Hayes when she called him.

"I want to see you, Tony."

"We have to wait, baby. Betsy's mother knows about us. She's going to go to court to try to keep me from inheriting, and she'll try to use our relationship against me, so we have to wait a while before we can see each other."

"I miss playing with you," Stacey said, pitching her voice to sound like a little girl's.

Carasco felt himself stiffen. "I miss you too."

"I need you tonight," Stacey pouted.

"Once the dust settles, we can be together all the time. You have to be patient."

"I'm too horny to be patient. I'm wet now just talking to you."

"Be reasonable."

"If you don't come here, I'll have to come to your house, and reporters might see me. You can get away after dark. Please."

Carasco imagined Stacey naked, and his mouth went dry. "Okay. I'll come over around ten."

"I can't wait."

Carasco hadn't made love to Stacey in a while, and he could barely think by the time he parked near her apartment. Stacey opened the door as soon as he rang her bell. Carasco had imagined that she would be naked or wearing sexy lingerie, but she was dressed in jeans and a man-tailored shirt.

"Come in, Tony. I have someone I want you to meet."

Carasco was confused. "We're not alone?"

Stacey walked into the living room without answering. Carasco followed her and saw a man sitting in an armchair in a corner of the room. He was wearing a tight black turtleneck that stretched over a bodybuilder's physique. The man smiled.

"Pleased to meet you, Judge. Stacey has told me so much about you, I feel like I've known you for a long time."

"Who is this?" Carasco asked Stacey.

The man stood up and halted inches from the judge. He was only slightly taller than Carasco but twice as wide. Thick black hairs covered his large, apelike hands, and his forearms strained the fabric that covered them.

"I'm Stacey's manager, and I have a bone to pick with you. Stacey is a valuable property, and you've stolen her from me without compensation."

"Stacey isn't property," Carasco stammered.

Carasco never saw the punch coming, but he felt the impact. One minute, he could breathe. The next moment, all the air left his body and he was flopping on the carpet like a fish that had been slapped on the deck of a boat.

Carasco looked at Stacey while he gulped in air. She was observing him without emotion, which hurt more than the punch.

"You're a lawyer," the man said while Carasco fought for air. "Lawyers love to argue. Me, I never learned the fine points of debate. I believe in a more direct approach."

"What do you want?" the judge managed when he could breathe again.

"Compensation."

Carasco got on his hands and knees, then struggled to his feet.

"What kind of compensation?"

"Two hundred and fifty thousand dollars."

"I don't . . ." Carasco started to protest. The man kicked him in the shin. Carasco doubled over from the pain and collapsed on the floor again.

"You seem to forget that I don't debate. You also forget that Stacey knows how much money you can get your hands on. That's one of the dangers of pillow talk, Tony. Oh yeah, you're also forgetting that Stacey can tell the district attorney that you took care of her warrants, which is illegal, and tricked poor Ian into being your alibi when your wife was killed. And in case you're thinking that it would be her word against yours, I'm pretty handy with surveillance equipment, and you are the star of several videos and audiotapes. Now, stand up and look at me."

The man waited while Carasco used the arm of a chair to help him stand. There were tears in his eyes from the pain.

"Do you want to argue about the money?" the man asked.

Carasco shook his head while whispering, "No."

"Good. Tomorrow night, you're going to bring my money to a location to be announced. Will you have the money by tomorrow night?"

Carasco nodded.

"I didn't hear anything, Tony. You got to say yes or no, and you need to know that *no* has consequences."

"I'll get it."

"Great! Now run along and wait for my call."

Carasco wanted to run, but his leg hurt too much. He limped out slowly in an attempt to salvage some dignity.

As soon as the door closed, Karl Tepper burst out laughing. "That was easy."

"I hope so," Stacey said.

"You're not worried about Carasco, are you? The guy is a pussy."

"I'm not worried about Tony. I'm worried

about people he might know. I think he set up that young DA so he would have an alibi when his wife was killed. If I'm right, Tony hired the guy who killed her."

Tepper's face darkened. "You think I can't take care of some meth heads he sent to beat up his wife?"

"No, Karl, but I had Tony wrapped around my finger, and I could have talked him into giving us the money."

"That would have taken time, and I want you back in the Bay, working. Now get naked, and let's get in bed. I want to celebrate."

CHAPTER THIRTY-FOUR

When Amanda was a block away from the Jungle Club, Robin saw a naked neon dancer twitching back and forth on a sign that promised GIRLS, GIRLS, GIRLS. Moments later, Amanda parked two spots down from several Harleys in front of a square, squat building whose garish pink-and-green walls were decorated with palm trees, parrots, and bare-breasted hula dancers.

"You're taking me to a strip club?" asked Robin, who had never been in one and considered them to be sexist cesspools.

Amanda laughed. "The ladies are not strippers. They're exotic dancers. Freedom of expression is protected by the Constitution. That's important to remember if you ever represent the owner of a gentlemen's club that the government wants to close down."

Then Amanda's smile disappeared. "Before we go in, there are a few things you've got to remember. We're going to meet with Martin Breach. He owns the Jungle Club. Martin doesn't look it, but he is very dangerous. I'm bringing you along because you're Joe's lead counsel, but you have to let me run the meeting. Don't say anything unless I tell you to. If Martin asks you a question, do what you tell your witnesses to

188

do; give the shortest answer possible, then stop."

Robin frowned. "Okay."

Amanda put a hand on Robin's shoulder. "Believe me. This is for your protection."

The bouncer at the door recognized Amanda and let the women into the dimly lit interior, where the overamped sounds of a ZZ Top song slammed into Robin like a runaway train. Amanda wound between tables packed with males gawking at a blonde with breasts the size of cannonballs who was rotating around a pole. Some of the men stopped staring at the dancer long enough to leer at Amanda and Robin. A man patted Robin on the ass, but she restrained her violent impulses, worried that the club owner would not tell them what they needed to know if she put one of his customers in the hospital.

Breach's office was in the back of the building at the end of a short hall. The massive guard at the office door was one of many clients that Breach had referred to Amanda and her father over the years.

"Here to apply for a job, ladies?" the bouncer joked.

"In your dreams, Tully," Amanda answered with a smile. "Is Martin in?"

"Yeah."

"How's his mood?"

"It's always good when you visit."

The guard opened the door, and Robin followed

Amanda into a tiny office decorated with pictures of naked women and an out-of-date calendar from a motor oil company. The furniture was rickety and secondhand because Breach wanted the club to look run-down so the IRS would not get a true picture of the money that was laundered through it. Breach was also paranoid. He had his office swept for bugs every day, and he ordered his dancers to disrobe to outrageously loud music to foil eavesdropping attempts by the DEA, FBI, or Portland police.

Breach had started out in the trenches breaking legs for Benny Dee, before staging a coup during which Benny disappeared, never to be seen again. Now Breach ran the most efficient and ruthless criminal organization in the Pacific Northwest.

Portland's most violent citizen was a shade under six feet tall, but his chubby legs and chunky upper body made him seem shorter. Thinning sandy hair, drab brown eyes, and a pale, vampire-like complexion made him look like a failed used car salesman. Today, the crime lord was wearing the type of tweed jacket with leather elbow patches a college professor might own, over an Aloha shirt and lime-green polyester slacks. His ghastly taste in clothes added to an impression of ineptitude that was a disguise for a genius IQ and a truly psychotic personality. Many of his rivals only figured this out when they found themselves strapped to a table, listening to Breach tell off-color jokes just before he went to work on them with a chain saw.

Breach flashed a big smile when he saw Amanda. Amanda couldn't help returning the smile. She had mixed feelings about Breach and no illusions, but she knew he cared for her in a weird way and had helped her survive more than one life-and-death situation.

"Long time no see," the gangster said.

"That's a good thing, Martin. It seems like the only time we get together is when you or a friend are facing serious jail time or my life is in danger."

Breach spread his hands. "I'm leading a virtuous life, so you must be in trouble."

"I'm safe and sound, but I need your help. This is Robin Lockwood, my cocounsel in a death penalty case."

Breach looked at Robin. "I'd be glad to help this little lady since she helped me make a few grand when she KO'd Mendez. A roundhouse kick to the head, followed by a wicked left hook. Am I right?"

Robin grinned. "You are."

Breach turned back to Amanda. "What do you need?"

"Some information that will help us with a death penalty case defense."

"The guy who offed the judge's wife," Breach said.

Amanda wasn't surprised that Martin knew she was involved in Joe's case. Breach had informants everywhere and knew about anything that involved crime in Oregon, which was why she was visiting him.

"We think he's innocent," Amanda said.

"Don't you think all of your clients are innocent?"

"Not if you refer them."

Breach threw his head back and laughed. "That's why you're my favorite mouthpiece. No bullshit. So, what can I do for you?"

"Our client is homeless. He used to box professionally, and he was approached by a person who was recruiting people who are down on their luck to participate in an illegal, no-holds-barred fight on a farm. Joe killed his opponent, and the people who ran the fight blackmailed him into breaking into Judge Carasco's house. He was told that he was supposed to steal something, but he found Mrs. Carasco beaten to death when he got inside.

"The body of Carlos Ortega, the man Joe fought, was found in a vacant lot. He'd been beaten to death. Joe wore hand wraps during the illegal fight. The police found them in the garbage at the Carascos' house. Mrs. Carasco's blood was on the wraps along with Ortega's. Joe swears that the man who ran the fight kept his hand wraps. We think this man was behind the murder of Mrs. Carasco and set up Joe to take the fall, but we have no idea who he is or who runs the fights. If you know who they are, it would really help if you clued us in."

Breach was quiet for a while, and Amanda let him think.

"How sure are you that your guy didn't kill Carasco's lady?" Breach asked.

"Knowing what we know, I'd vote not guilty if I were on his jury," Amanda told Breach.

"That's good enough for me, so I'm gonna tell you something, but it can't get back to me."

"Of course," Amanda said.

"A guy named Kevin Bash runs the fights, but there's someone behind him fronting the money and taking a cut. I don't know who that is, and I've never been interested enough to find out."

"Do you know where these fights are held?" Amanda asked.

"Last I heard, there's a farm out in Washington County."

"What can you tell me about Bash?"

"Not much. He has a Mercedes dealership in Hillsboro. It may be legit, or he may be laundering profits through it from the fights, backroom poker games, bookmaking, and some prostitution."

Amanda knew that Breach usually had a finger in any illegal enterprise in Oregon.

"You let him run this stuff?" she asked.

"He's too small to interest me, but I have people who keep an eye on him. I don't know much more, but I have ways of finding out when the next fight is going to be held and where they're holding it. The only problem for you is that the guest list is invitation only, so they can keep out undercover cops."

"Can you get us an invite?" Amanda asked.

"I can try, but I can't promise anything."

"Our client told us that he was recruited," Robin said. "Do you know how they go about finding the fighters?"

"The fighters are usually street people, homeless. Bash has people in the tent cities and people who look for fresh meat downtown or other places where the homeless hang out."

"Do you know any of these recruiters?" Robin asked.

"Why?"

"If we can't get invited to the next fight as a guest, maybe you can get one of the recruiters to get me in as a contestant."

Amanda's features darkened, but Robin didn't notice how upset her suggestion had made her friend.

"Let's not get ahead of ourselves," she cautioned Robin. Then she turned to Breach. "Thanks for the info, Martin."

"It's always a pleasure to see you. And say hi to Frank."

"Will do."

Breach opened a humidor that sat on a corner of his desk and took out two hand-wrapped cigars.

"Give these to your dad. They're Cuban. Totally illegal. He'll love them."

Amanda turned her back on Robin as soon as they left Breach's office and stalked out of the club at a brisk pace. Robin could see that her friend was angry, but she had no idea what she could have done to upset her.

"Wait up," she said when Amanda walked to her car.

Amanda didn't answer her and slammed her door when she was behind the wheel. Then she closed her eyes and took several deep breaths.

Robin looked puzzled. "What's got you so upset?"

"Didn't I tell you to let me run the meeting?"

"Yeah. I did."

"You have no idea what you did in there," Amanda said.

"I don't understand."

"Martin Breach has no boundaries. He is the most dangerous man in this city. When you asked Martin to find a recruiter so you could infiltrate the fights, you were asking him for a favor. You never, ever want to owe Martin Breach, because he will call in the debt, and that is never a good thing."

"You asked Breach for help."

Amanda sighed. "Martin and I have a very complicated relationship. My dad and I have helped him and Art Prochaska, Martin's only real friend, on a few occasions, and he's returned the favor by literally saving my life more than once. Sometimes I think he sees me as his daughter. But even with all that, I stay clear of Martin unless it's absolutely necessary. Saving Joe Lattimore's life is in that category.

"And there's another thing," Amanda continued. "This idea of being a contestant in these illegal fights is nuts."

"The women I fight will be out-of-shape amateurs. I won't be in any danger."

"You're forgetting something, Robin. You're famous. Martin knew who you were as soon as you walked into his office, and someone at these fights will recognize you. Once they figure out who you are, they'll know you represent Joe. If they beat Betsy Carasco to death, what do you think they'll do to you?"

"I may be a blonde, Amanda, but I'm not completely ditzy. This was just an idea. And if I decide to fight, I'll dye my hair and make myself look homeless. But I don't think it will get that far. Once we know where the fight is, we'll call the cops and have it raided."

"I want you to forget about going undercover. This isn't a movie. What do you think Jeff would say if he heard what you're thinking?"

Suddenly, Robin looked worried. "Please don't tell him. He's gotten very upset when I've put myself in danger. It's caused trouble between us."

Amanda softened. "Don't worry. Mum's the word. What happens in the Jungle Club stays in the Jungle Club."

Robin laughed, glad her friend wasn't angry with her anymore.

"And," Amanda reminded her, "we do have another lead—Kevin Bash."

CHAPTER THIRTY-FIVE

"Mr. Macklin?" Ian Hennessey asked when a man answered the phone.

"Yes?"

"This is the person you met last Thursday night at the bar. I might have something interesting for you, but I don't want to discuss it over the phone."

"Why not?"

"You never know who's listening."

"Like in wiretapping?" Macklin laughed. "My hope is that someday I'll be important enough to be under surveillance, but I don't think I rate that high right now."

"This isn't funny."

"Sorry."

"You'll understand why after we meet. Can you come to the same place we met at nine tonight? I'll be in a booth at the back."

"You mean—"

"No names!"

Hennessey heard Macklin sigh. Then Macklin said, "Okay, you've got me curious. Nine it is."

When Hennessey hung up, he was sweating and light-headed. It had taken all of his courage to make the call, and he hoped he wouldn't regret it.

• • •

Hennessey wore a baseball cap, dark glasses, old jeans, and a black-and-orange jacket with an Oregon State University Beavers emblem. He got to the bar early so he could commandeer a booth near the rear door, just in case he had to make a quick escape. When the waitress came for his order, he asked for a pitcher of beer so she wouldn't bother him for a while.

Ian was hanging on by a thread. He wasn't sleeping, he had no appetite, and he was convinced that a powerful judge and a ruthless woman were out to destroy him. While he waited for Brent Macklin, he sipped his beer, wishing it were something stronger, but he knew he needed a clear head for this meeting.

Macklin walked into the bar at nine on the dot. He waited until his eyes adjusted to the dim light before scanning the booths. Hennessey waved quickly, and Macklin sat down across from him.

"Bond, James Bond," Macklin said.

"This isn't funny," Hennessey snapped.

"Sorry, but it's all so cloak-and-dagger-ish."

"You'll see why when you hear what I have to say. First, though, you have to guarantee me that you'll never reveal that I was your source."

"You want to be a Deep Throat?"

"Yes. If I'm right, what I'm telling you can cost me my job. In the worst-case scenario, I could be killed."

Macklin studied Hennessey, who was sweating and twitchy.

"Okay, you're anonymous."

"And you'll go to jail to protect me?"

Macklin was going to argue with Hennessey, but he was too curious to walk away.

"We were never here," he said. "So, what's this big secret?"

"A man named Joseph Lattimore was arrested for the murder of Elizabeth Carasco, the wife of Judge Anthony Carasco. The judge and I very conveniently drove up to the judge's house just as Lattimore ran out.

"It was raining very hard when we turned into Carasco's street, and we saw Lattimore standing in our headlights. He was too far for me to make him out very well what with the wipers moving and the downpour. Carasco told the police that the man had a scar on his face. I don't know how he could see a scar under those conditions and from that far away."

"Where is this going?"

"Just listen," Hennessey said as he leaned across the table and lowered his voice. "Vanessa Cole is going to argue that Lattimore is homeless and killed Mrs. Carasco during a failed burglary. I don't know if Lattimore beat Mrs. Carasco to death, but I have a very strong suspicion that Judge Carasco hired Lattimore or whoever killed her."

Macklin's brow furrowed. "Do you have evidence to back that up?"

"It's all circumstantial."

"Why are we meeting?"

"I'm sure Carasco set me up, and I could lose everything."

"Talk to me about that."

Without using her name, Hennessey told Macklin about Stacey and the warrants, which had mysteriously disappeared. He explained that Carasco had arranged for him to appear in his court shortly after Stacey had blackmailed him, and he told Macklin how the judge had maneuvered him into being with him at the exact time Betsy was being killed.

"It's too many coincidences. I just know I was set up to be his alibi."

"I admit it sounds like it, but it really could be a coincidence."

"That's why I'm talking to you. If Carasco's innocent, I don't want to get him in trouble. But if he's guilty and you break the story, your career will be made. And if you can keep me out of the story, my career might be saved. I haven't done anything wrong, and I can't stand the idea that I'm being used to help a murderer go free."

"You've definitely made me curious."

"There's something else. When we talked the first time, you told me that you wanted to do a story about these illegal, no-holds-barred fights."

"I still do."

"There may be a tie-in between the Ortega

fight and Mrs. Carasco's murder. You've seen the YouTube video of Lattimore's fight with Ortega, so you know Lattimore killed him. What's not public knowledge is something that was discovered at the crime lab. Hand wraps like a boxer uses were found in a garbage can on Carasco's property. Mrs. Carasco's blood was on the wraps, but so was Mr. Ortega's.

"If Lattimore didn't kill Mrs. Carasco, then he was set up by someone who got those hand wraps, and the most likely place would have been where the illegal fight was held."

Macklin frowned. "You're saying that someone involved with the illegal fight was also involved with Mrs. Carasco's murder?"

"Yeah. And if the judge is behind his wife's murder, it means that he's also involved in some way with the illegal fights."

"Have the cops figured out who's running the fights or where they're held?"

"Not that I know, but I'm not part of the investigation or prosecution now that I'm a witness."

"Can you find out?"

"I can try, but I won't do anything that puts me in danger. I'm taking a big enough risk talking to you."

"I can accept that. And you'll tell me if you learn anything useful?"

"You can count on it."

CHAPTER THIRTY-SIX

Karl Tepper called Tony Carasco and told him to bring the money to a parking lot in downtown Portland at ten o'clock. Tepper told Stacey he'd be back for her once he got the money, and they would drive back to San Francisco. Then he opened the door to Stacey's apartment.

Tepper's mood changed from elation to horror when a fist the size of a ham mashed his nose. Tepper staggered backward into the apartment. A giant in a ski mask tased the pimp. Stacey screamed. The giant grabbed Stacey's cheeks and squeezed.

"Make another sound and I'll rip your tongue out."

Two more men wearing ski masks rushed into the apartment, and the giant locked the door behind them. He turned to one of the men, who was only slightly smaller.

"Take her into the living room."

The man grabbed Stacey's arm and hustled her onto an armchair.

"Help me move this piece of shit," the giant said to a light heavyweight in a leather jacket.

The light heavyweight slapped tape over Tepper's mouth. The giant grabbed the collar of Tepper's jacket, dragged him along the floor, and dumped him in the middle of the living room a few feet from Stacey.

"You're supposed to see what we do to your friend," the giant told Stacey. "So, get comfortable and enjoy the show."

While the giant stood next to her, the other men started beating Tepper with police batons. Stacey heard bones crack and closed her eyes to block out the blood and horror. The giant smacked her hard.

"This is educational, bitch. If you don't want us to start on you, keep your eyes on your boyfriend."

The men took turns beating Tepper until he was weeping. When the giant told his men to stop, he turned to Stacey.

"Do you understand that we're serious people?"

Stacey was too frightened to speak, so she nodded.

"That's good. Now, a friend trusted you, and you betrayed him. He believes that you have videos, audios, or other items that could embarrass him. Think before you answer. A lie will result in some of the same punishment your greedy friend suffered. You don't want to know what will happen to you if you lie more than once. So, do you have anything that could embarrass our friend?"

Stacey nodded vigorously.

"Is it in this apartment?"

"Yes."

"Show me where it is," the giant said.

Stacey got up unsteadily. When they were in the bedroom, Stacey pointed at a bookshelf that was across from the bed.

"The camera is hidden behind the books on the top shelf, and the recordings are in a hollow space in the books on either side of the camera."

Even though he was tall, the giant had to stand on his toes to see the camera, which pointed at the bed through a gap between two books on the top shelf. The giant opened the books. They had been hollowed out. Inside them were several DVDs and audiocassettes. The giant grabbed them and tossed the books on the floor. While the giant's back was turned, Stacey thought about going for the gun in her end table, but she was too scared to try for it.

"Is this everything?"

"Yes, I swear."

"You know what will happen if you're lying?"

"It's everything."

"It'd better be," the giant said as he scooped up the recordings. Then he turned to Stacey. "If you pulled this shit with me, you'd look like something out of a horror movie, but the man you betrayed is merciful."

The giant grabbed her arm and led her back into the living room. Tepper was moaning in agony. The giant knelt next to him and made eye contact.

"I checked with some friends in the City by the Bay. They told me you're a small-time punk. My friends owe me. If you ever show your face in Oregon or bother anyone in Oregon again, my friends will pay off their debt by making this beating seem like a spa treatment. Do you understand?"

Tepper nodded. Stacey collapsed on the sofa and tried to stop herself from shaking.

"Put this turd in the trunk of their car," the giant told his accomplices before turning to Stacey.

"Your boyfriend stays in the trunk until you're out of Oregon and in California, Washington, or wherever you decide to go. When you're over the border, do what you want with your pimp. If you go to a hospital, tell the doctor that your boyfriend was in a car accident. Under no circumstances do you try to put this on us. Understand?"

Stacey nodded.

"Good girl. We're going now. Wait twenty minutes, then you can go."

The two men carried Tepper outside, and the giant followed. One of the men returned and tossed Stacey the car keys. Stacey thought she might throw up, but she was too scared to run for the bathroom. Instead, she watched the clock tick off twenty minutes.

Stacey had packed for the return trip to California when she thought she would be leaving with Tepper and the money he'd extorted from the judge. As soon as the last second passed, she grabbed her valise and ran to the car. Washington was the closest state. She found the location of the nearest Washington hospital and headed north.

CHAPTER THIRTY-SEVEN

When Loretta Washington gave Robin and Amanda her draft of the juror questionnaire, they edited it and sent it to Judge Wright. The day after Robin and Amanda visited the Jungle Club, a pool of jurors was summoned to Judge Wright's courtroom and given the questionnaires. The next day, a messenger delivered the defense copies of the completed questionnaires to Barrister, Berman, and Lockwood, where Robin, Amanda, Jeff, and Loretta started ranking each juror in order of desirability.

Robin and Amanda spent three days questioning the jurors individually in Judge Wright's courtroom. Each side was allowed to exclude an unlimited number of jurors for cause. Cause could be shown if a juror had formed an opinion about Joe's guilt or innocence, if the juror was opposed to the death penalty or would always opt for death if a person was convicted of murder, if a juror had a prejudice against an African American defendant, or for any other reason that made it obvious that the juror could not be fair.

In addition to an unlimited number of challenges for cause, each side in an Oregon death penalty trial was allowed fifteen peremptory challenges. These challenges could be made for any reason and were used when an attorney could not show cause but did not want a juror sitting on his client's case. A defense attorney who had a gut feeling about a potential juror might use a peremptory challenge to exclude the juror even if she claimed that she could be fair to both sides. Similarly, a prosecutor might use a peremptory challenge to exclude an attorney who practiced criminal defense, who said he could be unbiased if selected as a juror.

Late Friday afternoon, after Robin and Vanessa used the last of their peremptory challenges and made no further challenges for cause, Judge Wright seated a panel of twelve jurors and six alternates. A death penalty trial followed by a sentencing hearing could go on for some time. In a long trial, it was not unusual for one or more jurors to become ill or to be excused for a valid reason. The alternates would hear the evidence the selected jurors would hear, but they would not take part in the deliberations unless a seated juror was excused.

Judge Wright admonished the jurors to avoid internet, television, radio, or newspaper accounts of Joe's case and told them that they could not talk about the case with anyone, including their families. Then he adjourned court until Monday morning.

Robin was exhausted when she returned to her office a little before five. As soon as she walked into the waiting room, her receptionist told Robin that Jeff wanted to see her.

"How did jury selection go?" Jeff asked when Robin had slumped onto a chair across from him.

"Okay," replied Robin. "I've got three jurors I'm pretty sure won't be able to sentence someone to death, so I'm feeling good about going to the sentencing phase if Joe is convicted, but I don't have a real feel for how we'll do in the trial."

"You look like you're wiped out."

"I am, but I have to work on my opening statement. Amanda's going to meet me Sunday afternoon to critique it."

"You're in no condition to create a great opening statement. You'll fall asleep unless you get some chow. Let me take you to dinner, and I'll tell you what I found out about Kevin Bash."

"Tell me now."

"Only if you'll promise to get some nourishment. A dead girlfriend is no fun."

"I promise."

"Okay. Remember what Erika Stassen did for a living before she moved back to Portland?"

"She investigated tax fraud for the IRS."

"Right. So, I asked Mark to ask her if she could help us out. She got back to me while you were in court. Kevin Bash is listed as the president of Irongate Inc. It's a shell company registered in the Cayman Islands. Irongate owns several properties in Oregon. One is a farm in Washington County."

Robin perked up. "We have to go out there. We can take pictures and show them to Joe to see if he can ID it as the place where the fight was held."

Jeff nodded. "I'll do that over the weekend. Right now, I'm going to feed you. Then you're going to get a good night's sleep."

Robin was going to argue with Jeff, but she was too tired. Jeff saw the fight go out of the woman he loved, so he told her the information he had saved for last.

"There's one more thing Erika discovered. Anthony Carasco is a member of Irongate's board of directors."

CHAPTER THIRTY-EIGHT

Jeff spent Saturday in the field interviewing witnesses. Robin spent Saturday morning in her office with Loretta, reviewing the set of jury instructions her associate had prepared. Robin could see that there was something worrying Loretta, but she decided Loretta would tell her what was bothering her if she wanted to. The moment came when they were on the last instruction.

"Can I ask you something?" Loretta said.

"Sure."

"How do you do it, take on a client when he could die?"

Robin had asked herself that same question the first time she agreed to take a capital case.

"Someone has to," she answered.

"But you don't. You can always pass."

"True, but that would be cowardly. There are innocent people who've ended up on death row because they had incompetent representation. I take being a lawyer very seriously, and I have a duty to make sure the system works. The case where the system has to work as perfectly as it can is a case where a client can die."

"I don't know if I could stand the pressure, knowing that a person's life depended on me being perfect," Loretta said.

"You will never be perfect, Loretta. All you can do is try as hard as you can to do everything you can think of. But you will always screw up somewhere along the line. That's why you have a cocounsel; someone who, hopefully, will tell you when you're going astray. And even then, with the best representation and the greatest will, you will fuck up, because humans aren't perfect. So, you just try as hard as you can and hope for the best."

"Have you ever seen an execution?" Loretta asked.

"No. And I hope I never will. And if it's a client of mine, I would pray that he was really guilty and that I did everything I could for him. And with that, I am ordering you to go home so I can start working on my opening statement."

On Sunday morning, Jeff programmed in the address Erika Stassen had discovered for the Washington County farm. The first part of the journey was on Highway 26, one of the main routes to the coast, but Jeff's GPS soon sent him into sparsely populated farmland. The weather was raw, and a light rain started falling when Jeff turned onto a two-lane country road that had been ravaged by the cruel winter weather. Stands of trees flanked the road as it wound up into low-lying hills. The road was pitted with potholes that caused Jeff's ride to bounce. This coincided with

Joe Lattimore's description of the final part of his ride in the windowless van. When Jeff neared the top of one of the hills, the navigation system told him that he was less than a quarter mile from his destination.

Jeff spotted a dirt track bordered by densely packed trees and bushes. He drove in a few car lengths, turned the car so it faced the road, and parked. His camera was in the back seat. He grabbed it and got out. The rain had started to come down hard. Jeff pulled up the hood on his rain jacket before hiking through the woods to the top of a hill that overlooked the farm. Jeff used his telephoto lens to scan the terrain. A driveway led off the country road through a white clapboard fence. Beyond the fence was a farmhouse, outbuildings, and a barn. An old pickup truck and a new-model, jet-black Mercedes-Benz stood in a gravel parking lot next to the barn. Jeff searched the property for any signs of life, but he didn't spot any people or livestock. Then a door in the side of the barn opened, and two men walked out.

Jeff had searched the Web for information on Kevin Bash. His picture was on the website for his car dealership, and Jeff recognized him right away. Jeff didn't need a picture to identify Andre Rostov. Bash was well built, but he looked like a child next to the massive human who was standing beside him.

Jeff snapped a series of pictures as Bash

and Rostov ran through the downpour to their vehicles. It dawned on Jeff that the road from the farm would pass his car. He hustled down the hill and jumped in the driver's seat. He could hear the cars coming as he started his engine and backed the car deeper into the woods. The Mercedes and the pickup drove by seconds after his car was out of sight of the road.

Jeff took a deep breath and leaned back against the headrest. He had no desire to meet Rostov or Bash, but he did want to find out where they were going.

Jeff let the men get enough of a head start so he wouldn't be seen on the deserted country road. He lost sight of the truck and the Mercedes until he topped a rise. The men were following the route he'd taken from Portland, so he gambled that was where they were headed and didn't speed up until he reached Highway 26.

It didn't take Jeff long to catch up to the two vehicles. When they were on the outskirts of the city, Jeff was faced with a choice. The Mercedes kept going toward Portland, but Rostov turned off and headed into another rural area.

Jeff knew that Kevin Bash worked at his Mercedes dealership. He could follow him home anytime. So, he decided to tail Rostov. The pickup truck drove past poorly kept-up homes and trailer parks before turning into the driveway of a house with a lawn that looked like a retirement home for weeds and an exterior that had not seen paint since the Dark Ages.

Jeff memorized the house number as he cruised past. Then he parked down the street and watched the house until some teenage boys, who had been sitting on a front porch, started walking toward the car. Jeff headed back to town.

Robin and Amanda looked up when Jeff walked into the apartment.

"How's the opening coming?" he asked as he shed his water-spotted jacket.

"We're done. We just finished up a review of the jury instructions, and we're talking about how we're going to cross-examine Vanessa's witnesses. How did your secret mission go?"

Jeff told the women about the farm and following Bash and Rostov.

"I was just at the jail. I showed Joe the pictures I took. He says that one of the men is the giant who drove him to the fight and Kevin Bash is the man who ran it. He's not certain, because he was there at night, but he said that this could be where they held the illegal fight. He remembered the gravel parking lot and the field where some other cars were parked, and the door at the side of the barn is where he remembered it being."

"Good work," Robin said.

"We want to get your opinion on something," Amanda said.

"Shoot."

"We've been debating whether we should call Joe as a witness. What do you think?"

Jeff's brow furrowed as he weighed the pros and cons. Contrary to what most people thought, it was usually a mistake to call a defendant to the stand in a criminal case. The state had the burden of proving that the defendant committed the crime he was accused of committing, and the state's burden was very high. To vote guilty, a juror could not have a single reasonable doubt about the defendant's guilt.

A defendant had no obligation to prove he was innocent. That meant that the defense was never required to put on evidence. If the state's case was shaky but Joe made a bad impression when he testified, he could erase any reasonable doubts harbored by a juror. The only time the defense had to call a defendant to the stand was when he was the only person who could explain away devastating evidence that would lead to a conviction.

"I think it would be a mistake to put Joe on the stand," Jeff said.

"Joe's fingerprints put him in Carasco's house, next to the body," Amanda said. "Don't we need his testimony to explain why he was there?"

Jeff was certain that the women had already decided on a course of action and were challenging him to see if he would come to the same conclusion.

"Joe sounds like he's telling the truth when we talk to him, but I don't know how he'll hold up under one of Vanessa's cross-examinations. He's told us that he has a bad temper. And Vanessa will rip apart his story about being blackmailed. Let's face it. It makes more sense for a homeless man to be burglarizing a home for money.

"And I see another problem. Didn't Judge Wright rule that evidence that Joe had killed Carlos Ortega in an illegal fight could not come in at the trial?"

"Yes."

"Won't that come out if Joe explains why he was in a position to be blackmailed?"

"Good point," Robin admitted.

Jeff shook his head. "You're probably going to have to wait until you see how the state's case comes across before you decide whether to call him."

CHAPTER THIRTY-NINE

In 1972, in *Furman v. Georgia*, the United States Supreme Court struck down all of the existing death penalty schemes in the United States. In the course of writing the opinion, the court established the principle that "death is different." Robin Lockwood knew that this was true in more ways than one. The rules governing death cases and the jurisprudence of capital cases differed from other criminal cases, but the emotional impact on lawyers who represented defendants in death cases was also different.

When Loretta asked her how she could take on a death case, Robin had given her an answer that was mostly philosophical. She hadn't talked about the way your gut reacted with every mistake and the fear that gripped you when you wondered if you had done everything possible to save your client's life, knowing that the failure to dot one i or cross one t could kill her.

Robin didn't know if there was an afterlife. If there wasn't, all a person had was the span of years allotted to her. Death ended the experience, and she knew that one mistake on her part could put an end to Joe Lattimore's existence. That was a very heavy burden, and Robin felt the pressure mount as the start of Joe's trial neared.

The night before she was scheduled to give her opening statement, Robin barely slept. Every time she started to drift off, she thought of something else she had to do. When she woke up at five, she felt groggy and a little nauseous. Strong coffee helped her combat her fatigue, but nothing could settle the butterflies that flitted through her stomach or quell the awful feeling that she wasn't up to the task of saving Joe Lattimore's life.

On Monday morning, Joe, dressed in a suit and tie Robin had purchased for him, was led out of the holding area and into the courtroom. Joe had always been a private person, and he hated being the center of attention. When he fought, the worst part was the walk from the dressing room through the crowds to the ring, when every eye was on him. Once the fight started, he was so focused on his opponent that he didn't hear the crowd, but having to sit in court, unable to move, with nothing to do with his hands, knowing that everyone was staring at him, was hard to handle.

As soon as he was out of the holding area, Joe looked for Maria. Robin had arranged a seat for her in the front row of the spectator section behind his chair at the defense table. Joe smiled when he saw his wife. He couldn't touch her, but they talked whenever they could, and she would tell him about Conchita, who was trying to stand and talk.

"How are you doing?" Robin asked Joe as Judge Wright called for the jury.

"I'm hanging in," Joe answered, trying to sound brave. He didn't want to think about what would happen if he was convicted. Locked in a cage forever or put to sleep like a rabid dog were the most realistic results. He trusted Robin Lockwood to do her best, but he found it hard to see a happy ending.

"Are both sides ready to proceed?" Judge Wright asked.

As soon as Robin and Vanessa said they were, the judge nodded to Vanessa. The prosecutor walked to the jury box. After a few minutes, Robin knew that she was going to lose the battle of the opening statements.

Vanessa told the jurors that circuit court judge Anthony Carasco would testify that he had received a call from his wife at seven fifteen in the evening and his wife sounded fine. The judge would then tell the jury that he had seen a man who resembled the defendant fleeing the scene of the crime a little more than an hour later. She promised to corroborate the judge's testimony by producing Ian Hennessey, a deputy district attorney who had been with the judge the evening that Carasco's wife was murdered.

Vanessa told the jurors that a forensic expert

would tell them that prints that matched the running shoes the defendant was wearing when he was arrested were found inside the Carasco home, and Joseph Lattimore's fingerprints and palm print were on a wall in proximity to the body of Elizabeth Carasco. The state medical examiner would testify that Elizabeth Carasco had been beaten to death. Vanessa promised that evidence would establish that Joseph Lattimore, who was homeless and desperate for money, was a professional boxer. She had concluded her opening statement by explaining that professional boxers used hand wraps to protect their knuckles and that hand wraps covered in Elizabeth Carasco's blood and stained with Lattimore's DNA had been found near the scene of the crime.

Vanessa's opening was loaded with facts. Robin had not decided whether she would call Joe to the stand, and she did not have any evidence that would prove that Joe was set up by Betsy Carasco's real killer, so she was reduced to talking in general terms about the burden of proof and a juror's duty to keep an open mind until he had heard all of the facts. When she sat down, she knew that most of the jurors were probably ready to convict.

Carrie Anders and Roger Dillon had been in the back of the courtroom during opening statements. They left when Vanessa called her first witness.

"Detectives," Brent Macklin said.

Anders and Dillon turned and saw a handsome young man approaching.

"Do you have a moment?" Macklin asked, flashing an ingratiating smile.

"That depends on what you want," Anders answered.

Macklin handed Roger a business card. "I'm working on a story about illegal, no-holds-barred fights. I understand that you're the detectives on Mr. Lattimore's manslaughter case, and I was wondering if I could talk to you for background about these fights."

"This is an ongoing investigation, so we can't comment on it."

"Do you know how frequently they're held, who runs them, or where they hold the fights?"

"I'm sorry, but we can't help you," Roger said.

The detectives started to turn away.

"I've heard rumors that Judge Carasco is involved," Macklin said.

The detectives stopped.

"Who told you that?" Anders asked.

"My source talked to me on the condition that I not reveal his or her identity."

"That's a serious accusation," Dillon said. "Do you have any evidence to back it up?"

"Right now, it's just speculation. I was hoping you could tell me if I'm on the right track."

"Like we said, we can't comment on an

ongoing investigation, but you should be careful about making unfounded accusations. Now, we have to go."

Macklin watched the detectives walk away. Then he returned to the courtroom.

CHAPTER FORTY

Vanessa filled the rest of the Monday court session with noncontroversial testimony from the police officers who had secured the crime scene. On Tuesday morning, Vanessa called Dr. Sally Grace, the medical examiner, who told the jury about the autopsy and the cause of death. On cross, Robin got Dr. Grace to admit that you did not have to be a professional boxer to beat someone to death and that a woman could have inflicted the injuries that killed Elizabeth Carasco.

Other than her brief cross of the medical examiner, Robin had not asked very many questions of the State's witnesses, and she noticed that Joe had gotten more depressed as Tuesday morning wore on.

"Why didn't you cross-examine those other witnesses?" he asked Robin when Judge Wright called the morning recess.

"You don't question a witness just for the hell of it, Joe. Everyone Vanessa called told the truth, and nothing they said proved you killed Betsy Carasco. Can you think of anything I should have asked?"

Joe thought for a moment. Then he shook his head.

Robin didn't tell Joe that his real problems would start after lunch, when the testimony of the prosecutor's next witness would go a long way toward convincing the jurors that Joseph Lattimore was guilty of murder.

"The State of Oregon calls Wendell Appleton, Your Honor."

Moments later, a narrow man with a washed-out complexion limped down the aisle toward the witness stand with the aid of a cane. Appleton was dressed in a tweed jacket, dull white shirt, dark slacks, and a drab brown tie. He reminded Robin of a civics teacher she'd had in tenth grade.

"Mr. Appleton," Vanessa asked after the witness was sworn, "how are you employed?"

"I'm a fingerprint specialist with the Oregon State Crime Lab."

"What are the duties of a fingerprint specialist?"

"I compare and analyze fingerprints that are submitted to the crime lab. By this, I mean I receive fingerprint evidence from crime scenes, and I compare them to fingerprints that are recorded at a jail or other place to see if they match."

"How often do you do this?"

"I work eight hours a day, five days a week."

"How long have you been working as a fingerprint expert?"

"It will be fifteen years, next February."

"Where did you start analyzing fingerprints, Mr. Appleton?" Vanessa said.

"I worked at the Federal Bureau of Investigation Fingerprint Identification Division in Washington, D.C."

"What was your job at the FBI?"

"I classified, compared, and analyzed fingerprint submissions in the criminal division of the identification division."

"Did you receive any educational training at the FBI?"

"Yes. We went through several months of training, followed by a one-on-one tutorship from more senior examiners. My probationary period was about a year."

"How long did you work for the FBI?"

"A little over four years."

"Where did you work after that?"

"I was at a private company that did background checks for school bus drivers, day care workers, things like that."

"This also involved comparing fingerprints?"

"Yes."

"How long were you there?"

"Three years."

"And after that?"

"I moved to Oregon after being hired by the crime lab."

"Other than your initial training with the FBI, have you had more training?"

"Yes. I go to thirty or more hours of training each year at a minimum. For example, I've attended seminars taught by the Royal Canadian Mounted Police and the Arizona, New Jersey, and Illinois State Police, among others. I've been all over for training."

"What are the two basic properties of fingerprints that make them useful for identification, Mr. Appleton?"

"First, they are unique. No two people have ever been found to have the same fingerprints, palm prints, or footprints.

"Second, they are permanent. Fingerprints begin to form on the skin in the womb, and they stay permanently until a person dies and the skin decomposes. The only exception would be if there was permanent scarring or a person had the prints surgically removed."

"How are fingerprints compared for purposes of making an identification?" Vanessa asked.

"We use ridge characteristics, and we look to see if a ridge characteristic on one print is identical to the ridge characteristic on another print. Some ridge characteristics end abruptly, and we call them *ending ridges*. Some divide, and we call those *bifurcations*. We also look at the ridge structure, the flow of the ridges. Is it straight or curved? We also look for anomalies within an individual ridge. Things like that."

"Mr. Appleton, I'm going to show you State's

Exhibit 13, and I'll put an enlarged photo of this on an easel for the jurors, so they can see what you're looking at. What is this?"

"That is a print that was taken from the defendant's right index finger when he was arrested."

"Do you have a full set of prints that were taken from the defendant when Exhibit 13 was lifted?"

"Yes."

Vanessa had the set marked and entered in evidence.

"I'm going to show you Exhibit 14. What is that?"

"It's the defendant's right palm print. It was also taken at the jail."

Vanessa introduced Exhibit 14 into evidence and placed a blowup of the palm print on another easel.

"What is a latent fingerprint, Mr. Appleton?"

"A latent fingerprint is created by the sweat and oil on the skin's surface."

"Can you see it with the naked eye?"

"No. Latents are invisible, and you have to use additional processing with chemicals or powder to make them visible."

"Were you called to the home of Judge Anthony Carasco and his wife, Elizabeth Carasco, on the evening Mrs. Carasco was murdered?"

"Yes."

"Where was Mrs. Carasco's body when you arrived?"

"She was lying on the floor in the living room of their home in proximity to the wall of the living room closest to the entryway of the home."

"Did you search the area surrounding the body for latent and observable prints?"

"I did."

"Did you discover any latent prints that were made by the defendant?"

Robin stood. "Objection, Your Honor. Whether any of the latent prints from the crime scene match Mr. Lattimore's prints is a decision the jury will have to make."

"Sustained," the judge ruled. "Ask another question, Mrs. Cole."

"Did you discover any latent prints in the living room?"

"I did."

"Were there many latents?"

"Yes. Most belonged to the victim and her husband."

"Did you find any latents in proximity to Mrs. Carasco's body that did not belong to her or her husband?"

"I did."

"Did you compare any particular prints to the set of prints that were taken from the defendant after his arrest?"

"Yes. Of special interest were a fingerprint I discovered on the living room light switch and a palm print on the wall near the light switch."

Vanessa handed Appleton two exhibits.

"Can you identify these exhibits for the jury?" she asked.

"Exhibit 29 is the fingerprint I lifted from the light switch, and Exhibit 30 is the palm print I found on the living room wall."

"I'd like to introduce State's Exhibit 29 and 30, Your Honor."

"Any objection, Ms. Lockwood?"

"No."

Vanessa put blowups of the two new exhibits on other easels.

"Can you explain how you went about comparing Exhibit 29 to Exhibit 13?"

"I placed them side by side and used a magnifying glass to find points that looked identical or any points that were not identical."

"If you found a point that was not identical, what would you have concluded?"

"I would have concluded that the two prints did not match."

"Did you find any points that did not match?"

"No."

"How many points did you find that did match?"

"Thirteen."

"What did you conclude?"

"That the known print and the print from the light switch were made by the same person."

"Are thirteen matching points enough to reach that conclusion?"

"Yes."

Vanessa repeated her questions with regard to the palm print, and the witness stated that he had found thirteen points of comparison on the palm print and concluded that it matched the print of Joe's palm taken at the time of his arrest.

"No further questions," Vanessa said.

"Ms. Lockwood," Judge Wright said.

"Mr. Appleton, I noticed that Mrs. Cole did not ask you about your formal education. Do you have a college degree in biology or any other branch of science?"

"No."

Robin knew Appleton would answer in the negative because she had done an in-depth internet search to determine his education, his personal life, and anything else that might help her client.

"Any graduate degrees in biology or any other branch of science?"

"No."

"I see. Now fingerprint identification is not a science, is it?"

"What do you mean?"

"You get some basic training about what fingerprints look like, then you use a magnifying glass or a microscope and you look at the prints. Anyone on the jury could do it with a little training, right?"

"They would need a lot more than a little training."

"But this isn't an exact science. It's not like math. It's subjective, like the judging in Olympic figure skating or boxing, where different observers can see the same thing and reach different conclusions?"

"Well, no. I have to be certain about the similarities."

"But you could be mistaken."

"No, I never make a mistake."

"That's amazing. You're saying that in fifteen years of analyzing prints, you have never been wrong?"

"I have never been wrong."

"You must make a killing at the racetrack."

"Objection!" Vanessa shouted out.

"Sustained," the judge ruled.

"Would you agree that other fingerprint examiners have made mistakes when comparing fingerprints?"

"I . . . Well, yes. I've heard of that."

"Are you aware of a study conducted by the United States Department of Justice in 2016 titled *Error Rates for Latent Fingerprinting as a Function of Visual Complexity and Cognitive Difficulty* that showed an error rate among experienced examiners as high as 9 percent?"

"I've read that study."

"What about the 2016 report of the Presidential Council of Advisors on Science and Technology titled *Forensic Science in Criminal Courts—*

Ensuring Scientific Validity of Feature Comparison Methods that quoted error rates as low as one in three hundred and six and as high as one in eighteen, or 5.55 percent? Are you aware of that report?"

"Yes."

"But you still want this jury to believe that you're perfect?"

"I have never made an error in any of my comparisons."

"Are you aware that fingerprint examiners in the Los Angeles Police Department erroneously matched two individuals in two separate cases to prints that did not belong to them and covered up the errors?"

"I did hear of that."

"Are you also aware that one of the worst examples of misidentification involving fingerprints was made right here in Oregon, when three FBI examiners hired by the court erroneously identified Brandon Mayfield, an Oregon attorney, as having left a print on the bag that held the detonators in a bomb that blew up a train in Madrid, Spain?"

"I am aware of Mr. Mayfield's case."

"These were three top FBI examiners with over thirty years of experience; maybe some of the FBI examiners who trained you. And they made a horrible error that led to the arrest and incarceration of an innocent man."

"Yes."

"But you have never been wrong."

"No."

Robin paused and looked at the jury before asking her next question. Some of the jurors were frowning.

"Mr. Appleton, you testified that you found thirteen points in Exhibit 14, the known palm print of Mr. Lattimore, that matched thirteen points in Exhibit 30, the latent palm print that was found on the wall in the Carasco's living room?"

"Yes."

"Your Honor, may I go to the blowups?" Robin asked.

"You may."

Robin studied the blowup of the palm print. Then she turned toward the witness.

"There are a lot of ridges in this palm print, aren't there?"

"Yes."

"Are there more than thirteen?"

"Yes."

"But you stopped after comparing only thirteen?"

"I was satisfied that I had found enough points of similarity to conclude that the palm print belonged to your client."

"Didn't you tell the prosecutor that you would conclude that there was no match if you discovered one point on the palm or fingerprint that did not match?"

"Yes."

"Was there a scientific reason you stopped analyzing these prints after you found thirteen points of comparison?"

"No."

"So, you just concluded in your mind that thirteen was enough?"

"Yes."

"You're telling the jury that there is no scientific reason you stopped. You'd simply made up your mind that thirteen was enough?"

"Yes."

"There are plenty of other ridge characteristics and end points and bifurcations on this palm print, aren't there?"

"Yes."

"If you had continued your examination, you might have found twenty matching points?"

"Yes."

"Or fifty?"

"Yes."

"What if point fifty-one did not match?"

"Well, I . . . Then the palm print wouldn't belong to the defendant."

"So, fifty matches and one mismatch would clear Mr. Lattimore's name?"

"Yes."

"You know that Mr. Lattimore could be sentenced to death, do you not?"

"I do."

"But knowing that, you decided, for no scientific reason, that thirteen was enough to send a man to death row?"

"Objection," Vanessa Cole said.

Robin turned her back on the witness. "I have no further questions of this man."

"That was pretty dramatic," Amanda whispered to Robin.

"Yeah," Robin agreed, "but it doesn't disprove Vanessa's contention that Joe's prints were found next to Betsy Carasco's body."

CHAPTER FORTY-ONE

"The State calls Ian Hennessey," Vanessa Cole told the court when it convened on Wednesday morning.

Ian had barely slept, and he felt sick when he walked to the witness stand. He had to fight to keep his hand from shaking when he took the oath to tell the whole truth, because he knew that he could not tell the whole truth. If anyone found out that he'd lied under oath, he would definitely lose his job. In the worst-case scenario, he would go to prison for perjury.

Moments after taking the oath, Ian was sitting in the witness-box answering questions about his education and how long he had been employed as a deputy district attorney.

"So, you're pretty new to the Multnomah County district attorney's office?" Vanessa asked.

"Yes."

"When did you start trying cases on your own?"

"About eight months ago."

"Did you try a case in Judge Anthony Carasco's courtroom recently where the defendant was represented by Robin Lockwood, Mr. Lattimore's counsel?" Vanessa asked.

"Yes."

"What did you think the result of that case was going to be?"

Ian turned red. "I thought I would get a guilty verdict."

"What was the actual outcome?"

"The defendant was found not guilty."

"Were you upset about losing the case?"

"Yes."

"Did you take any steps to find out what you had done wrong so you could do a better job in the future?"

"Yes."

"What did you do?"

Ian felt hot and dizzy. This was the point in his testimony where he was going to commit perjury, but he couldn't think of any way out of his predicament. His life would be ruined if he testified that he'd gone to see Anthony Carasco on the evening of the murder because he was being blackmailed by a prostitute.

"I asked Judge Carasco if he would tell me what I'd done wrong, so I would improve the way I tried cases in the future."

Ian prayed silently that the prosecutor or Robin Lockwood wouldn't ask why the mentoring session was over a week after the Stassen trial.

"Where did this discussion take place?"

"It was late—around six o'clock—so the judge suggested that we talk over dinner at Bocci's, an Italian restaurant."

"During dinner, did the judge receive a phone call?"

"Yes."

"What time did he get this call?"

"It was around seven fifteen."

"Who made the call?"

"The judge told me that his wife was calling."

"When did the call end?"

"A few minutes later."

"After dinner, did you drive the judge home?"

"Yes."

"When did you turn onto Judge Carasco's street?'

"It was sometime after eight o'clock, about eight fifteen, I think."

"Did you see anyone near the judge's home?"

"Yes."

"Tell the jury what you saw."

Ian's mouth was dry, and he took a drink of water. "There was a man standing in the street."

"What did this man look like?"

"It was hard to tell, because I wasn't close enough to make out any details."

"Could you tell his race?"

"Yes. He was African American."

"What about his build?"

"All I can say was that he looked average, normal."

"Did your headlights illuminate the man?"

"Yes."

"What did he do?"

"He stared at us for a second. Then he threw

up his arm to block his face and ran between two houses on the other side of the street."

"Did you go inside Judge Carasco's house?"

"Yes."

"Tell the jury what you discovered in the living room."

Ian swallowed. "It was Mrs. Carasco. She was lying on the floor in a pool of blood."

"No further questions, Your Honor," Vanessa said.

"I have a few," Robin said. "It was raining very hard by the time you turned onto Judge Carasco's street, wasn't it?"

"Yes."

"And your windshield wipers were going full blast?"

"Yes."

"And it was very dark?"

"Yes."

"You testified that you saw a man standing in the road near Judge Carasco's house?"

"Yes."

"How far was your car from the man when you first saw him?"

"Several house lengths."

"And the houses on the judge's street are big with lots of property?"

"Yes."

"Wasn't the man you saw wearing a coat with a hood?"

"Yes."

"And the hood was up because of the rain?"

"Yes."

"How far were you from the man when he threw up his arm to block his face and ran?"

"Still a few houses away."

"I've read the statements you gave to the police and the report of your reactions at a lineup in which Mr. Lattimore was one of the participants. Isn't it true that you cannot say that the man you saw near Judge Carasco's house was Mr. Lattimore?"

"I can't say he was the man."

"And that is because the distance between you and this man, the heavy rain falling on your windshield, and the action of your windshield wipers obscured your view."

"Yes."

"Judge Carasco was seated right next to you, wasn't he?"

"Yes."

"Was there any difference between what you could see through the downpour and what the judge could see?"

"Objection," Vanessa said.

"Sustained," Judge Wright ruled.

"No further questions, Your Honor."

As soon as Anthony Carasco was sworn, Vanessa asked him about his educational and professional background and the length of his marriage to Elizabeth Carasco. Then she moved to the night of the murder and established that his wife had sounded normal when he spoke to her at seven fifteen.

"After dinner, did you ask Mr. Hennessey to drive you home?"

"Yes. I'd taken Lyft to the courthouse that morning, so I didn't have my car."

"Approximately what time did Mr. Hennessey turn onto your street?"

"A little after eight."

"So less than an hour after you'd talked to Betsy, when she'd sounded fine?"

"Yes."

"What did you see when you turned onto your street?"

"I saw a man standing in the street in front of my house."

"Please describe this man for the jury."

"He was average height and weight, African American, and he had a scar on his right cheek."

"You are certain about the scar?"

"I am."

"We've had testimony that this man was wearing a jacket with a hood. If he had the hood up, how could you see his scar?"

"At one point, when he was illuminated by the headlights, the hood fell back far enough to expose his cheek."

"Does the defendant resemble the man you saw outside your house?"

"Yes."

"To be fair, can you say with certainty that the man you saw outside your house was the defendant?"

"No, I cannot."

"No further questions."

Robin didn't want to challenge the judge about seeing the scar, because she knew that his answer would just reinforce his direct testimony, so she told Judge Wright that she had no questions. It didn't matter anyway. Whether or not Judge Carasco had seen the scar on Joe's face, Joe's finger and palm prints were in the Carasco house right next to Betsy Carasco's corpse, where they had no business being.

When Judge Carasco stepped down, Vanessa called Carrie Anders to the stand to tell the jury about the raid on the motel and Joseph Lattimore's arrest.

"Detective Anders," Robin said when Vanessa was through with her witness, "other than asking you not to shoot him and asking you to make sure his wife, Maria, and Conchita, their baby, were safe, did Mr. Lattimore say much more to you or any other officer or detective?"

"No."

"Specifically, he never told you, or anyone else, that he had killed Elizabeth Carasco?"

"No."

"Isn't it true that one of the few statements he did make was an assertion that he did not kill Mrs. Carasco?"

"That is true."

"I'd like to turn to something that has been confusing me, and I'm hoping you can help me out."

Carrie had known Robin for several years, and she was well aware of how smart she was. When Robin asked her for help, it raised a red flag that was similar to the flags at the beach that warn swimmers that there are sharks in the water.

"Based on Judge Carasco's seven fifteen phone conversation with his wife at the restaurant and his discovery of the body roughly one hour later, the time of death has been narrowed down to sometime between seven fifteen and eight fifteen, hasn't it?" Robin asked.

"Yes."

"Judge Carasco told you that Mrs. Carasco sounded fine when they talked, didn't he?"

"Yes."

"And the conversation at the restaurant didn't end at exactly seven fifteen, right?"

"Yes."

"It lasted a few minutes more?"

"Yes."

"So, we can assume that some time passed

between the end of the conversation at the restaurant and the murder, can't we?"

"Yes."

"So, maybe a forty-five- or fifty-minute window for time of death?"

"That sounds reasonable."

"Now, Judge Carasco and Ian Hennessey testified that they saw a man outside the judge's house at about eight fifteen?"

"Yes."

"He was on foot?"

"Yes."

"Did they tell you that he ran away on foot between two houses down a lane that leads to the woods?"

"Yes."

"If he came by car, and the car was parked near the Carasco home, he abandoned it, right?"

"If he came by car and parked nearby," Carrie said.

"Am I correct that when Mr. Lattimore was arrested, there was mud on his clothing and the clothes were damp?"

"Yes."

"It was raining heavily, and that would make the ground in the woods muddy, wouldn't it?"

"Yes."

"Was that confirmed by officers who searched the woods for the man the judge and Mr. Hennessey say ran from the scene?"

"Yes."

"If the clothes had not dried out, that would indicate that he had returned to the motel shortly before his arrest, would it not?"

"Probably."

"So, if Mr. Lattimore was the man who Judge Carasco and Mr. Hennessey say they saw run from the scene, there is evidence that he was on foot and went through the woods on his way back to the motel where he was arrested?"

"Yes."

"How long does it take to run from the Carasco home, through the woods, and then go to the Riverview Motel?"

"I would have to guess."

"If I said that I had my investigator take the shortest route through the woods to the Riverview and it took him one hour and ten minutes, would that sound right?"

Carrie thought for a moment before agreeing.

"When did the first officer arrive at the crime scene?"

"About eight forty-five."

"When did the first reporter or other person not affiliated with the police show up?"

"Around nine twenty."

"So only the police knew that there had been a murder and that the victim was Mrs. Carasco until at least nine fifteen?"

"I can't say for certain. A reporter could have intercepted a police broadcast."

"Okay. But not before the judge called 911 at eight thirty-five?"

"Yes."

"How did you know that you would find Mr. Lattimore at the Riverview Motel?"

"We received a tip."

"When?"

"The call came to 911 at nine thirty-five."

"Do you know who made the call?"

"No. The caller wouldn't give his name."

"Did you try to trace the call?"

"Yes, but we were unsuccessful."

"It was a man?"

"It sounded like a man."

"What did the caller tell the police?"

"He said that Joe Lattimore killed Judge Carasco's wife and that he was in room 214 of the Riverview Motel and we should go there fast if we wanted to get him."

"Nine thirty-five would be right around the time Mr. Lattimore would have gotten to the motel if he ran there from the Carasco house?"

"Yes."

"Am I right that the caller had to know that Mrs. Carasco had been murdered in order to make the call?"

"Yes."

"And that Mr. Lattimore was staying in a particular room at a particular motel?"

"Yes."

"Since the call was made so soon after the murder at the Carasco home and so soon after Mr. Lattimore returned to the motel, doesn't that suggest that the caller had also been present at both locations when both the murder occurred and Mr. Lattimore returned to the motel?"

Carrie went quiet and the jurors focused on her, waiting for her answer.

"I would have to speculate to answer that," Carrie said.

"Isn't one possibility that the caller set up Mr. Lattimore by luring him to the Carasco home after he killed Mrs. Carasco and set up Mr. Lattimore's arrest by calling 911?"

"I'm not going to speculate."

"Don't you mean that you really don't have a good answer, Detective?"

CHAPTER FORTY-TWO

Thursday morning, Vanessa called a witness from the crime lab who testified about the running shoe print. She followed that with the testimony of Joe's trainer and manager, who established that Joe was a professional boxer with several knockouts on his record. Neither man looked at Joe when they testified.

Jeff had interviewed the men, so Robin knew that they were reluctant witnesses. During her cross-examination, she established that Joe did not enjoy fighting but did it to earn money. Both men testified that Joe was honest and hardworking.

After the testimony of the manager and trainer, Vanessa called Marvin Bradshaw, the police officer who had discovered the hand wraps in the Carascos' garbage can.

"Officer Bradshaw," Robin asked after Vanessa turned the witness over to her, "given that the victim in this case was beaten to death, these bloody hand wraps are very important and very incriminating evidence, are they not?"

"Yes," Bradshaw agreed.

"And you found them discarded in a trash can right next to the house where the murder occurred?"

"Yes."

"Aren't there woods across the street from the Carasco home?"

"Yes."

"Is there a sewer grate nearby?"

"Yes."

"And there are thousands of places in Portland far from the Carasco house where a killer could hide this evidence?"

"Yes."

"Wouldn't anyplace be better for hiding incriminating evidence a killer would not want the police to find than a trash can right next to the murder scene?"

"I guess."

"Now, say you were in possession of hand wraps with Mr. Lattimore's DNA on them and you wanted to frame him, wouldn't it be a clever thing to kill Mrs. Carasco, put her blood on the wraps, and stash them where the police were sure to find them?"

"Objection," Vanessa said. "She's asking the witness to speculate."

"No, I'm not. Your Honor, Mrs. Cole qualified the officer as an experienced professional who deals with crime and criminals on a daily basis. Obviously, she feels he's an expert in the field of criminal investigation, and that makes him qualified to answer my question."

Judge Wright thought over the arguments for a moment. Then he turned to Vanessa.

"I'm going to overrule your objection."

The judge had the question read back to Officer Bradshaw and told him to answer it.

"I guess you might do that if you wanted to frame your client."

"No further questions."

"Officer Bradshaw," Vanessa asked, "putting the hand wraps in the Carasco trash can would not be a smart thing for Mr. Lattimore to do if he killed Mrs. Carasco, would it?"

"No."

"In your years of dealing with criminals, have you often found them doing stupid things that led to their arrest and conviction?"

Bradshaw laughed. "I'd say that's more the rule than the exception."

"No further questions, Your Honor," Vanessa said.

"Ms. Lockwood?" the judge asked.

"Nothing more, Your Honor."

"May the witness be excused?" Vanessa asked.

Judge Wright nodded.

When Vanessa called her next witness, Robin sighed. Melinda Cortes, a forensic expert with impeccable credentials, had no trouble explaining what DNA was to people who didn't know anything about it. When Vanessa finished her preliminary questions, the jurors knew that no two people had the same DNA. After Cortes explained the tests she'd conducted on the blood and other matter found on the hand wraps and her conclusions after reviewing the results of those tests, she testified with confidence that DNA testing had established that some of the blood on the hand wraps was Betsy Carasco's and that DNA belonging to Joseph Lattimore had been found on the wraps.

Robin pulled out her bag of tricks for dealing with DNA, but she didn't feel that she'd done anything to blunt the impact of the expert's testimony.

"The State rests," Vanessa said as soon as Cortes stepped down.

"I assume you have motions for the court," Judge Wright said to Robin.

"Yes, Your Honor."

"It's getting late," the judge said. "Let's recess for the day. Unfortunately, I have a matter in another case I have to attend to that will take up the morning, so let's start up at one tomorrow."

Robin talked to Joe for a few minutes while Amanda collected their trial materials.

"What's the plan, boss?" Amanda asked as she, Robin, and Loretta walked down the curving marble staircase to the courthouse lobby.

Robin looked dejected. "I don't have one."

"Are you going to put Mr. Lattimore on the stand?" Loretta asked as they headed back to Barrister, Berman, and Lockwood under overcast skies as gloomy as Robin's mood.

"What would you do?" Robin asked her associate.

"Don't you have to put him on to explain why he was at Judge Carasco's house?" Loretta asked.

"Amanda?" Robin asked.

"I agree with Loretta. Joe's the only person who can tell the jury what really happened."

"He'll also be telling the jury that he killed Ortega," Robin said.

"Manslaughter doesn't carry a death penalty," Amanda answered.

The trio debated their next move on the short walk to Robin's building. They had just entered the lobby when Amanda's cell phone buzzed. Amanda looked at the caller ID and held up a finger to silence everyone. She looked grim when the short call ended.

"That was my 'friend,' " Amanda told Robin. "The next fight is tonight after sundown at the same place Joe fought."

Robin was lost in thought as they rode the elevator to her floor.

"I have to make a call," she said as soon as the elevator doors opened. "I'll meet you in the conference room."

When she was in her office, Robin closed the door and speed-dialed Carrie Anders. Carrie and Robin had grown to trust each other during a series of cases where they were on opposite sides but had shared information. Robin was hoping that the mutual respect that had developed would work in her favor tonight.

"Carrie, I just learned that there is going to be a no-holds-barred fight tonight, and I know where it's going to be held. I'll take you there, but you have to do something for me."

"Yeah?" Brent Macklin said when he answered his phone.

"It's me," Ian Hennessey whispered.

"Can you speak up? I can barely hear you."

"I'm in a stall in the men's room at the DA's office, and someone just came in. I can't risk anyone hearing me."

"Okay. So?"

"Anders and Dillon were talking with Vanessa Cole, and I overheard them. There's a barn in Washington County. It's where they hold the illegal fights. There's going to be a raid tonight."

"Where is the barn?"

"I don't know, but Carasco might go to the fight if he's a backer. Follow him, and he might lead you there."

CHAPTER FORTY-THREE

Jeff's pickup bounced as soon as he drove onto the unpaved country road that led to the farm. Every time the truck thudded down after going airborne, the holster at Robin's back bit into her spine.

"How much farther?" Robin asked between grimaces.

"Not much more. There's a side road in about a mile. The SWAT team can park there, go over a hill, and come down on the barn through the woods."

Earlier that evening, Carrie had told Robin that she had arranged a joint raid with the Washington County Sheriff's Office. Robin relayed the information about the side road to Carrie, who was leading a convoy of police vehicles. Shortly after Carrie acknowledged the message, Jeff spotted the narrow logging road where he'd hidden his truck on his prior trip to the farm. He pulled to the side of the road so the police caravan could hide.

"Let's get one thing straight," Carrie told Jeff and Robin when the raiding party was assembled. "You will lead us to the top of the hill and show us our objective. Then you will stay put until I tell you that you can come down. Is that clear?"

"Definitely," Robin said. "I have no problem staying safe while you risk your life."

Carrie raised an eyebrow. "I know you, and I am not fucking around."

"I'll stay put, but you've got to try to get the recording of Joe's fight."

"That was the deal, and I'll make every effort to keep my promise, if it doesn't involve breaking the law or screwing up the arrests."

Jeff led the raiders to the top of the hill. Carrie scanned the area around the barn with binoculars. Cars filled the gravel lot and the field, and they could hear an occasional roar from the barn.

A drone was scanning the area and sending pictures back to a van that was outfitted with communications equipment. After checking with the van, Carrie radioed the police cars that were hanging back on the road, waiting for the signal to follow the raiding party. Then she led the team down the hill.

Robin watched through her binoculars. The raiders were dressed in camouflage, and even knowing where the SWAT team was, she had a hard time following them as they drifted downhill through the shadows.

Robin shifted her focus to the area around the barn. Several people were standing in the parking area, smoking, drinking, and talking. A white van was parked near the side door to the barn where Joe and the other fighters had entered, but no one was around it. Robin guessed that the audience for the fights entered through another door.

She watched the raiders inch along the side of the barn toward the door near the van. They paused. Then Carrie wrenched open the door, and the SWAT team stormed in. Carrie had a bullhorn, but the walls of the barn muffled her message and the screams and shouts that followed it. People were racing out of the barn toward their cars, but the police had blocked the road, and the few cars that left the lot were stopped at a barricade.

Robin panned the area on the side of the barn farthest from the parking area. A man who vaguely resembled Anthony Carasco darted out a back door and drove away on a narrow track toward the back of the farm. He was followed by another man. Normally, Robin wouldn't have been certain of his identity from this distance, but few humans who didn't play on an NFL offensive line looked like Andre Rostov.

"Rostov is getting away," Robin told Jeff as she headed for the pickup.

"What are you doing?" Jeff asked.

"This is Joe's only chance. The night of the fight, Rostov told Joe his fight had been recorded. It will show him giving Bash his hand wraps. What if Rostov has the recording?"

"Tell Carrie. She can send someone after Rostov."

"It's chaos down there. By the time we can get

through to Carrie and the police can get someone to Rostov's house, he could have destroyed the recording and any other evidence he's hiding."

Jeff hesitated. Robin grabbed his forearm. "Joe could die if we don't act now! You know where Rostov lives. We've got to get there as fast as we can."

For a moment, Jeff didn't move. Then he pulled away and headed for the pickup.

Brent Macklin had followed Anthony Carasco when he left the courthouse. Instead of going home, Carasco had driven to Washington County and taken a country road to a farm. Brent had been in court when Judge Wright had ruled that evidence of the illegal fight could not be introduced in Lattimore's trial for the murder of Elizabeth Carasco, and he'd read the memos Vanessa Cole and Robin had filed. The farm matched the description of the fight venue in the statements of fact in the memos.

Carasco parked in a grassy area behind the barn, next to a pickup. Macklin drove a quarter of a mile past the farm. After parking on a side road, he scrambled up a hill until he had a view of the back of the barn through his binoculars. A narrow track led from the back of the barn across a field and onto the road a half mile from where Macklin was parked.

Macklin had brought a canteen and energy bars

to tide him over through his stakeout. As the sun set, vehicles began appearing on the road to the farm. Shortly before sunset, the parking area on the side of the barn farthest from Macklin was clogged with cars and pickups. Macklin was fascinated by the variety of people who had come to the fight. There were gangbangers and country club types, bejeweled women and men in business suits. Shortly after the lot filled up, a roar drifted up to Macklin on the wind, barely making it to his perch.

Then a caravan of police vehicles appeared, and Macklin saw armed men and women snaking down a hill and bursting into the barn. He swung his binoculars toward Carasco's car and spotted the judge and a gigantic man running from the back of the barn. Macklin ran back to his car and drove out of the woods, moments after Carasco's car and the pickup sped down the road.

CHAPTER FORTY-FOUR

Tony Carasco tore out of the barn faster than he'd run in ages. The adrenaline that had supercharged him started to wear off when he was in his car, racing away from the police. He laughed, relieved to have escaped. It had been a close call, but he was free. Then it dawned on him that Kevin Bash had not been so lucky. The last thing the judge had seen before he ran out of the barn was the police closing in on Bash. Fear gripped Carasco. Bash had a piece of information that he could trade for his freedom. He knew who had hired him to get rid of Betsy. And once he named Carasco . . .

The judge fought the sudden urge to throw up. He had to think. He couldn't stay in Oregon. Hell, he couldn't stay anywhere in the United States. But how would he get to a country without an extradition treaty? In theory, he was loaded, but Helen Raptis's attorneys had frozen his assets, and his attorneys hadn't had time to get him access to his money.

Using an ATM was out of the question. The police would swoop down as soon as he used a debit or credit card. And where could he go while he figured out what to do? The police would have his house staked out. Then Carasco remembered a place he could go where no one would think of looking for him.

Carasco slammed the door behind him and leaned against the wall. He tried to calm his breathing so he could think clearly. When his breathing was normal, he started to turn on the lights, but he stopped. Lights would be a giveaway that someone was in the apartment. So would his car, which he'd parked out front. He'd have to move it before dawn. There was visitor parking that couldn't be seen from the entrance to the complex.

When his eyes adjusted to the dark, Carasco went into the den, which did not have windows, and flipped on the lights. He dropped onto the chair behind the desk and rested his head in his hands. His plan had been foolproof. Everything had gone smoothly. Lattimore was on trial, the evidence against him was overwhelming. How had it all gone to hell so quickly?

Maybe Bash would keep his mouth shut. What if he didn't? Carasco had to plan for the worst-case scenario. He had to get away, and he needed money to do that, but where would he get enough money to . . . ?

Carasco sat up. Of course, it was the obvious solution. The judge laughed with relief. Then he made a call.

CHAPTER FORTY-FIVE

It was dark on Rostov's block, and there were only a few scattered streetlights. A light rain was keeping everyone inside. Jeff pulled to the curb down the street from Rostov's house. Robin couldn't see any lights, and no car was parked in the driveway.

"Maybe he went somewhere else," Jeff said.

"Damn, you might be right. He had a head start on us. If he were coming here, he'd be here by now."

"What do you want to do?"

"Let's watch the house. If he doesn't show up, we can leave or . . ."

"Or what?" Jeff asked, worried by Robin's tone of voice.

"We could search for the recording."

"That's called burglary, Robin. It can get you double digits in the state penitentiary."

"What if the recording is in Rostov's house and it shows Bash taking Joe's hand wraps? Joe would walk."

"I don't know."

"Well, I do. I will not let one of my clients die, even if it means breaking the law. Remember the old adage. It's better to beg for forgiveness and then ask permission."

"I hope you don't end up begging for a reduced sentence."

Robin kissed Jeff on the cheek and got out of the car. Jeff followed her across the street and up Rostov's driveway. Robin tried the front door, but it was locked.

"Let's go around back," she said.

The side yard and backyard was a mass of weeds and unmown grass. A rusted car was up on blocks near a back door. Robin peered through the glass pane in the upper half of the door.

"I can't see much. I think this opens into a living room."

She tried the knob. The door was locked. She hesitated. Then she used her elbow to shatter the glass. Jeff started to say something, then thought better of it. He'd learned long ago that Robin was going to do what Robin wanted to do.

Robin reached in and opened the door. "Give me your flashlight," she whispered.

Jeff handed it to her, and she moved the beam around an open space with a television, sofa, a recliner, and bookshelves. The bookshelves surprised her, as did the titles that filled them. Nietzsche and *Mein Kampf* weren't easy reads.

Robin heard a sound like the one a hammer makes when it smashes down on a melon. She turned just as Jeff's eyes rolled back in his head and he collapsed. Standing over him was Andre Rostov, who was brandishing the large handgun he had used to knock out Jeff. Rostov flipped on the living room light.

"Drop the flashlight and raise your hands."

Robin did what she was told.

"Who the fuck are you?" Rostov asked.

That question gave Robin an idea.

"I'm someone who'd kick your ass if you didn't have that gun."

Rostov stared, open-mouthed. Then he burst out laughing.

"You've got guts, but that won't save you or your boyfriend."

"I don't need guts to beat the shit out of a muscle-bound ape. Your size probably scares people. But I bet you've never been in a real fight."

Rostov looked angry. "I'd love to beat you to death, but I'm in a hurry."

Robin looked Rostov in the eye and smiled. "You have no idea who I am, do you?"

Rostov was about to say something. Then he stopped and stared.

"You're the lawyer who's representing Lattimore. The fighter."

"If we fought," Robin taunted Rostov, "I'd try to kick you in the balls, but I'm afraid I'd miss a target that small."

That did it. Rostov grinned and tossed his gun onto the easy chair that was at his elbow.

"This is gonna be fun. First, I'm going to beat

you until you beg me to stop. Then I'll let you discover just how big my dick is."

Robin pulled out the gun in the holster at her back and shot Rostov in his right kneecap. The giant screamed, collapsed on the floor, and rolled back and forth in agony.

Robin kept her gun aimed at Rostov as she edged around him and knelt next to Jeff. His breathing was shallow, and there was a bloody gash on the top of his head. Robin tamped down the urge to kill Rostov. She wanted to avenge Jeff, but Joe Lattimore's life hung in the balance.

Robin dialed 911 and asked for an ambulance and the police. Then she turned her attention to Rostov, who appeared to have conquered his pain enough to glare at her.

"Here's the deal, Mr. Rostov," she said in the businesslike tone she used when she was negotiating a plea. "You have a recording of Joseph Lattimore's fight. I want it. Give it to me or I'll blow out kneecap number two, and you can see how tough you are in prison with no legs."

"You stupid bitch," Rostov shot back. "You're the one who's going to prison for breaking into my house and assaulting me."

"I remember things differently, Andre," Robin answered calmly. "I remember you assaulting my investigator, then holding me at gunpoint and threatening to rape me. That's when I pulled out my gun and shot you. Who do you think the cops will believe?"

"Fuck you."

"I hope you have a good health plan," Robin said as she aimed at Rostov's undamaged kneecap.

"Wait! Stop!" Rostov shouted. "Let's make a deal. I know things that the cops will want to know."

"What kind of things?"

"Lattimore didn't kill Ortega. I know who did, and I know who killed Carasco's wife. If I tell what I know, your client will walk."

"You've got my attention. Keep going."

"I was just a bit player. All I did was drive Lattimore to the judge's house. But I can ID the man who beat the judge's wife to death and the person who sent him to do it."

"Your word won't be enough."

Rostov smiled through his pain. "I was the one who filmed your client's fight with Ortega."

"I've seen it on YouTube."

"But you haven't seen all of it. I kept filming when the fight ended. What's on the rest of the recording was my insurance policy if the people behind the fights and the murder of Mrs. Carasco tried anything with me. It's also my get-out-of-jail-free card."

"Where is the recording?"

"It's not here, but I can get it as soon as I get

immunity. Believe me, the cops will be drooling when they find out what I know and can prove."

"I'm not a cop. I can't promise you anything."

"But you know people who can. Make the call."

CHAPTER FORTY-SIX

When Jeff opened his eyes, the first thing he saw was Robin. She was sitting next to his hospital bed, holding his hand. Jeff blinked, unsure of where he was.

"You'll be okay," Robin said, choking up as she spoke. "The doctors say you'll be fine."

Robin could see that Jeff was having trouble focusing. She wasn't surprised. Jeff's doctor had told her that the concussion would make him disoriented and groggy.

"Where . . . ?" Jeff managed.

"You're in the hospital. You'll be okay in a day or so."

Jeff closed his eyes, laid his head back on his pillow, and went to sleep. Robin wiped the tears from her cheek, leaned forward, and kissed him.

The next time Jeff was conscious, he was more alert.

"How long have I been out?" he asked.

"A few hours. You came to for a minute, but you probably don't remember."

Jeff stared at Robin. "Have you been here the whole time?"

"Every second. I was afraid I'd lose you, and I didn't want to miss a moment."

269

Jeff squeezed Robin's hand, which had been holding his.

"I'm not that easy to lose."

A thought occurred to Jeff.

"What happened? I remember the police raiding the barn, then nothing."

"It was Rostov. He came up behind you after I broke into his house. He smashed you in the head with the butt of his gun."

"We broke into his house?"

Tears started streaming down Robin's cheeks. "I'm so stupid. I don't think. I just charged ahead, and when I turned around, you were lying there and I thought you were dead and I'd never talk to you again or be with you and . . . I'm so sorry. You tell me something I want to do is dangerous, and I don't listen."

Robin choked up and looked down at the side of the hospital bed.

"It's okay," Jeff said. "It's who you are. And your intentions are always good."

"But I can be so stupid." Robin looked up. "Can you forgive me? You could have died."

Jeff managed a weak smile. "Of course I forgive you. I love you."

Robin started to bawl.

"Hey, cut that out," Jeff said. "You said it yourself. I'm going to be fine."

"You're so good to me. I don't deserve you."

Robin stopped, wiped her eyes, and took deep breaths.

"There was a time when you were lying on the floor and Rostov was pointing his gun at me when I thought we would both die. And I realized right then that you are the most important person in my life. I always want to be with you, always."

Robin paused and took a deep breath.

"Will you marry me?" she said.

Jeff blinked. "Did you just propose?"

Robin laughed. "I think so."

"Oh my God!"

Robin flushed. "You don't have to answer right away. I mean, you can wait until the drugs wear off and you have a clear head. There are a lot of negatives. I know I'm a slob. I can try to be neater. And I have poor impulse control at times . . ."

"Are you changing your mind?"

"No, it's just . . . See? I just blurted that out without thinking, and I should have waited until—"

Jeff laughed. Then he winced from the pain.

Robin looked alarmed. "Are you okay? Should I call the doctor?"

"Yes, I am okay, and no, don't call the doctor, and yes, I do want to marry you, despite your many flaws."

CHAPTER FORTY-SEVEN

Andre Rostov had been lucky. He'd only suffered a flesh wound. Robin's bullet had hit his leg just above the knee, bounced off bone, and exited, missing all of his major blood vessels. The attending physician had given him some pain meds and sutured him up.

Two hours later, Rostov lay in a hospital bed with his damaged knee wrapped in a bandage. He looked a little groggy, but his doctor had assured everyone that the effect of the drugs had worn off enough for Rostov to be questioned.

Vanessa Cole, Roger Dillon, and Carrie Anders sat on uncomfortable metal chairs on Rostov's right. The edge of Carrie's chair was cutting into her leg, and she kept shifting her weight every few minutes.

Seated on Rostov's left side was Mary Garrett, who showed no signs of discomfort. Carrie didn't expect her to. The criminal defense attorney was famous for a laser focus that shut out anything that might distract her from winning a case.

Garrett, with her plain looks, overbite, dense glasses, and five-foot-tall stick-figure frame, resembled a tiny bird. Offsetting her height and appearance was a designer wardrobe straight out of the latest edition of *Vogue* and showy jewelry that cost as much as some people's cars. Garrett knew that she wasn't going to win a beauty contest, but she didn't care. What she did care about was destroying the case against her client. Even the most seasoned prosecutors dreaded going up against her in court.

"Robin Lockwood says that Mr. Rostov admitted driving Mr. Lattimore to the judge's house as part of a setup to frame him," Vanessa Cole said. "That makes him an aider and abettor in a capital case."

"That makes him a minor player in someone else's scheme, who had nothing to do with the actual killing," Garrett shot back.

Vanessa smiled. "Let's cut to the chase, Mary. What do you want?"

"Immunity."

"And what do I get in exchange?"

"A treasure trove. Mr. Rostov can tell you who killed Betsy Carasco, who paid for the hit, and who was involved in framing Joseph Lattimore. And, as they say in the infomercials, there's more. He can tell you all about a crooked judge and a bent DA."

"You've got my attention."

"You'll get the details once we get your offer," Garrett said.

Vanessa and Garrett went into the hall and battled back and forth over the benefits that would accrue to Rostov if he delivered on

Garrett's promise. Twenty-five minutes later, Mary Garrett spelled out what her client would tell a grand and trial jury.

"Kevin Bash runs the illegal fights, and Sal Benedetto recruits the fighters and is involved in several other capacities. Judge Anthony Carasco had been funding the fights secretly for a share of the profits. When his wife told him that she was going to divorce him, Carasco approached Bash with a plan he had devised that involved someone murdering his wife while he had an airtight alibi. Carasco made a down payment on the plan by forfeiting his share of the profits for the next two fights."

"Mr. Rostov will testify that Anthony Carasco arranged his wife's murder?" Vanessa said, using all of her self-control to keep from showing her surprise.

"He wasn't present when that happened, but he was in on part of the plan to frame Lattimore."

"Go on."

"Bash had Sal Benedetto find a patsy. Benedetto had people in the tent city where Joe Lattimore was living who found men and women who would participate in the illegal fights. Lattimore was perfect for the scheme. He was a professional boxer, and he was desperate to find shelter for his family.

"Next, Benedetto found Carlos Ortega. Right before Lattimore and Ortega fought, Bash drugged Ortega to make sure he would lose. Then Bash told Lattimore that he'd killed Ortega so they could blackmail him into going to Carasco's house on the night of the murder. What Lattimore didn't know was that Ortega was still alive after their fight. When Lattimore left the barn, Bash killed Ortega.

"Bash paid Benedetto to beat Elizabeth Carasco to death so it would look like Lattimore was the culprit. The judge arranged for Ian Hennessey, one of your deputy DAs, to have dinner with Carasco at the same time Benedetto was beating Mrs. Carasco to death. When the deed was done, Benedetto phoned the judge while the judge was eating, and the judge pretended that he was talking with his wife. After that call ended, Benedetto phoned Mr. Rostov and told him to bring Lattimore to the scene of the murder. They timed it so the judge and your deputy drove onto Carasco's street in time to see Lattimore run out of the judge's house."

"Does Mr. Rostov have any hard evidence to back up these allegations?" Vanessa asked.

"He has a recording that shows Bash murdering Carlos Ortega. In it, Bash takes Lattimore's hand wraps, so Lattimore couldn't have been wearing them when Elizabeth was beaten to death. Benedetto was, and he's the one who dumped them in the trash can."

"What evidence can Mr. Rostov provide

that supports his belief that Judge Carasco is a criminal?" Vanessa asked.

"Carasco owed money to Mr. Bash for arranging the murder of his wife, but he only paid part of what he owed. Bash was getting impatient. He demanded his money. Carasco came to that barn you raided on the night of the raid. Mr. Rostov was present when Carasco told Bash that Elizabeth Carasco's mother had filed a lawsuit that was tying up Elizabeth's trust fund. He said he would have plenty of money as soon as the case was dismissed. Bash told him he wasn't going to wait and would have Mr. Rostov take care of him if the money wasn't paid soon. He was in the middle of threatening the judge when you raided the barn.

"Mr. Rostov will also tell you that the judge hired him through Bash to take care of another problem involving a woman who was blackmailing the judge. This also involved Ian Hennessey, the DA who was with the judge when his wife was being murdered."

"Ian?" Vanessa said. "How is he involved?"

"Hennessey was sleeping with a prostitute named Stacey Hayes. Hayes was staying in an apartment that the judge owns. Carasco was paying her to be his mistress."

"Did Ian pay this woman?" Vanessa asked.

Garrett leaned over, and she and her client had a whispered conversation.

"Mr. Rostov doesn't know. What he can tell you is that an associate of Hayes named Karl Tepper tried to blackmail the judge. Carasco hired my client through Bash to go to Hayes's apartment, beat up Tepper, and get several sex tapes that Hayes was using to blackmail the judge and this DA.

"Mr. Rostov and two men went to the apartment and beat up Tepper, who had installed a hidden camera in a bookshelf across from the bed in the bedroom. Mr. Rostov got Miss Hayes to show him the location of the camera and to hand over the sex tapes. Then he told her to get out of the state."

"Does Mr. Rostov have the sex tapes?"

"No. He watched some of them, but he turned them over to Carasco at the fight."

"The judge wasn't in the barn when we raided it. Does Mr. Rostov know what happened to him?"

Rostov and his lawyer had another whispered conversation.

"As soon as your people broke into the barn, Mr. Rostov told the judge to run. They both went outside through a back door," Garrett said. "The judge drove away, and Mr. Rostov doesn't know where he went."

"Why did your client help the judge?" Vanessa asked.

"Carasco still owed Mr. Rostov for taking care

of Tepper. The judge wouldn't have been able to pay if he were in jail."

"This is all very interesting, Mary. I want to think about what you've told me. I promise to get back to you very soon."

Vanessa turned toward Rostov. "You're doing the right thing by cooperating. If what you've told us is accurate, good things will be coming your way."

CHAPTER FORTY-EIGHT

Kevin Bash, dressed in an orange jumpsuit, sat across from Carrie Anders and Roger Dillon. Bash was unshaven and had the exhausted appearance of a man who had spent a sleepless night in a jail cell. Max Weaver, Bash's attorney, sat next to him.

"You're in a lot of trouble," Carrie told Bash.

"Mr. Bash has no priors," Weaver said. "I doubt he'll go to prison for running an illegal fight."

"How much time have you spent with your client, Max?" Carrie asked.

"We just met twenty minutes ago."

"During your meeting, did he tell you that he beat a man named Carlos Ortega to death and conspired to have Judge Anthony Carasco's wife murdered?"

Weaver looked confused. "Those are serious charges. What's your proof?"

Carrie looked at Bash. "We bagged Ralph Knowland during the raid at the barn."

The color drained from Bash's face.

"Who's that?" Weaver asked.

"He's the doctor your client paid to attend the illegal fights he's been running," Carrie answered.

Then she addressed Bash. "Dr. Knowland says

Ortega was alive after his fight with Lattimore."

"Knowland's a junkie," Bash blurted out. "You can't trust anything he says."

Roger smiled. "You have a good point, Mr. Bash. Addicts are notoriously untrustworthy. Unfortunately for you, we can prove that the good doctor is telling the truth."

"I think it's time for a little show-and-tell," Carrie said.

A television was sitting next to the wall. Roger pressed Play on the remote he was holding. Weaver watched the screen intently as Lattimore and Ortega fought. Then Ortega was down, and Lattimore jumped up and yelled something. Moments later, Dr. Knowland knelt beside Ortega and examined him. Bash and the doctor talked for a few minutes, and Knowland left.

"Here's where it gets interesting," Carrie said.

On the screen, Joe handed Bash his hand wraps. Soon after Joe left the barn, Bash stripped naked, rewrapped Lattimore's hand wraps around his knuckles, and rained punches on Ortega.

"I've seen enough," Weaver said.

"I don't blame you," Carrie said. "I almost puked while I was watching."

"There's more, Max," Roger said. "We have a witness who can testify that Mr. Bash sent the man who murdered Betsy Carasco. Joseph Lattimore is facing the death penalty for that murder. Once Mr. Bash trades places with him, he'll be looking at spending what's left of his life on death row."

"Can I have a moment with my client?"

"We'll wait outside," Carrie said. "Take all the time you want."

Carrie turned to Bash. "Be smart. Listen to your lawyer. You have a small window to cut your losses. If you play hardball with us, we will charge you with aggravated murder for Ortega and Carasco, we'll go after you for running the illegal fights, and we'll charge you for every traffic and health code violation we can dig up."

Twenty minutes later, the door opened, and Max Weaver walked into the corridor.

"What would you offer if Kevin told you the name of the person who killed Mrs. Carasco?"

"We know his name," Roger said. "We have an APB out for him. What we need is the name of the person who told Mr. Bash to have Elizabeth Carasco murdered. We want the big baddie."

"What's your wish list, Max?" Carrie asked.

"You can see that Ortega was in really bad shape after Lattimore got through with him. He might have died anyway. Dr. Knowland probably told you that. So, manslaughter for the case with Ortega."

"The Ortega case is the least of your client's problems," Carrie said.

"Take death off the table and put on life with

the possibility of parole and Kevin can tell you what you want to know."

"He'll tell us who hired him *and* testify for the State?" Carrie asked.

Weaver nodded.

"We'll take your offer to Vanessa. She has the final say. But we'll need a proffer. Who does Bash say ordered the hit on Elizabeth Carasco?"

"Her husband, Anthony Carasco."

CHAPTER FORTY-NINE

When Harold Wright walked into the anteroom of his chambers at twelve thirty, he found Vanessa Cole, Robin Lockwood, and Carrie Anders waiting for him.

"What's up?" the judge asked Vanessa.

"Let's talk in chambers," the prosecutor replied.

The judge studied the attorneys and the detective. They looked grim. He frowned. Then he led everyone into his office.

"Okay, we're in chambers," the judge said when everyone was seated and the door was closed. "Why does everyone look so serious?"

"I'm going to dismiss all of the charges against Mr. Lattimore," Vanessa said.

The judge sat up. "I didn't see that coming. Do you want to tell me why?"

"He's innocent, Judge. He was set up. Late last night, Detective Anders phoned me. She'd just finished raiding the barn in Washington County where Mr. Lattimore engaged in an illegal fight with Carlos Ortega. I believed that Mr. Lattimore had killed Mr. Ortega based on a YouTube video that showed the fight. A cooperating witness has provided my office with the full video. It shows a doctor examining Mr. Ortega. We've interviewed the doctor. He told us that Mr. Ortega was still alive after the fight. A man named Kevin Bash organized these illegal fights. The full video shows Mr. Bash beating Mr. Ortega to death after Mr. Lattimore leaves the barn."

"Where is Mr. Bash now?" Judge Wright asked.

"In custody. We're finalizing a plea deal with him. What's relevant to the case before you is the section of the video that shows Mr. Bash taking Mr. Lattimore's hand wraps and wearing them while he's beating Mr. Ortega to death. The wraps were a major piece of evidence in our case.

"The cooperating witness who gave us the recording of the fight told Carrie that a man named Sal Benedetto dropped the hand wraps in a garbage can on the Carasco property after he beat Mrs. Carasco to death. The cooperating witness will also testify that he brought Mr. Lattimore to Mrs. Carasco's house after she was dead and abandoned him there to frame him for the killing."

"Do you have Benedetto in custody?"

Vanessa nodded. "The California Highway Patrol picked him up a few miles from the Mexican border."

"Has he admitted killing Betsy Carasco?" the judge asked.

"He's refusing to talk, and he's requested counsel. If he resists extradition, I'll send someone to interview him in California."

Vanessa paused. "There's more, and you're

not going to like this. Mr. Bash will swear that Anthony Carasco paid him to have his wife killed."

"You're shitting me!"

"I wish I were," Vanessa said. "But that's what our witness says."

"Is there anyone who corroborates his story?" Wright asked.

"No."

"What does Anthony say?"

"I would tell you if I knew, but the judge has disappeared."

CHAPTER FIFTY

As soon as the meeting in Judge Wright's chambers ended, Robin rode up in the elevator to the courthouse jail.

"I have wonderful news, Joe. The police have questioned the doctor who was at the fight. He says that Carlos Ortega was alive when you were hustled out of the barn. We have the full recording of your fight with Ortega. What's on it confirms what the doctor said. It shows you giving your hand wraps to Kevin Bash. Then Bash puts them on and kills Ortega. So, your conscience is clear. You didn't kill Carlos Ortega. Vanessa is dismissing the manslaughter indictment."

For a moment, Joe looked relieved. Then he sobered. "What about Mrs. Carasco?"

"That's the other piece of good news. Those charges are going to be dropped too. We know you didn't kill Mrs. Carasco, that you were set up. All of the charges have been dismissed. So, you're a free man. You'll be out of jail in a few hours."

Robin expected Joe to be ecstatic, but he didn't look happy.

"What's wrong?" she asked.

"I appreciate all you've done for me. I really do. You're fantastic. But Maria, me, and the baby are still homeless. At least with me in jail,

Conchita and Maria could stay in the shelter. Now, we'll be back on the street with no money and no prospects."

Robin smiled. "Did you think I was going to abandon you after the case was finished? I talked to Barry McGill. He remembered you. Barry's got work for you at the gym. It's mostly janitorial, but he said he can also get work for you as a sparring partner, and there are some young kids who could use coaching. That will give you an income while you look for a better job, and I'll use some of my contacts to see if I can line one up.

"And you won't have to live on the street. Barry invested in rental property over the years, and he's going to let you stay in one of his apartments. It's not fancy, but he'll hold up on the rent until you have a steady income."

"Does Maria know I'm free?"

"As soon as you're out, my associate, Loretta Washington, is going to drive you to the shelter. You can tell her yourself."

Joe began to sob. "I'm sorry," he said as he swiped at his eyes.

Robin placed a hand on Joe's shoulder. "Don't be. You've been through hell, and you deserve a good cry."

"One more question," Joe said when he had calmed down. "Do the police know who set me up?"

Robin nodded. "We're pretty sure Betsy's husband, Judge Carasco, was behind the plot to have his wife killed."

"Is he under arrest?"

"No. The police are looking for him. It's just a matter of time before they find him."

After she left the jail, Robin walked back to the law office. As soon as she'd checked her messages, she found the contact number Helen Raptis had left for her.

"Mrs. Raptis, this is Robin Lockwood. I have news for you. We know what happened to Betsy. Joe Lattimore is completely innocent. You were right; Judge Carasco paid to have your daughter killed."

"I knew the sick son of a bitch killed her. Is he in jail?"

"No. The police are looking for him. Sal Benedetto, the man who did the actual killing, is being held in California. Two other people who were involved in the plot are in custody and have agreed to cooperate with the prosecutor."

"Thank you for letting me know. How did the police find out that Carasco killed Betsy?"

"I'll let the authorities give you that information. There are confidential sources involved, and I don't know how much I'm allowed to tell you."

"How much do I owe you?"

"Not a cent. Joe is my client. I just wanted you to know what was happening. I hope it brings you some peace of mind."

"I'll have peace of mind when that bastard is executed."

PART FIVE

THE WAGES OF SIN

CHAPTER FIFTY-ONE

"That's all anyone's talking about," Portland police officer Marty Webb said as he pointed his bacon cheeseburger at the television over the bar where he and Paul Reese were taking their break.

On the screen, a female talking head was asking a male talking head where he thought the Honorable Anthony Carasco would be found. The male talking head said that the judge was rumored to be in Mexico, Eastern Europe, or dead.

"He forgot outer space," Reese answered as he polished off his BLT.

"And Easter Island," Webb said.

It was four in the morning on Saturday when the officers walked out of the bar. A cold front had swept in shortly after midnight. Webb hunched his shoulders and cursed the weather. His partner didn't seem to mind the frigid air. Reese started the engine moments before the dispatcher told them that there had been a report of a dead body at the Grandview apartments. Fifteen minutes later, their headlights illuminated a security guard who was pacing back and forth next to his car in the parking lot. He looked stressed. Reese parked next to the guard.

"You the one who called in a body?" he asked.

"Bert Solomon. I work for Northwest Security.

We patrol several apartment complexes in the city on a rotating basis. A woman named Stacey Hayes lives in number 5, but her car hasn't been in her spot for a while, and the place has been dark. When I got here just before midnight on Thursday night, I saw a car driving very slowly through the parking lot. It looked suspicious, so I drove over to talk to the driver. As I approached, the car sped up and drove away.

"Moments later, I noticed a light on in number 5 and a car parked in Miss Hayes's spot. It wasn't the one that was usually there, but I thought she might have bought a new car. I stopped in front of the door. It was closed, so I drove on.

"I didn't look that closely again at number 5 until tonight. That's when I noticed that the door wasn't completely closed. I knocked. When no one answered, I called for Miss Hayes. There was still no answer, so I took a few steps inside. That's when the odor hit me. I've been in combat, and I knew the smell. When I went into the bedroom, I saw a man lying on the floor. It was the guy everyone is looking for."

Vanessa Cole walked around the lab techs who were working in the living room and followed Anders and Dillon to the bedroom entrance. She stopped to study Anthony Carasco's corpse, which sprawled facedown on a bloodstained carpet. Then she shook her head.

"I thought we had this case gift wrapped and secured with a nice red bow."

"Someone wants to keep us employed," Roger quipped.

"What's Sally say?" the DA asked.

"Two shots," Roger answered. "One to the body and one to the head. The blood spatter patterns suggest that the head shot was administered when he was on the floor."

"Did we find the murder weapon?" Vanessa asked.

Carrie shook her head. "We've searched everywhere in the apartment. It looks like the killer took the gun."

"What about time of death?" Vanessa asked.

"Sally's guessing he's been dead a few days," Roger answered. "The car parked in front of the apartment is registered to Judge Carasco, and the security guard says it showed up late Thursday night."

"So, shortly after we raided the fight."

Roger nodded.

"Did the guard see anyone going into or out of the apartment?"

"No, but he did say that there was a car driving in the Grandview complex when he pulled in on Thursday night. He started driving toward it, and the guy peeled out."

"Did he get a good look at the driver?"

"So-so. It was through the driver's-side

window, and it was pretty quick. But he did get the license. He's going to give it to us as soon as he gets to his office."

Vanessa skirted the body and walked around the bedroom. There were no clothes in the closet, and all the drawers in the dresser and nightstands were empty. A bookcase stood across from the bed. The top shelf was almost empty, and several books were scattered around the floor in front of it. Carrie saw where Vanessa was looking and pointed at the top shelf.

"There's a camera up there that's aimed at the bed. It was probably hidden by some of the books. You can just see it now that the books are out of the way."

"The sex tapes Rostov said Hayes was making?" Vanessa guessed.

Carrie nodded. She pointed at two of the books that lay on the floor. There was a hollowed-out cavity in each one.

"The tapes were probably hidden in those books."

Vanessa walked around the bathroom. There was nothing on the sink or in the medicine cabinet. Vanessa looked around the bedroom once more. Then she headed toward the front door.

"Any idea who killed Carasco?" Vanessa asked when they were outside.

"Just theories right now," Roger said.

"Hit me with them."

"There were always rumors that Carasco was fixing cases," Roger said. "A few of the criminals he was friendly with might have been worried that he would name names to cut a deal when he was caught."

"Sal Benedetto might have wanted to shut up the judge for the same reason," Carrie said.

"We can eliminate Joe Lattimore," Roger said. "He might have wanted revenge, but he was still in jail Thursday night."

"What about Betsy Carasco's mother?" Vanessa asked. "Helen Raptis was certain that Carasco was behind her daughter's murder. She has that spooky bodyguard for heavy lifting, and she knew about the Grandview. When Raptis met with me, she showed me pictures of Carasco with Stacey Hayes in this apartment. She told me that her daughter was going to file for divorce because she found out about his affair. You should talk to her."

"Will do," Roger said. "And Hayes is someone we should check out."

"Rostov said he chased her out of Oregon after he beat up her pimp," Vanessa said.

"She had to hate the judge for siccing Rostov on her," Roger said. "She could have come back."

"Do we know anything about her?" the DA asked.

"No," Carrie said. "But we'll probably find her prints in the apartment. I'll run them."

"Ian Hennessey met Hayes at the Grandview, and he was the judge's alibi," Roger said.

"Okay. Question him. Let's get on this fast."

What Vanessa didn't say was that she couldn't afford another screwup like Lattimore. The press was having a field day roasting her for prosecuting an innocent homeless man, and she had dropped six points in the polls.

CHAPTER FIFTY-TWO

At nine the next morning, Roger Dillon settled onto a chair on one side of a scarred wood table in the interrogation room in the detective division.

"Have a seat," Roger told Ian Hennessey. Hennessey looked terrified, and Roger felt sorry for him.

"Do you mind if I record our conversation?" Roger asked.

"I guess not. Am I in trouble?"

"What do you think?"

Hennessey's eyes dropped to the tabletop. "I don't know why I'm here," he said, stalling for time.

"Let me give you a hint. Does the name Stacey Hayes mean anything to you?"

Hennessey looked like someone who'd just seen his pet puppy run over by a truck.

"I . . . Yeah. I know her."

"Ever been to her apartment at the Grandview?" asked Roger.

"Yes," Hennessey answered, his voice barely above a whisper.

"Been in her bedroom?"

The young DA looked like he was going to throw up.

Roger flashed a grandfatherly smile. "I apologize

for busting your balls, Ian. I have a very open mind when it comes to sex. The problem is that prostitution is against the law, which you have sworn to enforce."

Hennessey's head snapped up and he looked at Dillon.

"It wasn't that way. She set me up."

"I'm confused."

"I was only in bed with Stacey twice, and I never paid her. You've got to believe me. I never broke any laws. I was just stupid."

"Okay, Ian. Calm down and explain this to me in an orderly manner. Pretend you're giving a closing argument to a jury. Convince me you're not guilty of prostitution."

"I'm not. It was Judge Carasco, and I didn't have anything to do with his murder," Hennessey blurted out.

"Why would we think you might?"

"Because he was killed in Stacey's apartment, and I hated him for trying to ruin my life."

"The judge was killed late Thursday night or early Friday morning. Do you have an alibi for that time period?"

"No. I was home, alone."

"Okay. Let's get back to you and Miss Hayes."

Ian told Roger how Carasco arranged for him to have dinner with Stacey at Bocci's and how he ended up in her bed at the Grandview after the second date.

"After that weekend, she disappeared. Then, a week later, she called me at the courthouse in the morning and said she wanted to make love at the apartment. My next court appearance wasn't until late afternoon. It was supposed to be in front of a different judge, but it was mysteriously switched to Judge Carasco's court that morning. Since I didn't have anything scheduled for a few hours, I went to the Grandview. This was the second and last time we were in bed. I never went back to her apartment after that."

"Why is that?"

Hennessey turned red with embarrassment. "After we had sex, Stacey told me that she had been arrested in Portland for prostitution a few years ago and had outstanding warrants because she'd skipped town. She asked me to make the warrants disappear. I told her that was illegal. That's when she said she'd tell Mrs. Cole that I'd paid her for sex if I didn't get rid of the warrants."

Hennessey hung his head. "I'm such a sucker. I never suspected that I was being set up for blackmail. There was a bookcase across from the bed. A camera was hidden between two books on the top shelf. Stacey said she had a sex tape of us she'd send to Vanessa if I didn't help her. When I got upset, she pulled a gun on me and told me to get dressed and go to my office and fix the warrants. I left right away. I wanted to get out of there as fast as I could."

"Did you get rid of the warrants?"

"No. That's the crazy thing. Remember, I drove the judge home and we found Mrs. Carasco?"

Dillon nodded.

"He couldn't stay in his house because it was being processed, so I drove him to a hotel. After I dropped him off, I went home and tried to sleep. But I couldn't, so I went to the office real early and looked for the warrants."

"What were you going to do with them?"

"I honestly don't know, and it doesn't matter. They're gone."

"What do you mean?"

"There's an order from Judge Wilma Malone dismissing the cases and the warrants, but it makes no sense. Why would she get rid of the cases? She wasn't involved with them."

"What do you think happened?"

"I know you won't believe me, but I think Judge Carasco slipped Malone the order and she didn't know what she was signing."

"I do believe you. We have evidence that Judge Carasco hired the men who murdered his wife."

Hennessey's hand flew to his mouth. "Oh god. That's why the judge had my case switched to his court. He set me up to be his alibi, didn't he?"

"It looks that way. I don't know if we'll need you, but if we do, would you be willing to testify at a grand jury and at trial?"

"Definitely. This whole ordeal has been a

nightmare. I love my job, and I never broke any laws. I never paid Stacey, and I didn't do anything with those warrants."

"I believe you."

"What about the prostitution case? I swear I didn't do it. I'll take a polygraph."

"I don't think that will be necessary."

"Can I still stay in the DA's office?"

"I'll talk to Vanessa. She may want you to take some time off while this investigation is active, but I'm going to tell her that I don't think you did anything wrong. Carasco's murder plot was very complex, and it looks like you were an unwitting piece of it."

"Thank you so much, Detective Dillon. Thank you."

CHAPTER FIFTY-THREE

"We've got some interesting stuff for you," Carrie told Vanessa when she and Roger were seated in the DA's office. "First, we found Stacey Hayes. She used a credit card at a motel in Bellingham, Washington. A friend in the state police has her under surveillance. We're driving up as soon as we finish here.

"Second, Sally has fixed the time of death to sometime late Thursday to sometime early Friday morning. Helen Raptis says she was in her hotel from dinnertime Thursday until Friday morning, and her bodyguard agrees."

"Can anyone else vouch for her?" Vanessa asked.

"She ordered room service around nine, but that's the latest she has covered."

"So, they're each other's alibi?"

"Yup, and the alibis aren't very good, because there were a lot of times they weren't together."

"Go on."

"Here's the most interesting thing we came up with. We used a drone to scope out the farm before and during the raid. We reviewed the pictures it took. As we went in, two men ran out the back and drove off the property—one in a pickup and one in a car. We blew up the pictures and we were able to read the plates. Andre Rostov was driving the pickup, and it's registered to him. The car that left before the pickup is registered to Carasco. It's the car that was parked in front of apartment 5 at the Grandview."

Vanessa frowned. "How long after the raid did Robin have her encounter with Andre Rostov?" she asked.

"Why?"

"Find out how long it would take for Carasco to drive to the Grandview from the farm. Then figure out if Rostov would have been able to follow him, kill him, and drive home in time to get there when Robin captured him. If Carasco owed him money, that's a motive."

"Will do," Carrie said. "But there's something else. A car drove out of a logging road about a quarter of a mile from the farm and followed the car and the pickup. We ran the plates. It's a rental, and the number on the plate matches the number on the plate the security guard wrote down."

"The car that was cruising the lot at the Grandview?" Vanessa asked.

"Yes."

"Who rented the car?"

"Brent Macklin," Carrie said.

"Who is Brent Macklin?"

"That's a good question," Carrie said. "Roger and I met him in the courthouse during the Lattimore trial. He said he was a reporter who writes stories about UFC, boxing, combat sports, and he was working on a story about illegal fights. He wanted to know who was running the one where Lattimore and Ortiz fought."

"Oh, right. He tried to interview me," Vanessa said.

"We're pretty sure Macklin is lying about a lot of things," Roger said. "We haven't been able to find any article he's written. And Macklin isn't really Macklin."

"What do you mean?"

"When he talked to us in the courthouse, he gave me his card, and I kept it," Roger said. "It dawned on me that his prints might be on the card, so I had the lab check it out. The prints don't belong to anyone named Brent Macklin, but we did find a match.

"Carlos Ortega had a son named Luis Ortega. Luis has been masquerading as Brent Macklin. He's been trying to find out who was responsible for killing his father and sponsoring those fights, which makes Macklin a prime suspect."

CHAPTER FIFTY-FOUR

Bellingham is a coastal city in Washington State near the Canadian border, where a tourist can catch a ferry to Alaska or drive east to ski on Mount Baker, a huge, snowcapped volcano. The motel where Stacey Hayes was staying was not mentioned as a tourist attraction. It was situated near a dive bar, a tattoo parlor, and a body shop, and its chief attraction was that it was cheap.

As Dillon and Anders approached Hayes's door, they could hear the drone of a television coming from the room. Hayes opened her door moments after Carrie knocked. She was dressed in a faded Alcatraz T-shirt, dirty jeans, and sweat socks. Her hair was uncombed, and there were dark circles under her eyes. Roger thought that Hayes would be a knockout under other circumstances, but her rumpled clothes and the absence of makeup had erased any traces of glamour.

"How are you doing, Stacey?" Carrie asked as she held up her badge.

"What is this?" Stacey asked. She sounded frightened.

"Nothing scary. We just want to talk."

"About what?"

"You and Judge Anthony Carasco."

"The drive up from Portland is pretty long, and

we're starving," Roger said. "And you look like you could use a cup of coffee and a good meal. There's a Denny's across the street. We could talk there or in your room. Your choice."

"Do I have to talk to you?"

"You can refuse," Carrie said. "Then we'd ask Washington to hold you in jail as a material witness until we could extradite you. That will take quite a while."

"A material witness to what?"

"Haven't you heard? Anthony Carasco was murdered in apartment number 5 at the Grandview."

"Do I need a lawyer?" Hayes asked as soon as the server left with their order.

"Have you committed a crime?" Carrie asked.

"I didn't kill Tony," she answered. "You said he was found in my apartment. I haven't been there for days."

"Why did you leave?" Carrie asked, knowing what Rostov had told them.

"To save my life. Tony sent three men to my apartment. They beat the hell out of Karl and told me to get out of Oregon or they'd do the same to me."

"Who's Karl?"

"Karl Tepper. He's . . . an acquaintance."

Carrie let that pass. "What did you do when the men left?"

"I dropped Karl at the emergency room at

308

a hospital in Vancouver. Then I just drove."

"Why did the judge send men to beat up Karl?"

"I'll tell you if you promise you won't charge me."

"With what?"

"Look, what I did, it was bad, but Tony made me do it. I'll tell you everything if you let me go."

"I can't promise anything until I know what you did. Talk to me and I *will* promise that I won't use what you tell us now against you."

Anders let Hayes think. After a few minutes, she looked across the table.

"I'm a professional escort. Karl was my manager. I started in Portland and was busted twice, so I left the state and moved to San Francisco. Tony was in San Francisco for the bar convention. We met in a hotel bar, and he paid me to come to his room. After we slept together, he asked me to move to Portland. He said he'd put me up in the Grandview and give me money every month and get rid of the warrants for failure to appear.

"Before I accepted Tony's offer to move to Portland, I asked Karl what I should do. He said we'd caught a cash cow, and we should milk him for everything we could get. Karl set up this hidden camera in a bookcase across from the bed in my apartment at the Grandview, and I filmed Tony every time he came over.

"One day, Tony told me to come to the

courthouse and wait until the case he was hearing ended. He said this redheaded DA was going to go into his chambers, and I should wait a few minutes after the DA went in. Then I should walk in. He told me he would set it up for me and the DA to go to dinner. Then I was supposed to seduce him."

Hayes looked down. "It was a rotten thing to do, making Ian fall for me. He's a decent guy, and I didn't like doing it. I asked Tony what the deal was, but he said that I didn't have to know and promised me extra money to do it.

"When I told Tony I thought Ian was hooked, he told me to disappear for a few days, then lure Ian to the apartment on this particular weekday. That's when I was supposed to ask him to get rid of my warrants or I'd tell his boss he was paying me for sex."

"What happened when Ian came over?" Carrie asked.

"As soon as he came inside, I took him to the bedroom, and we screwed. Then I told him I had outstanding warrants and asked him to get rid of them."

"Did Ian say he'd do it?"

"No. He refused. He said it would be a crime."

"What did you do?"

Stacey hung her head. "I threatened him. I said I had a sex tape and I'd show it to his boss if he didn't do what I said."

"Was there a tape?"

Stacey nodded.

"What happened next?" Carrie asked.

"Ian was really mad. I had to hold a gun on him to protect myself. Then I told him to go to his office and get rid of the warrants. He got dressed and left, and I told Tony that Ian was really upset. He sounded pleased.

"I didn't know why Tony wanted me to pressure Ian. Then I found out Mrs. Carasco had been murdered that night and Ian had been with Tony when they found the body. I put two and two together and decided that I'd helped Tony get an alibi.

"I was scared that I was somehow involved in the murder, so I called Karl to ask what he thought I should do. Karl said he was driving up to Portland and I should get the judge over to the Grandview and we'd blackmail him. When Tony showed up, Karl threatened him with the tapes and told him how much money he wanted. Karl thought we had it made. Then these guys showed up and beat Karl bad."

"Can you identify any of these men?"

"No. They had masks. They were all big, but one of them was huge, like an NFL lineman."

Roger was pretty sure she was describing Andre Rostov.

"What did the men want?"

"The tapes. The giant made me show him where I was hiding them."

"Where were they?"

"The camera was hidden by two books. Karl had hollowed out the books, and the tapes were in the books. The big guy took them and told me to get out of Oregon. That's all I know."

"Where is the gun you used to threaten Ian?"

"I don't know. It was in my nightstand, but I didn't take it with me when I ran."

"What caliber gun was it?" Carrie asked.

"A .38."

The same caliber as the bullets that ended Anthony Carasco's life, Carrie thought.

"Do you still have the key to your apartment?" Roger asked.

"No. I tossed it."

The server appeared with their order. Stacey inhaled her food as soon as her plate hit the table. Roger guessed that she was low on funds and was not eating three squares a day.

"How much trouble am I in?" Stacey asked when she came up for air.

"If Ian wants to press charges, you could be in a lot of trouble, but I don't think he will. It would be embarrassing and not the type of thing he'd want going public."

"Are you still going to hold me as a material witness?"

"It would be easier if you rode back to Portland with us. Again, it's your choice."

"What if the guys who beat up Karl come after

me? They said they would if I showed my face in Oregon."

"You told us Tony sent them," Roger said. "The judge is dead, and men like that don't work for free. I think you're safe. But just to be sure, I'll see if we can put you in a safe house."

Stacey took a sip of her coffee, and the detectives let her think.

"Okay," she said. "I'll go back."

CHAPTER FIFTY-FIVE

After suffering a rash of thefts, the company Luis Ortega rented from had installed trackers in their cars. Two hours after Anders and Dillon arrived back in Portland, the company manager told them the current location of Ortega's car, and the detectives found it parked in the lot of a hotel near the airport.

Ortega's room was on the first floor near a door that opened into the parking lot. Carrie knocked on the door. Ortega opened it, and Carrie displayed her badge.

"Good afternoon, Mr. Ortega." Luis felt sick when he realized that Carrie had used his real name. "I'm Detective Carrie Anders, and this is my partner, Roger Dillon. I don't know if you remember, but we met in the courthouse. We'd like to ask you some questions. Can we come in?"

Ortega hesitated. Then he stepped back and waved the detectives inside. Roger looked around the room. A suitcase lay open on the bed, and it looked like they'd caught Ortega in the act of packing.

"What's this about?" Luis asked.

"It's about you calling yourself Brent Macklin."

"That's not a crime."

"It is if you're concealing your identity as part of a plot to murder someone."

"Whoa, hold on. I haven't killed anyone."

"Not even Anthony Carasco, the man who had your father murdered?"

"I didn't know the judge did that," Ortega said, but he didn't sound convincing.

"You didn't follow Carasco from a barn in the country to the Grandview apartments on Thursday night?"

"Where?"

"The Grandview apartments. They're on the Columbia River."

"I don't know what you're talking about."

"We think you do, Luis."

"I've never been to those apartments."

Carrie looked at Roger. Roger started to pull out his handcuffs, and Ortega punched him in the shoulder. The blow moved Roger aside. When Ortega started for the door, Carrie put all of her two-hundred-plus pounds behind a punch that sent Ortega to the floor. Roger snapped on the cuffs.

"Luis Ortega, I am placing you under arrest for the murder of Anthony Carasco," Carrie said. Then she read Ortega his Miranda rights.

CHAPTER FIFTY-SIX

Robin was experiencing post-death-case depression. While Joe Lattimore's life hung in the balance, Robin didn't have one restful night. She knew that Joe could die if she wasn't perfect. Exhausted from lack of sleep and plagued by doubt, adrenaline had gotten her through each day.

Once Joe was free, the exhaustion she had fought for weeks swept over her like a tsunami. Now that she was no longer responsible for Joe's life, Robin slept like a dead person. When she woke up, she wanted to stay in bed, but she knew it was important to get back into her routine, so she forced herself to grab her gym bag and run the five miles to McGill's gym, where she battled weights for an hour.

Robin's muscles ached, but she felt refreshed after taking a shower and making the leisurely walk to her office. She had a slow day and no desire to plunge back into her cases, so she sipped a latte and wasted an hour reading the *Oregon State Bar Bulletin* and a few issues of a magazine dedicated to mixed martial arts that she had not had the time to read while Joe's case was occupying her every waking moment.

After the pressure she'd been under, Robin was

grateful that her caseload consisted of several briefs that were not due for months, a shoplift, two DUIIs, and a he-said-she-said domestic violence case that would probably be resolved by a plea. None of her trial-level cases contained a complex legal issue.

Robin was reading about a teen phenom who had won his first five UFC bouts, when her receptionist buzzed her.

"You have a collect call from the jail."

"Tell the caller I died."

"You may want to take this one."

"Oh?"

"He says you've met him."

"What's his name?"

"Brent Macklin."

It took her a minute before she remembered the handsome reporter who was writing a story about illegal fights.

"Why is he calling from the jail?"

"He says that he's just been arrested for murdering Anthony Carasco."

Robin swore under her breath. The last thing she wanted to take on was another murder case, but she told the receptionist to put through the call anyway.

"Good afternoon . . ." Robin started as soon as the guard left the contact visiting room at the Justice Center jail. Then she stopped.

"Should I call you Luis Ortega or Brent Macklin?"

Ortega looked embarrassed. "Luis Ortega is my real name."

"On the phone, you said you were arrested for killing Anthony Carasco."

"I didn't do it. They have the wrong person."

"That's good to know, but the police must not believe you, and I assume one of the reasons is your snooping around using an alias. Why did you do that?"

"I wanted to find out who was responsible for my father's death."

"Tell me a little about him," Robin said.

"It's really sad. My dad was in the military. He did several tours in war zones and came back stateside all fucked up. We got him in rehab a few times, but he would fight, and they wouldn't let him stay. Once he was back on the street . . ."

Ortega shrugged. "Mom took him in again and again, but finally, she'd had enough. The last time Mom told him to leave, we didn't make an effort to find him. We were exhausted. Then the police told us he was dead."

Ortega shut his eyes for a second. Then he took a deep breath. "I saw the video of the fight. It was horrible. I didn't blame Lattimore. I blamed the people who were running the fights. Trying to find out who was really responsible for his death was my way of making amends."

"I'm sorry about your father," Robin said, "but revenge is a strong motive for murder."

"I swear I didn't kill Carasco. I would have told the police what I knew if I had proof Carasco was behind the fight that killed my dad."

"The police must have something stronger than your use of an alias if they've charged you. Can you tell me what it is?"

"I found out when the next illegal fight was going to be held. I had some information that Carasco was involved in the fights, so I followed him and staked out the site. I was hidden in some trees with a good view of the barn when the police made the raid. I saw Carasco run out the back and take off in his car. I followed him to the Grandview apartments, but he was far enough ahead of me so I didn't know which apartment he was in. By the time I drove into the lot, he was nowhere in sight. I was driving around, trying to spot his car, when a security guard drove up. I got scared, and I drove off.

"I was living in a hotel by the airport. I held off going home, because I wanted to find out if the police had arrested the people responsible for the illegal fight. When I heard that Carasco was murdered at the Grandview, I worried that I might have been seen. I was packing to go to my plane when two detectives showed up. They asked me if I'd ever been to the Grandview, and I lied and said I hadn't. That's when they started to arrest me. I panicked and hit one of the officers. The other one arrested me."

"Something puzzles me, Luis. The location and date of these fights is a well-kept secret. I only found out there was going to be a fight Thursday afternoon. How did you learn there was going to be a fight?"

Ortega looked conflicted.

"Luis?"

"This is tough. The person who told me . . . I promised I would keep him out of it."

"That's nice, but you're facing a possible death sentence, so I'd say that outweighs any promise you may have made."

"Will you keep him out of it, unless it becomes absolutely necessary?"

"That would be up to you. You're the client. The attorney-client privilege prevents me from revealing anything you tell me without your permission. Now, who told you where the fight was going to be held?"

Ortega took a deep breath. "He's a deputy DA named Ian Hennessey."

"Hennessey? But you knew he was Carasco's alibi?"

"He suspected that Carasco set him up to be his alibi, but he was afraid his career would be ruined if he went to the police. He thought I was writing a story about the illegal fights, and he told me Carasco might be involved with them.

He wanted me to expose Carasco if I found he was behind his wife's murder."

"Why did he think his career would be ruined if he took what he knew to the police?"

"Hennessey had been sleeping with a woman who was a prostitute. He said he didn't know that until she told him that she'd been arrested in Portland for prostitution and had outstanding warrants. She threatened to tell Vanessa Cole he had paid for sex if he didn't get the warrants off the system. He was sure he'd be fired if his boss learned about the prostitute."

"How did he learn about the fight?"

"He overheard something that was said in the DA's office. He called me with the information on Thursday afternoon. He didn't have a location, but he said I could follow Carasco."

"Did he know the judge was going to attend the fight?"

"No, but it was the only way he could think of to help me get to the fight."

"This is good to know."

"Will you have to tell Ian I broke my word?"

"I'm not sure. It depends on whether or not revealing his involvement will help you."

CHAPTER FIFTY-SEVEN

"Come in," Vanessa told Carrie and Roger, whom she'd summoned to her office to discuss the case against Luis Ortega.

"Can we go to a grand jury with what we have?" Vanessa asked when the detectives were seated.

"The case isn't as strong as we'd like it to be," Roger said, "but he was using an alias and asking questions about the illegal fights, so there's a strong argument that Ortega was in Portland to avenge his father's death. That's motive.

"Then, he was at the Grandview during the time period when the judge was killed. That's opportunity. And he fled the scene, which is evidence of guilt."

"Has the lab come up with any trace evidence that puts Ortega in apartment 5?"

"Not yet. And there is one complication," Roger said.

"Oh?"

"We did what you suggested and timed the shortest route from the barn to the Grandview, then from the Grandview to Rostov's house. If Rostov followed Carasco to number 5, killed him right away, then drove home, he could have arrived home in time for Lockwood to have her confrontation with him."

"Why is that a complication?"

"Rostov's prints are in the apartment. They were probably placed there when he beat up Hayes's pimp, but you can't date fingerprints. Ortega can argue that Rostov had as much opportunity to kill Carasco as he did, and Rostov's prints were inside the apartment, and his weren't."

"Damn. Were there any other latents found in number 5?"

"Only what you'd expect: Hayes, Hennessey, Carasco, Tepper, and two men who are known associates of Rostov."

Vanessa was about to ask another question when her intercom buzzed.

"Put her through," Vanessa told her receptionist.

"That was Robin Lockwood," Vanessa told the detectives when the call was finished. "She's been hired by Luis Ortega, so we'd better get all of our ducks in a row."

CHAPTER FIFTY-EIGHT

"Hi, Amanda," Robin said. "You'll never guess why I'm calling."

"I'm afraid to ask."

"I've just been hired by Luis Ortega, Carlos Ortega's son. He's been charged with murdering Anthony Carasco, and I need a second chair. And before you say no, you need to know that he swears he didn't do it, and he sounds like he's telling the truth."

Amanda sighed. "Have you checked to see if Mike is prosecuting?"

"Of course. I wouldn't have called if he were. But this is Vanessa's case. Are you in?"

Robin studied the crime scene photographs that had been taken in the bedroom of apartment 5 at the Grandview. After a few minutes, she put them down, closed her eyes, and rubbed the lids.

Robin and Amanda had been seated across from each other at the table in Robin's conference room for hours. In front of the attorneys was the discovery Vanessa had sent over in the Anthony Carasco homicide investigation. It included the photos, the autopsy report, the crime scene report, reports on the raid at the barn, and transcripts of interviews with Andre Rostov, Ian Hennessey,

Stacey Hayes, Luis Ortega, Bert Solomon, Helen Raptis, and others, as well as duplicates of all of the reports from Joseph Lattimore's prosecution.

"What do you think?" Robin asked her cocounsel.

"The case against Ortega is thin."

"Because?"

"They have him in the lot at the Grandview, but there's no DNA, fingerprints, and so on that put him in apartment 5," Amanda said. "Then there's the gun. They don't have it, so there's no evidence that connects Luis to it."

"He lied and ran when the detectives confronted him, and he ran when the security guard confronted him," Robin said.

"True, but he stayed at the airport hotel for a few days after Carasco was killed."

"And there's the alias," Robin said.

"Yeah," Amanda answered. "We won't be able to deny that he was in Portland hunting for his father's killer, but the police didn't know that Carasco was behind his wife's murder until after Kevin Bash and Rostov were interrogated. So, when he followed him to the Grandview, Luis wouldn't have known Carasco had devised a plot that resulted in Carlos's murder."

"Hennessey had given him reason to believe the judge might have been involved, and Luis followed him to the fight. Vanessa will argue that Luis confronted Carasco and got him to confess."

"That would be pure speculation without evidence that Luis was in apartment 5," Amanda said.

"Do you see any other suspects?" Robin asked.

"Rostov jumps out. Dillon and Anders figured out that he could have followed Carasco to the Grandview, killed him, and driven home just after you got there."

"What's his motive?" Robin asked.

"Maybe the judge didn't pay him for beating up Tepper, or he was afraid that Carasco would sell him out if he was arrested."

"What do you think about Stacey Hayes?" Robin asked. "They seem to be handling her with kid gloves."

"You think she might have killed Carasco?"

"I can make a case for it," Robin said. "The murder was in apartment 5, and her gun is the same caliber as the murder weapon."

"She told Dillon and Anders that she didn't have the gun when she left the apartment."

"We only have her word for that. Doesn't it make more sense that she'd take the gun with her for protection against Rostov and his goons? And she has plenty of motive. After seeing Tepper beaten to a pulp, she might want revenge on the man who ordered it. Plus, she could lure Carasco to the apartment, and no one knows where she was from the night Tepper was beaten until she was spotted in Bellingham."

Amanda yawned.

"Don't do that," Robin said. Then she yawned, and the women laughed.

"My brain has turned to mush," Amanda said.

Robin leaned back and rubbed her eyes again. "I'm ready to pack it in. Shall we call it a day?"

"I won't fight you."

"Okay. Let's call it quits."

"What's next?" Amanda asked.

"I'm going to request a bail hearing. You're right. The state's case is thin, and this way, we can force Vanessa to tell the court why she thinks she's got enough to keep Luis in jail."

That night, Robin fell asleep, exhausted, and soon found herself wandering through damp, dark, and narrow passages lined with the thick, slime-covered gray rock found in medieval prisons. She was desperate for a way out, and she knew that there was a door that would let her escape, but it was hidden somewhere in the maze of intersecting corridors, and she couldn't see where it was.

Jeff was home from the hospital. Robin was tossing, turning, and moaning so loudly that she woke him, and he shook her shoulder. Robin's eyes snapped open, and she sat up. Her heart was beating rapidly, and she was soaked with sweat.

"Sorry I woke you, but you were having one hell of a nightmare."

Robin took a deep breath and fell back on the bed. "It was a doozy," she said, and she told Jeff about her unsettling dream.

"Do you think you regret taking the Ortega case and you're subconsciously searching for a way out?" Jeff asked.

"I don't know, Dr. Freud, but I guess it could be a reaction to being sucked into another life-or-death prosecution when I should have gone on a long vacation."

"That will teach you to have empathy and a sense of civic duty," Jeff said.

Robin laughed.

"Can you get back to sleep?" Jeff asked.

"I think I'll go in the living room. My heart is still pounding. Sorry I woke you."

"Let me know if you figure out why you were wandering around a spooky castle. But do it in the morning. I'm going back to sleep."

Robin closed the door to the bedroom and walked into the living room. She stood in front of a window and looked down at the street through a rain-streaked pane. A homeless man huddled under the protection afforded by a doorway. No one else was out. The pale glow from the interior of a store across the street illuminated the raindrops that bounced off the pavement. It was a peaceful scene, and Robin watched the city lights, waiting for her eyes to grow heavy.

While she stood in the window, she couldn't

help wondering if her nightmare was a reaction to something in the police reports. She'd had a nagging feeling that there was something wrong or out of place in one of them, but she had no idea what it was.

Her eyes closed for a moment, and she felt her body grow heavy. She walked back to her bed and slipped under the covers. This time when she fell asleep, she didn't dream, but she remembered the dream in the morning and vowed to reread every report to try to see if her unease was justified.

CHAPTER FIFTY-NINE

The bail hearing in Luis Ortega's case had been assigned to Harold Wright because he was familiar with the Lattimore case and there would probably be some overlap. Luis came into court wearing a suit and looking like a young professional. He took a seat at the counsel table between Robin and Amanda, and Robin handed him a pen and a legal pad so he could take notes.

"If there's anything you think I need to know, write it down and make sure to tell me during a break in the testimony. If it's really important, tell Amanda, and she'll interrupt if she agrees. You're a smart guy, Luis. Use your brain and help us out."

"Got it," Luis said just as the bailiff called the court to order and Judge Wright came out of his chambers and took his seat on the dais.

"Mrs. Cole, Ms. Lockwood, and Ms. Jaffe, welcome back. I feel like I'm in a movie sequel."

"We hope it has a similar ending," Robin said, and even Vanessa smiled.

"Mrs. Cole, for Mr. Ortega to be held without bail in an aggravated murder case, the state must establish that the proof is evident or the presumption strong that Luis Ortega murdered Judge Anthony Carasco. You want to hold Mr. Ortega without bail, so the ball is in your court."

"Thank you, Your Honor. I'm going to let homicide detective Roger Dillon tell you why we think the proof is evident or the presumption strong that Luis Ortega murdered Anthony Carasco. There's a lot that you heard when you presided over the Lattimore case that is relevant to this hearing, but I'm going to have Detective Dillon go back to the beginning of the events that led up to Judge Carasco's murder to give you a complete picture of our case against Mr. Ortega."

"I'm listening," Judge Wright said as soon as the detective was sworn and had taken a seat in the witness-box.

"This case really started many months ago in San Francisco during the American Bar Association convention," Roger Dillon told Judge Wright. "That's when Judge Carasco met a prostitute named Stacey Hayes. They spent the night together, and he became infatuated with her and asked her to move into apartment number 5 at the Grandview complex in Portland. Hayes agreed, and the judge began spending a lot of time there. So much time that his wife, Elizabeth Carasco, discovered the affair and started divorce proceedings.

"Our witnesses will testify that Judge Carasco

had been bleeding his wife's trust funds dry. Other witnesses will tell you that the judge was using some of these funds to finance illegal, no-holds-barred fights. Kevin Bash was promoting the fights, and Carasco got a share of the profits Bash made from gambling and the fee spectators paid to attend.

"When the judge learned that his wife was going to divorce him, he devised a plan to have his wife murdered. He went to Bash and asked him to hire someone to kill his wife. Carasco offered to pay Bash with cash and by forfeiting his share of the profits from the next two fights.

"Part of the judge's plan involved providing himself with a cast-iron alibi. A few years before the judge met Stacey Hayes, she had been arrested for prostitution in Portland. When she failed to appear for her trials, warrants were issued for her arrest. Carasco introduced Hayes to Deputy District Attorney Ian Hennessey and ordered her to seduce him. Once the young DA was hooked, Carasco ordered Hayes to tell Mr. Hennessey, on a specific date and time, that she would tell Mrs. Cole that he was paying her for sex if he didn't erase her cases and warrants from the system. Mr. Hennessey didn't want to fix the warrants and went to Judge Carasco for help.

"On the day Hayes threatened Hennessey, Judge Carasco had one of Hennessey's cases transferred to his court for a four o'clock hearing, figuring that Hennessey would run to him because he had introduced Hennessey to Hayes. The judge invited Hennessey to dinner, and they were eating in Bocci's, an Italian restaurant, at the same time a man named Sal Benedetto was beating Elizabeth Carasco to death in the Carasco home.

"As you know from the Lattimore case, Joseph Lattimore was tricked into believing that he had killed the defendant's father, Carlos Ortega, in a no-holds-barred fight hosted by Bash. Benedetto phoned the judge at dinner to tell him that his wife was dead and phoned a man named Andre Rostov, who forced Mr. Lattimore to break into Carasco's house just as the judge and Hennessey drove onto Carasco's street. Mr. Lattimore was arrested for killing Mrs. Carasco and Carlos Ortega.

"The evidence will show that the authorities notified Carlos Ortega's wife that Carlos was dead. Mr. Ortega's mother told her son what had happened. Soon after, a video of the fight showing Mr. Lattimore fighting with Carlos was aired on the internet.

"The defendant came to Portland using the alias Brent Macklin. He claimed to be a writer working on a story about illegal, no-holds-barred fights. The evidence will show that he was really trying to find out who was behind the fight that ended in his father's death so he could exact revenge.

"On the Thursday evening Judge Carasco was murdered, Mr. Bash held another illegal fight in the same location, where the defendant's father was killed. We learned about the fight, and a raid was authorized. Judge Carasco was at the fight. We don't know how the defendant found out about the fight or its location, but photographs taken from a drone used to assist the raiding party show the judge fleeing the scene around eleven on Thursday evening and the defendant following him.

"A security guard entered the Grandview complex to begin his rounds around midnight on Thursday. He saw a car driving slowly through the parking lot. When he drove over to confront the driver, the car sped away. The guard wrote down the license plate number, and the vehicle turned out to be a rental car registered to Brent Macklin, the defendant's alias. The medical examiner will testify that the defendant was in the complex during the time span the medical examiner determined that Judge Carasco was murdered.

"We discovered that the defendant was staying at a hotel near the airport. When we questioned the defendant, he denied ever being at the Grandview apartments. Then he struck me and tried to escape."

"That is our case, Your Honor," Vanessa said. "We can establish a revenge motive and show that the defendant was at the Grandview apartments during the time period when the victim was killed."

"Do you have any questions of the witness, Ms. Lockwood?" the judge asked.

"I do. Is Bert Solomon the security guard who told you he saw Mr. Ortega's rental car driving through the Grandview lot?"

"Yes."

"Did he know if the car had just come into the lot, was leaving the lot, or was simply driving around looking for something?"

"He just said he saw the car driving around the lot."

"Didn't Mr. Solomon tell you that he checked the door on apartment 5 after Mr. Ortega drove away and found the door closed?"

"Yes."

"Didn't he also tell you that he looked at the door a day or so later, shortly before discovering the judge's body, and found that it was not completely shut?"

"Yes."

"Doesn't that indicate that someone entered, left, or did both after Mr. Ortega drove out of the Grandview complex?"

Dillon hesitated. "That could be one interpretation."

"Isn't it possible that Mr. Ortega drove into the Grandview complex looking for Judge Carasco and was spooked by Mr. Solomon before he figured out what apartment the judge was in?"

"That's possible."

"The medical examiner's estimate of the time of death spans several hours, doesn't it?"

"Yes."

"Isn't it also possible that another person entered apartment 5 after Mr. Solomon completed his rounds, killed the judge, and left the door ajar?"

"Yes."

"And this could have happened at any time between the time Mr. Ortega drove away, the time Mr. Solomon found the door to apartment 5 closed, and the time Mr. Solomon found the door to apartment 5 ajar, as long as it was within the time span when the murder occurred?"

"Yes, but Mr. Ortega might have returned."

"You can't prove that, can you?"

"No, it's just a possibility."

"Isn't it really groundless speculation?"

"It's a possibility," Dillon insisted.

"Detective, isn't it true that no trace evidence belonging to my client, such as fingerprints, DNA, hairs, and the like, was found inside the apartment?"

"Yes."

"But prints belonging to a man named Andre Rostov were found in the apartment?"

"Yes."

"Mr. Rostov ran out the back of the barn and drove away at the same time Judge Carasco ran out, didn't he?"

"Yes."

"And they both drove away in the same direction?"

"Yes."

"I conducted a citizen's arrest of Mr. Rostov at his house on the evening of the fight, didn't I?"

"Yes."

"Didn't you conduct an experiment to see if Mr. Rostov could have driven from the barn to apartment 5, then to his house?"

"Yes."

"You concluded it was possible, didn't you?"

"Yes."

"Mr. Rostov is a criminal with a record of violence, isn't he?"

"Yes."

"Have you recovered the murder weapon?"

"No."

"Did you find a key to apartment 5 on my client?"

"No."

"Do you have any witness who will testify that Mr. Ortega threatened to kill Judge Carasco?"

"No."

"Am I correct in concluding that you have no proof that Mr. Ortega expressed a desire to kill Judge Carasco, no proof that he was inside apartment 5 or possessed a key to apartment 5 or the weapon that killed the judge?"

"I . . . Yes."

"Nothing further, Your Honor," Robin said.

"Mrs. Cole?"

"Detective Dillon, is there evidence that Andre Rostov had been in apartment 5 before the date of the murder?"

"Yes."

"Please tell the judge what made him go there."

"Mr. Rostov will testify that Stacey Hayes had a pimp named Karl Tepper, who set up a hidden camera in the bedroom of apartment 5. Every time Hayes had sex with the judge, the event was recorded secretly. On the two occasions when Hayes and Ian Hennessey had sex, two more sex tapes were made.

"Tepper told the judge to pay him or the tapes and his relationship with a prostitute would be made public. The judge paid Rostov to go to apartment 5 and beat up Tepper. Rostov forced Miss Hayes to show him where the camera and the tapes were hidden. The camera was hidden on the top shelf of a bookcase that was across from the bed, and the tapes were concealed in two hollowed-out books that hid the camera from view. Mr. Rostov took the tapes out of the books. Then he told Miss Hayes to get out of the state and not return. Mr. Rostov gave the sex tapes to the judge at the fight."

"This incident occurred while the judge was still alive and before the illegal fight?"

"Yes."

"Nothing further, Your Honor," Vanessa said.

"Any more questions of this witness, Ms. Lockwood?"

"No."

"Any witnesses?"

Robin was about to tell the judge that she didn't have any witnesses when she remembered something Roger Dillon had just said. She froze. That was when she figured out what her subconscious had been trying to tell her in her dream!

"Ms. Lockwood?" Judge Wright said.

"Your Honor, can we take a recess? I might have a witness."

"Very well. Will twenty minutes be enough?'

"It should be."

Judge Wright left the bench, and Robin waved Jeff to the front of the courtroom.

"What's up?" Amanda asked.

"I'll tell you after I take another look at the discovery."

"You rang?" Jeff said.

"I need you to serve a subpoena right now."

"Who's the victim?" Jeff asked, and Robin told him. Then she took a look at the crime scene photograph of the bedroom in apartment 5 and reread one of the interviews.

CHAPTER SIXTY

"Good morning, Mr. Hennessey. I apologize for serving you with a subpoena on such short notice, but I need your testimony to clarify a few points."

"Okay."

"Do you feel that Anthony Carasco set you up when he asked you to take Stacey Hayes to dinner on the day that we tried a case against each other?"

"Definitely! He hired a man to kill his wife, and he suckered me into being his alibi."

"How did he do that?"

Hennessey flushed and looked toward the floor.

"Stacey played me. She pretended to like me. When we were in bed together, she taped us. On the day Mrs. Carasco was murdered, Stacey asked me to come to her apartment. Then she threatened to tell Mrs. Cole that I was paying her for sex if I didn't get rid of her outstanding warrants, which I never did."

"Get rid of the warrants or pay her?" Robin asked.

Hennessey blushed. "I didn't do either one," he said.

"Okay. What happened after she threatened you?"

"The judge had switched one of my cases to

his court for a late-afternoon hearing. He knew I'd run to him for help, and he engineered it so I would be with him when his wife was killed."

"You aren't involved in Mr. Ortega's case other than as a witness, are you?"

"No."

"So you haven't seen the police reports, crime scene photographs, autopsy reports—all the stuff Mrs. Cole gave me in discovery—have you?"

"No."

"I'm sorry if this is embarrassing, but I have to ask you. You were only in Miss Hayes's bedroom twice, right?"

"Yes."

"Was the first time on your second date?"

"Yes."

"Was the second time when she threatened you?"

"Yes."

"Were you in bed, naked, when Miss Hayes threatened you with her gun?"

Hennessey's pale features flushed bright red, and he nodded.

"You have to answer out loud so the court reporter can put your answer in the record," Judge Wright reminded the young DA.

"Yes."

"Can I assume that your eyes were glued to that gun?" Robin said.

"Yes."

"Can I also assume that you dressed and got out of that apartment as fast as you could?"

"Yes."

"And that was the last time you were in apartment 5 at the Grandview?"

"Yes."

"Then I'm confused, Mr. Hennessey. Do you remember being interviewed by Detective Dillon?"

"Yes."

"May I approach the witness, Your Honor?"

"Go ahead," Judge Wright said.

Robin handed Hennessey a copy of his interview, which had been turned to one of the pages.

"Did you tell Detective Dillon, and I quote,

"I'm such a sucker. I never suspected that I was being set up for blackmail. There was a bookcase across from the bed. A camera was hidden between two books on the top shelf. Stacey said she had a sex tape of us she'd send to Vanessa if I didn't help her. When I got upset, she pulled a gun on me and told me to get dressed and go to my office and fix the warrants. I left right away. I wanted to get out of there as fast as I could."

"Yes, I said that."

Robin paused and looked directly at Hennessey. "How did you know that the camera was hidden between two books on the top shelf of the bookcase?"

Hennessey looked confused. "She said she had a tape of us having sex. There had to be a camera."

"That would be a reasonable deduction, but the camera was hidden from view on the two occasions you were in Miss Hayes's bedroom. Can you explain to Judge Wright how you knew the exact location of the concealed camera?"

"I . . . She . . ."

"Let me help you. Isn't the answer that you learned where the camera was hidden on your *third* visit to apartment number 5, when you murdered a man you hated; a man who was trying to ruin your life?"

"No, I . . . I didn't kill the judge."

"Carasco knew that Kevin Bash would talk to get out of his legal troubles, and Bash's ace in the hole was his knowledge that Carasco had paid him to have Elizabeth Carasco killed. So, Carasco was on the run and needed money fast. He knew you had a trust fund, because you'd told Stacey Hayes. At the fight, Andre Rostov gave the sex tapes with you and Hayes on them to the judge. The tapes were not in apartment 5 when the judge's body was discovered.

"I think Carasco was hiding at the apartment and ordered you to come over. He knew you'd do anything for the tapes, including getting money when your bank opened on Friday morning. What he didn't count on was how much you hated him.

344

"When you came to apartment 5 the third time, Andre Rostov had knocked the books that had concealed the tapes to the floor, exposing the location of the camera. That's when you learned where the camera was hidden.

"You also knew that there was a gun in Stacey's nightstand. I think you killed Anthony Carasco with that gun and left with the sex tapes. Did I get that right?"

Hennessey's mouth opened, but no words came out. He looked at Vanessa Cole. Then his head swung back to Robin.

"Well, Mr. Hennessey. We're all waiting for your answer," Robin said, but all the young prosecutor did was look down and begin to sob.

Luis Ortega walked out of the jail elevator, and Robin walked over to meet him. As soon as she was near enough, Luis wrapped her in a hug.

"I don't know how to thank you," he said when he let go. "You literally saved my life."

"How are you feeling?"

Luis paused before answering. "You know, I thought I'd feel great when the people who were responsible for my father's death were punished, but I just feel empty. And I feel really bad about Ian. This was all Carasco's doing. Ian is an innocent victim of Carasco's horrible plot. I know he killed someone, but I wish there were some way he could be saved."

"I talked to Vanessa, and she feels awful about having to prosecute Ian. Mary Garrett is representing him. She's the best. She and Vanessa will work something out."

"Tell her I'll testify about Ian's mental state. It was obvious to me that he was at the end of his rope."

"I will. So, are you headed home?"

"After I make arrangements to have Dad's body sent back for burial."

"How is your mom doing?"

"She's sad that Dad's life ended the way it did, but I think she's finally found peace knowing he's at rest."

Robin took Luis's hand and gave it a gentle squeeze. "Have a safe journey home—you and your dad."

"We will, thanks to you."

CHAPTER SIXTY-ONE

Robin's cell phone rang, and Jeff grabbed it. They were lying on lounge chairs at the pool of a very expensive resort on Maui.

"Didn't I order you to turn that thing off?"

"You're not the boss of me," Robin said with a smile.

"I am definitely the boss of you on this vacation, and you may not communicate with anyone on the mainland for the next seven days. Now sip your piña colada or there will be no conjugation this afternoon."

Robin laughed. "I don't think that's the correct term for what we've been doing."

"Then where does *conjugal visit* come from?"

"I don't have the energy to argue about your vocabulary."

Robin held up her hand and smiled as she studied the diamond engagement ring Jeff had given her on their first night at the resort.

"Do you still like the ring?" Jeff asked.

"I'd like it even if it were plastic and came in a Happy Meal. How did you know how to size it?"

"I'm an ace detective."

Robin laughed and studied the ebb and flow of the ocean for a while before taking another sip of her drink.

"Say, I've been meaning to ask you about your dream," Jeff said. "Amanda told me that the nightmare helped you solve the case. How did that work?"

"When I was wandering through the spooky corridors in my nightmare, I thought the important thing was finding a hidden door that would let me escape. But that wasn't what my subconscious was trying to tell me.

"Roger told the judge that Rostov forced Hayes to tell him where the camera was hidden. That meant that Rostov couldn't see it, even though he's really tall, just like I couldn't see the hidden door. That made me wonder how Hennessey could have seen the camera during the two times in Hayes's apartment.

"When I looked at the crime scene photo, it showed the top shelf of the bookcase without any books and the two hollow books spread on the floor after Rostov got the tapes. That's when the position of the camera would have been exposed, and that's when I figured out that Hennessey had to have been in the apartment a third time."

"And you got all this from a dream?" Jeff said.

Robin shrugged. "What can I say? My mind is like a Rubik's Cube. Once I get a problem, it keeps tumbling around until all of the sides are the right color."

"Based on what our apartment looks like, I'd

say your mind is like a washing machine that's tumbling around a load of dirty laundry."

Robin fixed Jeff with a playful glare. "One more crack like that and you won't be conjugating any verbs or parsing any sentences for the rest of this vacation."

Jeff laughed. Then he leaned over and kissed Robin.

"You're the best," he said.

"Yes, I am," she answered with a big grin.

ACKNOWLEDGMENTS

When I do a Q&A at a book signing, I am often asked how I got the idea for my book. In the first section of *A Matter of Life and Death*, Robin Lockwood represents a man who is going through a sex change operation on a charge of prostitution. Transgender issues have featured prominently in the media in recent years, but I came in contact with them as a young lawyer in the 1970s when I represented a man who was transitioning to a woman who was charged with prostitution. One of the leading experts in the field was an Oregon doctor. His testimony was the key to getting a not guilty verdict.

To defend my client, I had to learn what a person who changes his or her sex goes through. It's quite an ordeal, and I developed a lot of sympathy for people who go through the procedure. When I decided to revisit my case in this book, I contacted Amy Penkin at the Transgender Health Program at OHSU. She brought me up to speed on the changes that have occurred since the 1970s. I really appreciate the time she took to meet with me.

Later in *A Matter of Life and Death*, Robin cross-examines a fingerprint expert. In September of 2019, the Oregon Criminal Defense Lawyers

Association held a seminar on forensic science. Gentry Roth of Mach 1 Forensics gave me a lot of the information about fingerprint identification. Thanks, Gentry, for taking the time to tell me what I needed to know to write this trial scene.

Dr. Don Girard and Dennis Balske, dear friends, also helped me with my research.

As always, I am extremely grateful to Jennifer Weltz, my agent and first reader, and to the terrific team at the Jean V. Naggar Literary Agency.

My books are always joint endeavors, and my brilliant editor, Keith Kahla, gets a lot of the credit if you thought *A Matter of Life and Death* was an enjoyable read. If you didn't, the fault is mine alone. I also want to thank Hector DeJean, Martin Quinn, Sally Richardson, Alice Pfeifer, Ken Silver, David Rotstein, Chris and Sara Ensey, and everyone else at St. Martin's for their fantastic support.

Finally, I want to thank my fabulous wife, Melanie Nelson, for making me happy every day.

Books are produced in the United States using U.S.-based materials	Books are printed using a revolutionary new process called THINKtech™ that lowers energy usage by 70% and increases overall quality	Books are durable and flexible because of Smyth-sewing	Paper is sourced using environmentally responsible foresting methods and the paper is acid-free

Center Point Large Print
600 Brooks Road / PO Box 1
Thorndike, ME 04986-0001 USA

(207) 568-3717

US & Canada:
1 800 929-9108
www.centerpointlargeprint.com